Visit Carolyn Miller at www.carolynmillerauthor.com

Copyright © 2023 by Carolyn Miller

All rights reserved.

No part of this book may be reproduced in any form or by any electronic or mechanical means, including information storage and retrieval systems, without written permission from the author, except for the use of brief quotations in a book review.

Cover Art by KT Design

Edited by Elizabeth Lance

# MUSKOKA SPOTLIGHT

CAROLYN MILLER

# CHAPTER 1

Jacqueline O'Halloran paused at the window of the beige hallway of Golden Elms, as sunlight reflected off the calm surface of Lake Muskoka. Early summer showcased this area in all its beauty, and the residents of the retirement community near Muskoka Shores were blessed with one of the best views in the area. Most people who could afford similar views were the very rich, movie or music stars, or professional athletes like hockey star Dan Walton, who owned a lakeside cottage not too far away. But a generous donor had gifted this parcel of land and turned a basic home into a state-of-the-art residential community for the elderly. Golden Elms specifically catered to those who were unable to afford those more expensive private facilities that were usually the domain of those who could afford the astronomical summer rents of the usual celebrities who dotted this part of the world each summer. No, instead of egos and demands for caviar and oat milk there was gratitude for the facilities and for the services of employees like those offered by Jackie and the other nursing staff and carers at Golden Elms. Well, from most of them, anyway.

"Enough." She turned from the magnificent view and moved to the next room on her list. Since his wife's death two years ago, Mr. McKinnon had rarely had visitors; his family lived on the west coast, or so his paperwork said. Which was a shame, as a more positive elderly man she had yet to encounter.

"Knock, knock." She suited actions to the word, tapping on the open wooden door, waiting for Dominic McKinnon to lift his gaze from his crossword.

"What's a nine-letter word for famous person?"

"Super star?" she offered.

"It's one word, not two."

Jackie thought, as she toed his worn slippers into a neat pile under the bed. "Celebrity?"

"No. The E fits. But nothing else."

"Any other clues?" she asked.

"Starts with a P, ends with another E."

"Maybe you should come back to it," she suggested.

"No." His frown grew more pronounced. "I know I know it. It's there at the tip of my tongue..."

Like it was for so many people at Golden Elms. This place might be in a beautiful location, but there was an element of frustration here too, as people learned to deal with the physical and mental challenges of older age. Dom McKinnon—or Mac, as he preferred to be known—wasn't the only person challenged by crosswords, sudoku, or remembering a simple word or person's name.

"How are you feeling today?" she asked him. It was a pointless question really, as it was obvious to all that he remained in dwindling health. His mind, which had always been sharp, had dulled of late, accompanying his mostly bed-ridden state since his most recent fall. Despite this, his attitude remained positive, even though the doctor's recent diagnosis of a stroke had altered other aspects of his personality and behavior. Mac was a sweetheart, someone she regarded almost like her own grandparents, even though they lived far away in Grand Falls, two provinces east in New Brunswick.

"Eh, what's that?" he asked, still studying his crossword as though his life depended on it.

"How are you feeling today, Mac?"

His gaze finally snapped up to meet hers, his bright blue eyes incongruous with the many lines feathering his weathered features. "I still can't get used to this thickened water stuff."

She winced sympathetically. "I hope it's only for a little while, then you'll be back to normal."

Although how 'normal' normal could ever be after a life altering experience like a stroke remained to be seen. One of the more challenging aspects of his ill health: being unable to drink water from a cup, instead, needing it to be thickened so he could swallow. Numbers of the older residents here struggled with dysphagia, their difficulty with swallowing meant food or liquid might enter the airways instead of the esophagus, which could result in the threat of aspiration. Sometimes this meant the liquid's thickness was altered through the addition of a gum-like thickening agent added to water. Mac wasn't one to complain, but his experiences had been unpleasant to say the least, resulting in recent weight loss.

She completed her usual questions, writing the answers on the chart at the end of his bed. This part of Golden Elms wasn't as high-needs as the hospice / nursing wing, but her role meant she needed to be aware of his progress—or lack thereof.

"Is there anything I can get for you?" she asked.

"Apart from a visit from my son?" he asked.

Her smile wavered. "He hasn't replied to the last message you sent?" The message that she'd sent last week at Mac's request on his phone.

Mac shook his head. "He's always too busy."

Shame on him. "And your daughter?" she asked, half-dreading to ask.

"Too far away."

"She's in Vancouver, right?"

"Near enough. Surrey, actually. But it's all too far from here."

"I'm so sorry," she said, touching his age-spotted hand.

"I know. Sometimes when you look at me with those big brown eyes it's like I can almost feel it."

Her throat grew tight, and she had to swallow to remove the lump. "Would you like me to send them another message?"

"Would you?"

"Sure."

He pointed to his phone, and she retrieved it then typed a repeat of the message she'd sent before. She'd had to carefully craft the words as Mac hadn't liked how a message sent to his family requesting a visit suggested he was desperate, but she'd assured him that the words "Love to see you if you're ever in Ontario" had been easy enough, not too guilt-inducing. But perhaps it was time for a less subtle approach.

"Are you sure you don't want me to say something more direct?" she asked him, her finger hovering on the green send key.

"No. Let it be. I don't want them to feel obliged to visit an old man. I know they are busy. Just send it."

She nodded, even as her heart ached. How many other elderly people never saw their families, under the assumption that they were too busy? Mac's resignation to his family's indifference only made her more determined to visit her grandparents in the Maritimes soon. From all that her mom had said, Grandpa seemed to be in the grip of dementia. Maybe she could visit next month, in her vacation time. But as for right now...
"I'll be praying they come see you soon," she promised.

"Thank you," he said gruffly.

She wasn't supposed to talk about faith-based things, but she'd known Mac long enough to know he wasn't opposed to her occasional fishing expeditions about matters of God. He stored his wife's Bible in his bedside drawer, though she figured that was more for sentimental reasons than anything else. From all she'd seen, he didn't have a relationship with God, and he didn't attend the chapel services Joel Wakefield ran here on some Sunday afternoons.

"So," Mac cleared his throat. "Have you found yourself a fella yet?"

Okay. How not to do a segue. "Uh, no."

"What? Still not? I would've thought all that attention from a few months ago would've seen one man at least ask you out."

Her nose wrinkled. "I did get asked out," and even scored her first marriage proposal, among some of the more bizarre results of her brush with fame back in February. "But it's kind of weird to have people reach out who I've never met before, just because they think I'm some kind of hero."

"But you were," he protested.

"Please. I only did what anyone else would've done in the circumstances. And if I'd known anyone was filming…" She shuddered. Her friend Rachel's video had gone viral.

"Are you saying you wouldn't have saved the day like that?"

She shrugged. "I was just in the right place at the right time."

Even though everyone else seemed to want to see it differently. But it was hard to argue and explain how truly it was just a split second—she believed God-given—decision to visit the snowy deck to find her friend Toni Wakefield and baby Ethan and boyfriend Matt Vandenberg at the mercy of a madman. Then for Jackie to have lifted that wooden chair was a miracle even she could not explain. Perhaps it wasn't so surprising people still talked about it four months on.

"As far as we're all concerned, it made you a heroine, so the fact others see that too and want to know you more really shouldn't be a shock."

"I'm just not used to it, that's all." She'd always been the plain one. The studious one. The one whose love for God seemed to earn her the badge of being too religious. She'd never been the one that boys paid attention to. If she was completely honest, she'd never really had a boyfriend, not even in high school or in grade school. That 'sweet sixteen and never been kissed' thing? Yeah. She might be close to finishing her third decade and it remained the same. Not that she worried about it. It just was. And she and Jesus were tight, so it really was okay.

"Hmm, well I don't know why you don't want to give it a try," Mac persisted.

"I had people write to me from as far away as China, Mac. They obviously saw the footage and thought they knew me."

"Mebbe. But I don't see how it's any worse than that thing where you go on a date and don't know the other person. What do you call it?"

"A blind date?"

"That's it."

She shrugged. Maybe answering one of those messages instead of deleting them all would have led to someone genuine. But judging from the creepy messages that had stalked her social media and email until she'd had to close or switch accounts, it appeared that Mr. Genuine hadn't been the one writing.

"I hear people go on the internet these days to find love," Mac said.

"Some do," she acknowledged. "But I'm not looking. Believe it or not I'm actually happy with who I am."

"Huh. You can say that, but I don't believe you."

"You don't have to believe it for it to be true," she countered.

"Sassy gal." He chuckled. "But I'm betting you ain't a fussy one, are you?"

"I certainly don't need tall, dark, and handsome, if that's what you're saying."

"What about rich?"

She raised her eyebrows and just looked at him, which earned her another raspy laugh.

"I'm taking that as a no. So, I guess that means you don't care what kind of job he has."

"I really don't." He could be a plumber or a pastor for all she cared. She just wanted someone genuine, someone who loved Jesus and would love her. "But like I said, I really don't need a man to complete me or anything."

"Good," he said firmly. "Women who need a man always seem a little too needy, know what I mean?"

"Yes." She hated to admit it, but her friend Anna Morely sometimes came across that way. Jackie prayed a micro-prayer that God would comfort Anna, that she'd find her identity and contentment in Him. "I've always felt that if God wants me to get married, then God would have to bring along the right man to cross my path."

"Hmph. And would you recognize him as the right man if he did cross your path?"

"I'd hope I'd get an inkling that if he's the right man for me then I'd know somehow."

His grin revealed stained teeth. "So God would need to tell you in a big booming voice, huh?"

"No. But I guess I'd feel a peace about it."

A sigh escaped him, as he looked past the curtains to the lake beyond. "I still remember when I saw Nancy for the very first time. Love at first sight it was. For me, anyway. She took a little longer to convince, but I managed."

"And then you were married for fifty-seven years, right?"

"Nearly fifty-eight," he said proudly. "And never a cross word between us. But that might've been because I knew she was always right, and she knew that too, and didn't mind pointing it out on occasion."

Jackie laughed. "You know she adored you."

"I know." Wistfulness crossed his features. "And I adored her too." His head tilted, his gaze swinging back to Jackie. "You remind me of her, you know."

"How so?"

"You're both direct and can be practical, but you've also got a wholesome kindness that Nancy had in spades, too."

Her heart hiccupped at the sweet description, and she had to blink away sudden moisture. Nancy had been a complete sweetheart, a Godly woman that Jackie had looked up to. Jackie had often imagined that if she was to ever get married, then Nancy would be the kind of woman Jackie would hope to be: strong, fearless, keeping a thankful spirit even in the face of cancer. Her death had proved a gaping loss in the emotional equilibrium of this tight-knit aged community.

Mac's lips pursed, his fluffy eyebrows lowering as he studied Jackie. "Back in my day we would've said you're a catch."

"Well, in this day, I think we could say the same, as I rather believe I am, too."

His lips twitched. "So, what is it? You're too fussy? Too busy? Are you still making those website things at night?"

"When I get a moment." Between that, and running Bible studies, and attending soirees with Serena and the girls. Although since Serena's February wedding there'd been fewer of their girls' get-togethers lately. Anna, the other single girl in their group, always bemoaned that it was because the others had coupled up, and it did seem that there'd been a spate of recent changes in the relationship status of their friends. Serena marrying Joel in February. Their author friend Staci and her doctor boyfriend seemed to be getting closer to an engagement every day. Toni had accepted a proposal from her city-based boyfriend Matt, and while Jackie was thrilled for her, she couldn't help but notice a mild level of anxiety about what this would mean, where they'd live. No more baby Ethan to cuddle and be Aunty Jackie to? She knew her identity wasn't found in such things, but sometimes it seemed little Ethan would be the closest she'd ever get to having a family of her own. Maybe their upcoming get together would finally see some answers.

"You know," Mac's voice intruded in her thoughts. "You really should meet that grandson of mine."

"Hmm." She made a non-committal noise as she quickly hung up Mac's clothes in the closet. If she had a dollar for every patient who had ever offered to fix her up with one of their relatives she could probably afford a Lakeside cottage of her own. It was obviously time to go.

"He could do with some more plain-speaking in his life instead of that fool—oh!" His expression cleared. "Personage!"

"I beg your pardon?"

He ignored her and grabbed his pencil and fitted the letters into his crossword. "It fits!"

"Well done," she said, moving to the doorway, her thoughts stretching to the next patient under her care. "Well, if that's everything, I shall see you on the morrow."

"I've got you in my sights, you know," he warned, before pointing at the ceiling. "I'm gonna have a word with the big fella upstairs about you and Mr. Right."

Dear heavens. While she was glad to see Mac was willing to be on speaking terms with God she'd prefer it to be about something important. "Thank you, Mac, but I really don't feel the need for a boyfriend."

"Who said anything about a boyfriend?" he demanded, before grinning a yellowed-teeth old man grin. "I'm gonna ask him to send you a husband." He nodded slowly. "And I have a—what was that word you said? Inkling, was it?" At her nod he continued. "And I have an inkling just who it might be. Go on, I know you want to ask me."

She had little choice but to play his game. "And who might that be?" she asked.

"My grandson. He's an actor. In Hollywood."

Sure he was. If he was an actor—which was highly doubtful,

Mac seeming to have similar thoughts to Mavis next door who believed her husband had been an astronaut, which definitely wasn't true—then he probably did community theater, or had done a skit in church, maybe, once upon a time, in some backwoods town somewhere.

"See you tomorrow, Mac," she said firmly, smiling as she closed the door.

Poor man. Mac was a dear, but it was clear he was becoming delusional. Good thing she wasn't looking for a man.

"Lincoln! Lincoln! Please, would you take a photo with us?"

Lincoln Cash paused on the red carpet and waved a hand as the flash of photographers dazzled his eyes. He smiled, ears hurting at the screams of adoring fans, his headache ramping up to eight on the Richter scale. Sure, his migraine meant he could've canceled, but today was all about playing nice, proving he was a team player, was trustworthy, was exactly the right man for the job so director Victor Drewe would pick Lincoln as the star of his next movie. He drew close to a bunch of teenage girls and accepted the phone held out in an outstretched hand. "You want me to take a photo of you?" he teased.

"No! Take a selfie with us," they pleaded.

He forced up his cheeks and acquiesced, then, amid meaningless chatter, handed it back and continued to walk into the film festival where he was air-kissed by a dozen actresses—and some actors—who were increasingly all starting to look the same. Tanned skin, tawny hair, teeth bleached even whiter than his own. Padded, hair-extended, fake nails, surgically enhanced and smoothed. He might love acting, but he hated this part of pretense. And it wasn't just the looks part he despised. He hated pretending this was his life calling, that he was supposed to care—to know—about a million different causes, everything from children's literacy to water wells in Burundi. Where the heck was Burundi, anyway? And why should an actor's opinion carry more weight than a scientist or teacher's? Just because he was in an industry that actively treadmilled the fifteen minutes of fame for as long as possible didn't mean he was anymore cluey than the next guy. He just had a so-called 'platform' to speak from. Or so that's what his agent, Richard Kneever said, and Jolene Hamburg, his publicist, agreed.

His heart dipped. Jolene was always trying to get Lincoln's profile out there—although where exactly 'there' was always seemed a little vague. How many followers was enough? How many likes meant he was loved? Sometimes he took a step back and could see this industry for the huge money-spinning game it was, the giant popularity contest that meant he'd one day be chewed up and spat out along with every other Tom, Brad, and Ryan. Fame wasn't real, which was why it was "Best to make your millions while the sun shines," as Jolene liked to say.

Because one day Linc would lose his looks as much as any starlet. And he knew that if anyone truly knew him, they'd discover he'd never be good enough to truly be loved.

"Lincoln, darling. Come stand here."

Natasha Ericsson, the star of tonight's screening of *The Man Without a Word*, drew him to stand in front of a giant poster that featured them in a passionate embrace. Not so passionate that he'd been able to ignore the stale cigarette taste of her mouth, and definitely not so passionate that he'd ever given the 'intimacy coach' a moment's concern. His left eyelid twitched, as a thud began behind it. Yeah, this wasn't exactly the kind of film he'd dreamt of doing when he was back in acting school. And after the tension on set, he was glad this publicity was the last time he'd have to deal with most of these people. But it had paid the bills, and it gave the public what they wanted, even if he'd long dreamed of something more gritty and real.

His phone buzzed and he waited until the roar of photography passed before drawing it from his pocket. Mom. Great.

*Good luck, honey,* the text read.

"Lincoln!" one of the publicists hissed.

He shoved the phone back in his pocket and posed and smiled some more. Exchanged banter with some of the other actors in the film. Nodded as if he was listening when one of the producer's wives talked at him with words he really couldn't hear. Lifted a hand to wave to the crowd one last time before finally, finally, they made their way indoors where the decibels halved and the warp-speed of frantic busyness hitched back to normal hectic rates.

"Mr. Cash?" A curvy blonde with enormous blue eyes—exactly his type—batted dark lashes at him as she offered a tray of filled champagne flutes and small caviar-dusted croquettes. "Would you care to eat something?"

"Thanks, but I'm good."

For a moment, his grandmother's voice twisted through his head: *No-one is good except God.*

He blinked, straightened, and snatched a glass and drained it. Where had that come from? Gran had been dead these past two years. Exactly the last time he'd gone to a church or even thought about God.

"Mr. Cash?"

Oh, the woman was saying something else. "Pardon?"

"Are you sure there's nothing I can offer you?" Her gaze looked less innocent now, especially as it traveled down the length of his shirt and lingered before slowly making its way up.

"Nope. Excuse me."

He hurried away, wishing for a shower—why did nobody ever talk about the way women objectified men?—as he moved to the side room of the theatre where tonight's film premiere was being held. They were supposed to have done press earlier today, but a bout of food poisoning affecting the director had caused a reshuffle until tonight. He suspected that had put a dampener on the styling pretensions of Natasha and Chlolinda and some of the others, but being a man, a suit, some hair product, and a smile was all Linc really needed to be camera-ready. There were plenty of blessings to being male.

"There you are!"

Victor Drewe, the film director of two dozen mainstream films, glad-handed him before gesturing to the stage. "Natasha is still outside swanning it up for the cameras, so we need to get ready if we're going to start the film on time. Do you mind answering a few questions with Chlolinda while we wait for Tash to arrive?"

"Sure thing."

Best to stay on the famous director's good side, even if his daughter was a bit naïve. But hey, this was her first film, and they'd all been green once upon a time.

He followed yet more publicists and assistants to the stage where spotlights caused him to blink as he settled into a seat and grabbed some water. Maybe he shouldn't have had that champagne before. Taken with the pain meds from before, it now felt like his head was swimming.

Chlolinda arrived in a rush of feathers that made his nose itch. She hadn't grasped the art of air-kissing, smacking his cheeks with purple-hued lipstick that meant he had to grit his teeth as he smiled while she laughed and rubbed it off. He drew his phone from his pocket, glancing at the time. How much longer before he could get out of here?

"Oh my gosh, this is so exciting!" Chlolinda murmured, wiping on more lipstick.

"Just relax and have fun," he murmured back.

"'Just relax,' he says." She sighed, then picked up a bottle of water, struggling to open it. "Would you mind?" she asked, holding out a bottle of water. "I'm so nervous, so my hands are sweaty."

"No problem." He undid the blue plastic lid and handed it to her.

"You're so sweet." She fluttered her eyelashes, and his stomach tensed.

Okay, so it hadn't exactly been a picnic starring in this movie with this girl. Chlolinda—her name was a hybrid of Chloe and Linda, he'd now heard her explain a dozen times—seemed to have eyes for him in a way that made him uncomfortable, but in an age of #MeToo he suspected a man talking about females sexually harassing him wasn't going to go down too well. He subtly shifted his chair away, glanced at his phone again.

Another message lay there. His mom. Again. *You're in New York. Have you got time to swing by Toronto on your way home?*

That was a solid no. After this he had a flight to the west coast then he'd soon be into rehearsals for his next audition, a space adventure that would basically echo his role in last year's cop-buddy movie. And while the material wasn't ground-breaking, at least he'd be working with Victor again, although he'd be even happier if there was a guarantee that Chlolinda wouldn't be jumping on her daddy's dime once more and snatch a role a more talented actress deserved. Once was more than enough as far as Linc was concerned.

"Ready?" Chlolinda placed a red-talon-tipped hand on his arm.

He was tempted to shake it away. He subtly eased away his arm instead. "Sure. Let's go." He shifted closer to the microphones, pasted on his working smile. "Hey everyone, thanks for coming out tonight. It's good to see you."

The film's publicist gave a short spiel then introduced them before a microphone was handed to Lola Jenkins, an entertainment reporter from the Post.

"Lincoln, we'd love to begin with you and your thoughts on your role."

Oh, right. His role. What was the name of his character again? He nodded, gazing out to the sea of cameras and microphones. "It's not every day a man gets to play the role of someone like Nehemiah Buzzard. I thoroughly enjoyed the deep dive into a character of such complexity, who had been misunderstood for so much of his life." Perhaps because he could relate so well. "I'm really grateful that Victor chose me to take this role, and I hope the author feels like I've done his Nehemiah proud."

"It's quite a different role to your usual action-man types. Did you enjoy the chance to be a bit quieter in this piece?"

"I have to admit it's a lot easier to be quieter when you're the man without a word." He waited for polite laughter—yeah, it wasn't the first time he'd made that joke—then talked a bit about his inspiration for the role, how he'd interviewed people suffering trauma and how they'd dealt with it. And yeah, that after years of roles that demanded he live up to the buffness of a leading man, he'd enjoyed the chance to actually act, rather than simply look like eye candy. He managed to say it better than that, though.

The questions kept coming, interspersed with ones asking about his opinion of his co-stars, and his thoughts on the acting newcomer from movie royalty he was sitting beside.

"It's been a real pleasure," a real pain, "getting to know Chlolinda," and how needy for approval she was, "and I can't wait to see her in her next film."

Which hopefully would be filmed in a location far away from him.

"Can't wait," he repeated. For this to be over. To never see Chlolinda again. To stop the artifice and noise and endless go-go-go. What he'd give to take a month off and have a real break. He glanced at his phone again. Maybe he could swing a trip to Toronto, see the lakes, catch up with friends. When did rehearsals have to begin, anyway?

"And how do you think viewers are going to respond to this film?"

How was he supposed to answer that? Everyone knew an audience viewed a movie based on their own perspective. A sleep-deprived person might see a movie one day and hate it, then see it another and think it an Oscar contender. A cocktail or three before a movie made for a very different film-going experience than when one saw it sober. Art was subjective. Everybody knew that.

He managed to screw together enough intelligible-sounding words that he hoped passed for intelligent then sat back, face fixed in assumed pleasantness as his headache thumped and the reporters turned to Chlolinda and asked the director's starlet daughter for her opinion on starring in her first film.

"It was like a fairytale come true, you know?" Chlolinda gushed. "You know, like, I was Cinderella, and here was my handsome prince." She squeezed Linc's bicep. "I felt like a princess, except it was a movie, right? A real movie. Like, one you'd see on the big screen, you know?"

Lincoln sucked the inside of his bottom lip as he struggled to hold in a laugh. Okay, there was young and naïve, and then there was whatever this was. Had she been drinking? Taken weed? Something harder?

Judging from the ripple of amusement floating around the room he might not have been the only one who found her answer startling.

"So, Lincoln, have you got any response to that?"

"To being a handsome prince or to starring in a *real* movie?"

Whoa, he hadn't meant to say that like that. Regret at his quick tongue tightened his stomach.

"Huh?" Chlolinda turned to him, head tilting, her smile fading.

Man. He pasted on a smile. "I'm always grateful for the opportunities directors like Victor give us. I'm looking forward to working with him in the future, too. After years of seeing her father's work on the big screen I'm sure that's why Miss Drewe is excited. Who wouldn't be, right?"

Judging from the smirks being shot his way he wasn't sure he'd completely covered his slip up, but it'd have to do. Where the heck was Natasha, anyway?

A sequined pink gown glimmered into view. Thank goodness. "And would you look who's here," he murmured into the microphone.

Phew. As heads turned to gaze at the leading lady he took another swig of water. His head was killing him. He nodded to the publicist's assistant who immediately drew close to the table. "Yes, Mr. Cash?"

"Got any ibuprofen?" he asked.

"Have you got another headache?" Chlolinda asked.

"Yeah. I'm afraid so." 'Headaches' had been the excuse he'd often used on set when the director's daughter had gotten a little too pushy with wanting to invade his space or practice their kissing scenes. No, thank you. Maybe it was a coward's excuse, but he preferred to not go there. He'd learned enough in this industry over the past seven years to know a guy didn't encourage the director's daughter. Not if you wanted the director to cast you in his movies again.

"Here, I'm pretty sure I've got some." She opened her gold mesh bag as Natasha took to the stage and offered a dramatic wave hello, making a show of kissing Chlolinda and Lincoln. His nose wrinkled. He could smell the cigarettes she'd smoked before coming here. Chlolinda wasn't the only one he'd feigned headaches with to avoid unnecessary closeness.

"What is she doing?" Natasha hissed as Chlolinda continued rummaging through her bag.

"Looking for ibuprofen," he muttered out of the side of his mouth. These microphones had an uncanny way of picking up everything.

"And for a braincell. I couldn't *believe* what she said before," Natasha murmured. "Like we all know the only reason she got cast at all is because she has Daddy twisted around her little finger."

A titter raced around the room.

What? He kept straight face on as he glanced around. Beside him, Chlolinda continued searching through her bag, her focus entirely on that and not on the fact their every move was being scrutinized. Or that the microphones had picked up Natasha's comment. He swallowed a word his Grandma wouldn't have liked.

"Miss Drewe?"

Her head bobbed up. "Huh?"

"What do you have to say to that allegation?" Zeke Sinclair, an MTV and podcast host with a talent for posing tough questions asked.

"Here it is!" Chlolinda handed Lincoln a silver packet of white pills.

His stomach tensed. This *was* ibuprofen, right? He wouldn't put it past spacey Chlolinda to have other pharmaceuticals of both legal and non-legal status in there.

"Thanks," he muttered, placing it on the table. He might just wait to visit a drugstore on the way home later.

"What was it, Zeke?"

"What do you have to say about Miss Ericsson's comment that the only reason you got the film role was because you're the daughter of the director?"

"You said that?" Chlolinda's eyes widened. "Really?"

"I didn't mean it," Natasha protested.

Yeah, but she had. The rumors of tension on the set had been based on fact. He could only be glad this particular truth hadn't spilled from his own mouth.

"Come on, you know I love you, Chloe," Natasha continued.

"It's Chlolinda," she sniffed, before picking up the water bottle. "I should've known you would be jealous of me."

"Excuse me?" Natasha's head cocked, as if she was spoiling for a fight.

"You've always been jealous of me. Ever since Lincoln slept with me—"

"What?" His voice was louder than he'd anticipated. Shock did that to a man.

"Come on, baby. You can admit it," Chlolinda wheedled. "It's not like we're not both adults."

Lincoln held up his hands. "Whoa. We did *not* do what you said. I don't know what you've been smoking, but this is not a movie scene. This is real life and right now you're telling lies."

She pouted. "It's not a lie if it's true."

Except this wasn't. But judging from the barrage of questions being thrown his way he wasn't going to get a chance to have his side heard. How could he tell the world the director's daughter was delusional? The pain in his head sharpened and he rose, shrugging off her hand as his head swam. He needed a drink of water. He was so dizzy. He needed to escape. From this place. From New York. To Toronto? Maybe further north, to see his grandfather in Muskoka.

But before another thought could sharpen into clarity he staggered back, and fell off the back of the stage.

# CHAPTER 2

"Oh my gosh! Can you believe it?"

"Believe what?" Jackie asked Anna, her gaze not shifting from the lakeside view.

Around them the quiet of Serena and Joel's house was filled with the kind of peace that settled over Muskoka in early summer before the tourists came and loud music and parties traveled across the lake and stole tranquility. Now, as the last of the sunset melded into golden pools, Jackie drew in a breath and inhaled serenity. It was like a blanket of calm lay across the world, the hazy golden red rays easing into dark blue.

The tranquil scene in front of her was snatched away as a phone was thrust in front of her face. "This. Did you see this?"

Jackie leaned back and had to squint a little, before accepting Anna's phone as Anna clearly intended, and read the news article.

*Drunken Movie Star Fail.*

Her nose wrinkled. "Exactly why do you think I need to see this? You know I'm not a fan of gossip."

"But it's Lincoln Cash," Anna whined.

"Who?"

Anna rolled her eyes at Serena who joined them with a tray of antipasto. "I can't believe she never knows about the movie stars we do. Tell me you know who Lincoln Cash is, please."

"I can tell you that, but it wouldn't necessarily be true," Serena said, with a wink at Jackie.

"Ugh! You two are hopeless. Just wait until Rachel gets here. She'll know who I mean. Actually..." She snatched the phone back and tapped on it a few times then thrust the screen back at Jackie again. "Look. Remember the *Incitement* movie we watched last year? That one in New York about a wise-cracking handsome cop and his older buddy? Well, he's the young one with the muscles."

"Sorry. Still don't recall." Although, she frowned at the screen, something about the picture was familiar.

"Oh my gosh, Jackie. It's like you never watch anything except *The Chosen*."

"Hey, don't knock it."

"I'm not knocking it, but honestly, sometimes it seems you're stuck in a rut and have no idea about what else is going on in the world."

"I know enough," she protested.

"Do you? Really?"

"Look, I get that you're into movies and stuff, but it's just not for me."

"You'd rather sit at home and cross-stitch, right?"

"I don't think that's something to mock, either. Honestly, I don't know why you're getting so worked up about this."

"Because Lincoln Cash is hot, and he had an accident and everyone is talking about it."

"Well, clearly not everyone," Serena said, with a small chuckle.

And Jackie was supposed to care about this man... why?

The front screen door opened with a wheeze and a bang amid a call of "Hello!"

Seconds later in came Rachel, followed by Toni and baby Ethan. Jackie's heart leapt. Okay, maybe it was weird, but it was like she had this bond with Toni's child—Ethan would be a year old soon—but there it was. She liked nothing more than to babysit, and already he was starting to call her Aunty Jackie. She was pretty sure that's what his baby mumbles meant, anyway.

"Now we're here let's get the party started," Rachel sang out, passing a bottle to Serena then offering air kisses to all before plopping onto the sofa next to Anna. "Ooh, look, food I didn't have to cook, and not a piece of macaroni to be seen." She cut a wedge of cheese, shoved it on a cracker and ate it as she sank against the leather lounge. "Oh, I needed that."

Ethan's bright eyes widened as he saw Serena, but his face lit in a grin as he saw Jackie. "Hello, little man," she said.

Toni chuckled. "Hello, Jackie."

Oops. "Oh, and hi to you too." She pushed to her feet and gave her friend a hug. "How are you?"

Toni flashed a grin as sparkly as the rock anchoring her ring. "Pretty good."

"Have you got news? You look like you have news."

"I have some news," Toni admitted.

"Hurry up and sit down, then," Rachel commanded. "She refused to tell me when we walked up the path just now."

"So, you've been waiting years, then?" Jackie teased.

Rachel threw a grape at her, which bounced off Jackie's unsubstantial chest and into her lap. She ate it anyway.

Serena did a final check about drinks, then set her own glass on the coffee table as she took the final chair. "It's been so long since we've done one of these gatherings. It's good to be back together again."

"It's a shame Staci couldn't be here," Jackie observed.

"She's no doubt having fun on her book tour. I sure would be," Rachel said, stretching one hand above her head. "I'd love to see New York again."

"You could go," Serena said.

"Yeah, right. Just abandon the kids and Damian and have a girls' weekend. Wouldn't that be a dream?"

"Sure would," Anna said, her face and tone holding similar wistfulness.

"You could go with Damian," Jackie said. "How long have you two been married for now?"

"We must be getting close to ten years."

"You were a child bride," Jackie teased.

"Obviously." Rachel smirked. "But hey, ten years deserves a trip to New York, right?"

"Absolutely," Toni said.

"Hmm. I might see if I can convince him to take some time away from the business. That's the problem of running your own business. The only way you stop thinking about it is if you really get away."

Damian ran a local small construction company, and Rachel helped with the administration when she wasn't ferrying her three small children around to various activities.

"Has anyone got vacation plans?" Serena asked. "Or will you all be here for Canada Day?"

Muskoka Shores always held a fun celebration on July first. It was a great opportunity to relax and celebrate and feel like summer had really started. "I think I'm working that day," Jackie admitted.

"Again? Girl, you work too hard," Rachel said, eyeing her over her wineglass.

"Somebody needs to," she said. "And I'd rather do it than deprive someone of time with their family, so I really don't mind. The home always does something nice for the residents, anyway. We're going to spend some time at the park during the day."

"Yeah, but not as nice as if you're at the beach, eating barbecue."

Regret twinged. Okay, it probably would not be as good as that. "I really don't mind," she said firmly. Perhaps if she said it often enough, her heart might start believing it was true. "And I hope to still make the fireworks at night."

"That's something. We'll see you then, at least," Toni said.

"When was the last vacation you had?" Serena asked, her brow pleated.

Hmm. Was it bad she couldn't quite remember? "A while ago," Jackie confessed. Two, three years?

"You need to take time off," Anna said. "Nobody functions well if they're always on the go."

Serena held up a hand. "Truth."

"Okay, okay. I hear you. And I had wondered about going east in the next month or two. See my family again."

"How is your mom doing back in New Brunswick?"

"Mom doesn't complain, but I know it tires her out." Guilt panged. "My grandfather has dementia, and it seems Mom is struggling to deal with their clutter."

"Wait," Rachel straightened. "When you say you are going there for vacation do you mean you're actually going to help out your mom or are you actually going to be taking time off?"

Ah. For all Rachel's abruptness she could be plenty insightful. "I miss them."

"Jackie, honey, if you're only going to provide respite for your mom you know that's not a true vacation, right?" Serena asked softly.

"I do. But it wouldn't be all toil. I do actually love my grandparents, and my mom," her dad had left years ago, "so it's not a sacrifice. You know that, don't you?"

"We know," Anna said. "But we also know that you can be a martyr sometimes."

"I beg your pardon?" Okay, so offended wasn't her go-to, but Anna thought her a martyr?

"No, I don't mean you complain about what you do, but you

help so many people I don't think it'd hurt for you to just have fun occasionally."

"I have fun," she said, indignantly. "Are you suggesting I'm boring or something?"

Rachel sighed. "Not boring. Just..."

Jackie's heart quavered at the way Rachel's nose wrinkled. Did her friends not like her?

"Just rather... worthy."

"I beg your pardon?"

"Come on, Pastor Jackie."

Pastor Jackie?

"You're very good. *All* the time. And it's like you—"

"Are you actually saying you want me to be bad?" she interrupted.

"Not bad," Rachel soothed. "Just try things out of your comfort zone. You only get one life, and if all you do is go to work or church or sit at home and design websites or cross-stitch then is that really you living life to the full?"

Jackie blinked, as words from Joel's recent sermon strode into mind. Wasn't that what Jesus had said? That He'd come to give His people life, eternal life, and to have it to the full? What did 'to the full' actually mean, anyway? Sure her friends might tease her about being Pastor Jackie, but was she narrow-minded? Had she slipped into a rut of familiarity? And was this actually all that God wanted for her life?

"I don't think Jesus meant for us to be living wild like one of Anna's movie stars," Serena objected.

"Do you think I'm boring?" Jackie demanded.

"No. Not at all. But..."

"But what?"

"But I can see Rachel and Anna's point. I don't think it hurts to try new things occasionally, either."

Hmm. Serena was the poster girl for trying new things. A year ago she had dumped her long-time boyfriend and started a course of personal transformation that had seen her change her diet and start running and shed fifty pounds, gain a fantastic haircut and a boyfriend—Joel Wakefield—who was now her husband. Yeah, Serena wasn't averse to trying new things.

So maybe Jackie could afford to do a few things differently. She had a choice: go with her initial reaction of offense, or take her friends' words on board.

"You know we love you, right?" Serena said.

Jackie nodded, her lips rolled flat. And because she did know that, she could perhaps go with option two. "Fine. I'll go east to see my folks, but I'll also arrange a vacation where I do nothing but sip mocktails and swim in the pool."

"I think you'd have more fun with cocktails, not the fake variety," Rachel said slyly.

Jackie caught the way Serena and Toni exchanged smiles, which reminded her. "Didn't you have something to share, Toni?"

"Ooh, how did your new exhibition go?" Anna asked.

Finally, the attention was off Jackie. She settled back in her seat, chewing over her friends' words, while internally bracing for whatever Toni might say next.

"That's going well," Toni admitted, with another small smile at Serena. "The resort has agreed now the trial period is up that they'll keep the exhibition space. We've actually earned enough now that we've paid back the resort for the renovations, so that's exciting."

"Yay! Congrats, girl. You've earned it. That was a lot of hard work." Rachel lifted her glass and clinked rims with Toni.

"She sure has," Serena agreed. "I know Adrian has been thrilled. He and the rest of the management team are talking with other resorts about the possibility of doing similar art galleries in their resorts."

"Ooh! Maybe you'll have to go on a tour like Staci, showing other resorts how it's done," Anna teased.

"Actually…"

"Is that what you've been asked to do?" Jackie asked.

Toni nodded, to the congratulatory squeals of the others.

Ethan seemed to notice their excitement as he blew a raspberry on the colorful floor mat.

Jackie's heart panged. "What will you do about Ethan?"

Toni sighed, her fingers playing with her ring. "Good question, although nothing is quite settled yet. Now being peak vacation time is hardly the time to leave the resort, but I hoped we could get away when things calm down after Thanksgiving."

"October is a long time to wait," Anna said.

"What's this 'we' business?" Rachel asked.

Toni's cheeks pinked. "See, that's the thing. Matt has a trip to London—"

"London, England?" Anna clarified.

Toni nodded. "And he, uh, well, wondered whether we could combine that with a honeymoon—"

"Ooh! Are you two finally talking about dates?" Serena interrupted.

So clearly this was news to her too. That made Jackie feel slightly better.

"I don't know," Toni confessed. "There's a lot to get my head around. Like where we'd live, and how we could make this work, because I really don't think I could live in the city anymore. And I know Matt would prefer to live here in Muskoka."

"I thought you'd once said something about wanting a long engagement?" Anna asked. "Doesn't anyone believe in long engagements anymore?"

"It's probably not so necessary when you are in-laws to a wedding planner," Jackie pointed to Serena.

"And when you're both Christians, and wanting to get busy with you-know-what," Rachel said with a wink.

"Stop it!" Jackie reached down to cover Ethan's ears. "Someone's too young to hear about such things."

"Hey, there's nothing to be ashamed of in wanting to enjoy marital relations with your husband, is there, Serena?" Rachel demanded.

Now Serena's cheeks were pink, but she shook her head. "And if you know you've found Mr. Right, and you're both wanting to not invite temptation, then getting married is better than burning with lust."

"Oh my gosh!" Anna slapped her hands over her ears. "I can't believe you said that."

Rachel laughed. "It's like she's turning into Joel, right? I bet he shares his sermon ideas as pillow talk."

Toni laughed, which spurted Jackie's own amusement, and triggered a wave of laughter from the others, even from poor Serena who was bright red. "You girls are bad."

"Not bad. Just real," Rachel said. "So, Toni, what are you saying? Do you have a wedding date? Is Matt really going to take you on a work trip?"

"We don't have a date yet, but we're thinking about October. And the work trip would be after. That just needs to be finalized too."

"Do you need someone to look after Ethan when you're gone?" Jackie asked. "I could." She glanced at Serena, who was regaining her composure. "Well, we could, between us. If you wanted."

"Especially seeing Serena and Joel are going to have to learn how to care for a baby for when they have their own," Rachel teased.

"Like I said, I don't know details," Toni's cheeks were pink, "but knowing that could be a possibility makes it easier to figure out other things."

"So you're saying you could be looking at a Fall wedding,

and then visiting other resorts, then maybe taking a trip to England as part of a honeymoon," Jackie clarified.

"There's a lot to be confirmed, but that's the gist of it, yes," Toni confirmed.

"Wow. Everyone's getting married," Anna's words held a strain of dejection.

"Not everybody," Jackie clarified, waggling her empty fingers. "No man on the horizon for me."

"What about that nice policeman?" Toni asked. "He was so helpful when Bryant was threatening me. And judging from some of the things he's said, I think Tom is a Christian."

"I don't think a cop is really my speed," Anna said. "Besides, I can't imagine my folks coping with that."

Anna's family was one of the more prominent ones in the local community. "Tom seems really nice," Jackie countered. "You shouldn't let someone's prejudice stop you."

"Says the woman who once said she didn't want to marry anyone who was handsome, rich or famous," Anna shot back. "Prejudiced, much?"

"Nope. Just practical. It's not like I'm going to meet anyone like that anyway. And it's not like I'm looking or needing or even wanting a boyfriend. So there." She didn't know why she added those last two words. It made it sound like a middle-school challenge, when really this discussion was pointless. "Besides, Tom the nice policeman is real, so maybe you could talk with him."

"If he's so nice why don't you talk with him?"

"I have talked with him." After the February incident she'd talked with Tom and many, many others, both in police and other interviews. "He seems nice, but I didn't sense any attraction there."

"Yeah, that's hardly the way to make me say yes," Anna grouched. "I can see that as unlikely as you falling for Mr. Cash."

"Mr. Cash?" Rachel had the instincts of a bloodhound. "Who's Mr. Cash?"

"Lincoln Cash." Anna got out her phone and the picture of a man the others called hot flashed before them again.

"Oh my gosh, could you imagine?" Rachel fanned herself. "I've told Damian that Lincoln is my hall pass."

"Your what?" Serena asked, as Toni giggled.

"Lincoln Cash is my hall pass. Like, if he ever asked me to run away with him then I'd say yes."

Serena's mouth swung open, much like Jackie's own.

Rachel laughed. "Not really. But kind of really," she added with a wink. "Although after his drunken press conference, I don't think I'd really want to take him up on that now."

"I can't believe you'd ever say such a thing," Serena said.

"Would you want to take up with a drunk?" Rachel asked.

"No! I mean, well, no, but I can't believe you would even say such a thing. Marriage means commitment. It means making vows that *last*."

"You know I love Damian more than anything," Rachel said. "But if a hunk of spunk like that was to smile at me, then I'm only human."

"You're married!"

"But not blind." Rachel laughed. "Come on. You all know I'd never actually do anything. But I have to say he looks like someone who knows how to have fun."

"I don't think he's a Christian," Jackie said, her words sounding prim even to her.

"So he needs saving." Rachel winked at Jackie. "And we all know that Pastor Jackie is the best one to do that."

WIND ROARED over the hood of the Mercedes as Lincoln roared up Highway 400, slumped in his seat, sunglasses on, baseball cap pulled down so low it hurt his ears. But he had no wish to be recognized. No wish to deal with cameras or phones or the thousand ridiculous questions since his stupidity from four days ago. Who would've thought a simple tumble off a stage could escalate to a place where there were now calls he should be put into rehab?

Rehab? He *never* drank unless a promotional opportunity demanded it. Bernie, his trainer, didn't allow it. Empty calories she called them, making all his hard work in the gym void. She, at least, was one person who believed he'd only had that one glass of champagne. Even his own mother had expressed her doubts.

"But Lincoln, you know it's unwise to drink so much, and then to mix it with medication."

He grimaced. At least she'd believed him when he'd talked about the pain meds. Other people... not so much. How anyone could think he'd suddenly turned into a heroin addict was beyond him, but apparently that was just one of the stories floating around the gossip channels. It was insane, but he really didn't have anything he could say except the truth. And when people seemed more inclined to believe a lie than to believe the truth it made him question a lot of things. Like whether people thought he really was that untrustworthy. Like who his real friends were. Like whether he should even be in this industry.

Victor Drewe had told him in no uncertain terms that if it wasn't for a signed contract then he would *not* be working with Lincoln again. Whether that was due to his own slip of the tongue or Natasha's rather more unfortunate remarks which had somehow transmuted and were now ascribed to him Lincoln didn't know. But he hoped that at least it meant he wouldn't have to worry about working with Chlolinda any time in the near future. Not when her father was outraged enough on her behalf.

A delay in the rehearsal schedule—that had made him

wonder if Victor was looking for an escape clause and wanting time to find another leading actor—had opened up a spare few weeks. So, instead of returning to hide in California he'd obeyed his mom's directive and had spent the past few days in Toronto, before hiring a car to take him two hours north.

"Go see your grandfather," Mom had pleaded on the phone. "Peter forwarded me Dad's latest message. Apparently your grandfather is desperate for family to see him, and you know I can't leave my work here."

Mom was a school principal and now was peak busyness as they finished the school year. Her vacation time would begin on Canada Day, in two days' time, and Dad's surprise vacation plans to take her to Hawaii meant they wouldn't be heading east anytime soon. Lincoln figured a quick trip—two days max—would be long enough to do his duty and see Granddad, then go stay in a cottage somewhere out of the spotlight and under the radar until either rehearsals began or the next poor sap's Hollywood scandal meant it was safe to reappear.

Easy.

In. Out. Done.

A bird swooped and he jerked the steering wheel, narrowly missing a black GMC truck with a bald driver who owned a meaty fist and a temper. Good thing this convertible had its roof and windows up. He pressed the accelerator and the car took off, and he relished the escape, the adrenaline, the sense he could finally be unknown.

Until he noticed flashing lights behind him. Some non-Mom approved words fell from his mouth as he moved over to the verge, and slowed then stopped the car.

Nerves prickled as the police officer drew in behind him, then after a minute exited his vehicle. Man. Exactly what he didn't want to happen.

The GMC passed, complete with laughing bald man with upraised middle finger.

Lincoln looked away, gripping the steering wheel, flexing his fingers as a foolish thought darted through his brain about gunning the car and speeding away. Nope. This wasn't the movies, and he might like adrenaline but he was no stunt man.

A tap came on the window, and he obeyed the officer's gesture to lower it.

"Sir, are you aware you were speeding?"

Lincoln nodded. "Sorry."

The police officer frowned at him. "Can you please remove your cap, sir?"

"Uh, sure." He did so, and anticipating the officer's next question, reached into his pocket for his wallet.

"Keep your hands where I can see them," he was warned.

"Just getting my license, sir."

"No sudden movements, then."

He picked it out of his leather wallet and showed the officer.

"John Lincoln Cash?"

Here we go, he thought, bracing for the inevitable, hoping for the best.

"You live in Vancouver?"

When he wasn't in LA. "I'm here to see family."

"Uh huh. Are they dying, or something?"

"I beg your pardon?"

"Is that why you were speeding? Did you know you were speeding twenty kilometers over the limit?"

"No. I mean, my grandfather is old, but that wasn't why I was speeding. I don't really have an excuse. But I am sorry."

A wry chuckle passed the man's lips. What—even the police didn't believe him?

Maybe something of his feelings showed on his face, for the officer leaned closer to the window. "It's been a long time since I've met someone without an excuse."

"Today's your lucky day then."

"Huh. We'll see if it's yours." He tapped Lincoln's license on the window. "I'll be back."

Not sure if the man was shooting for a *Terminator* vibe, Lincoln kept his mouth shut, fidgeting as the minutes ticked away. Whatever the fine was he'd pay it. He just wanted to be away from the rubberneckers, many of whom were slowing to see the policeman book the driver and count their lucky stars it was him and not them.

Traffic passed, and he wondered how much longer it would take when he noticed the officer approach again.

"Lincoln Cash?"

"Yes, sir?"

"Well, well, well. I didn't realize today would be *my* lucky day."

And here it was. The downside of fame. What was the guy going to do? Book him and boast about it? "Like I said, sir, I'm very sorry. It won't happen again."

"Have you been drinking?"

"No. I never drink and drive."

"You can blow into this anyway."

He obeyed. Sure enough the reading was clear.

"Uh huh. So that incident in New York the other day—"

"Involved ibuprofen and a headache, not a vehicle, sir."

"Right." The officer studied him. "Can you remove your sunglasses, Mr. Cash?"

"Uh, okay."

He did, and the officer nodded, checked the license again then handed it back before flashing a smile. "My wife will never believe this."

Linc braced. Was he going to fine him or what?

"Hey, I don't suppose you want to take a selfie with me?"

"Excuse me?"

"Come on. Just one. Just to prove to my wife that I actually met you. Otherwise she's never going to believe me."

"Uh, okay."

"You better step out of the vehicle."

Great. Hold him up even longer. But if it meant not getting a ticket…

The next minute was spent grinning awkwardly at the camera, recording a short video where Lincoln waved hello to the man's wife, and assured her it was really him.

"While I've got you, the boys in the station would love it if you could do a short message about road safety."

Really? He was now doing free publicity for Ontario highway patrol? Apparently so.

He stood smiling as the officer held out his phone on selfie video mode and introduced Lincoln, and Lincoln saluted the camera. The officer then advised people to obey the road rules, and Lincoln closed it with a "Drive safe, everyone," before saluting again.

The officer held out a hand. "Thanks."

Lincoln gripped it. "Thank you."

"Now get going, and follow the speed limits and don't make a liar of me—or yourself, Mr. Cash."

"Yes, sir."

He got back inside, and exhaled, clicking on his seatbelt as he waited for the police car to move. When it didn't he figured maybe it was waiting for him, so he slowly eased out in the next break in traffic. Whew. That was something he needed like a hole in the head.

By the time he got to Golden Elms his head was aching again, the sun was sinking lower in the sky, and he wondered if visiting hours would still be open. It had to be, right? Especially if Granddad was wanting to see him. Not that Granddad knew Lincoln was the self-nominated family representative.

He parked the hired car, popped some pain meds, then rubbed a hand through his hair. He probably should have shaved before seeing his grandfather for the first time in over two years. Still, the fact he was here at all would hopefully mitigate his scruffy appearance which he kept for the sake of anonymity.

At the front desk he waited, before noticing a small sign that said visiting hours had concluded an hour ago. He swallowed a mild expletive.

"Can I help you?"

He pivoted to see a brown-eyed, flat-chested brunette of indeterminate age dressed in the attire of nursing staff everywhere. "Hi." He pasted on his warmest smile. "I know it's late but I was hoping to see one of the inmates here."

It took him a second before he realized what he actually said.

Judging from the widening eyes it took her less. "Inmates?"

What was the correct term? A hasty glance at a nearby sign brought clarity. "Sorry, it's been a big day. I meant residents."

She lifted a brow and pointed to the sign. "Visiting hours are over—"

"I know, but I hoped you could make an exception. I've come a long way, and—"

"I'm sure you have."

Her tone held such a patronizing quality that he barely noticed her interruption. Wait, did she mean—?

"But our *residents*," she emphasized the word, "have meal and sleep schedules that we abide by so they are not agitated."

"Yeah, I get that." Man, he didn't mean to sound so curt. "But I've come a long way and I really feel like Granddad would like to see me."

"Then you should make sure you're on time tomorrow then."

His fingers clenched. She seemed to notice as her gaze dropped to his hands then trickled back. Her face leached into further professional impassivity.

"Have you got a problem, sir?"

Oh, he had more than one. But right now his major one was this slight creature who seemed determined to make his evening nearly as pain-filled as that of four nights ago. He gritted his teeth. "No."

"Then you are welcome to return tomorrow when it's visiting hours. Your Granddad will no doubt be pleased to see you then."

He could bet his next pay packet that while his grandfather might be happy to see him she sure wouldn't be. A flicker of perverseness hoped she would be here tomorrow so she'd see him prove his awesome grandson skills. Which made him a solid nine out of ten on the pathetic meter, didn't it?

She hitched a brow. "Was there anything else?"

Frustration swelled through him, the headache from earlier swirling to the front of his face and making it impossible to think clearly, let alone say anything more than a simple "No."

"In that case, goodnight, sir," she said impassively.

"Goodnight," he muttered, before stalking out.

Great. Well, he'd just return in the morning, show up, see Granddad, then return to the lakeside cottage his agent had found for him, even if it had meant paying out the previous renting vacationer way above market value before paying a second time the astronomical rents for guaranteed privacy.

He could lay low, stay off the radar, avoid the spotlight in Muskoka. And no-one—except his grandfather and his agent — would ever need know he was here.

# CHAPTER 3

"avis, how are you feeling today?" Jackie adjusted the pillows as the elderly woman complained about the lack of oxygen, the lack of privacy, the lack of visitors. Patience was certainly a necessary quality in this field, and she'd seen many people enter the industry only to quit when they realized that their compassion and ideals were no match for the steady routine of work that some called drudgery, and dealing with clients who were at times prickly, depressed, or confused. How thankful she was to have an endless supply of patience thanks to the well of God's Holy Spirit inside of her.

Some might question why she chose this field to work in. It certainly held little of the glitz and glamor attached to careers like Staci's internationally published books, or Toni's art, or Serena's work with the rich and famous doing celebrity weddings at Muskoka Shores resort. But Jackie saw her role here as more than a paycheck, instead it was more a ministry where she could offer light, life, and hope, and a measure of peace and joy. At least, that's what she hoped others saw in her, through her encouraging words and actions and smile. Even if some people like Mavis—and that man last night—made it hard.

"Well?" Mavis's face squeezed tight like a pincushion, her hair on the pillows like a gray wreath of tiny twigs. "What do you have to say about that? A woman has to breathe, you know."

"Of course she does. I think we both know that you get as much fresh air and sunlight as you need, and as for oxygen, well, the doctors are the ones who prescribe exactly what you need. Now if you would like me to open your windows to let more fresh air in, then you only need to say—"

"Don't be a fool, girl."

"Now, Mavis, you know I don't appreciate it when you start calling me names."

"I don't care what you appreciate," Mavis snapped. "I need you to leave. Now."

"Very well," she soothed. "I'll send someone to check on you later."

"I don't want anyone to check on me! I just want to be left alone."

Her heart wrenched. Poor Mavis. She'd been struggling with her loss of independence for some time now. Jackie prayed silently for her before heading to the next room.

Bernard was a dear, even if he rarely spoke. His dark eyes seemed to hold almost tangible conversations. "Good morning, Bernard. And it is a good morning, too, isn't it?"

He nodded, and she could almost hear the, "Yes, ma'am." He'd been in the military, once upon a time.

"Would you like me to open the curtains a little wider? The lake looks very beautiful today, all shimmering in the sunlight, like diamonds dancing on the water." At his nod she tugged the curtains away to maximize the view. "It sure is pretty, isn't it?"

His lips eased wider.

"Your flowers are looking good." She fingered a soft-as-silk petal on an African violet. Staci's grandmother, Rose, also had a shelf of these furry-leaved plants.

By the time she left Bernard's room she was almost back to a feeling of normalcy. Normalcy that fled when she saw who was walking down the hallway, dressed in a battered leather jacket with a baseball cap pulled almost to his ears. His jeans looked worn, and although she was no expert they looked way more expensive than the usual clothes she usually passed in the men's section at Target. His face was still covered in dark scruff, and his firm lips were flat, as if he was heading into something unpleasant.

His whole appearance was so intimidating that her chest tightened, just as it had last night, and she had to actively force herself to smile. "Good morning."

He glanced at her, and she got an impression of glittering dark blue eyes under thick dark lashes as he jerked a nod and kept walking.

Something squeezed behind her lungs, but whether it was a jolt of recognizing the man owned a Henry Cavill-like handsomeness, or whether it was the snub of near indifference she didn't care to explore.

"Are you here to see your grandfather again?" She winced at the stupidity of the question. Of course he was. Why else would he be here?

He paused, and she could almost see the agitation as his booted foot twitched, as if she was an unnecessary interruption, and he couldn't wait to leave her presence. "It *is* visiting hours."

"Sure is!" Ugh. Remorse at sending him away yesterday—even though it *had* been out of hours, and Dana, her supervisor, was adamant that protocols must be followed—now made her sound like a peppy cheerleader. She needed to tone it down. "May I ask who your grandfather is?"

His brow lowered. "Dominic McKinnon."

Oh! Was this the man Mac had called an actor? Just as she'd

thought, he looked like an out-of-work drama teacher. But still, he'd come. She'd give him points for that. "I'm sure Mac will be delighted to see you."

"Mac?" He barely pivoted, but somehow she sensed his attention on her.

She shivered. She wasn't used to men who looked so big and truth-be-told a little fierce paying attention to her. But now that his gaze was on her she was aware of her figure-shrouding blue uniform, the fact she hadn't brushed her hair or put on makeup this morning, the utter ordinariness of herself compared to this handsome specimen of manhood. She winced. Now she was starting to sound like Anna.

"Mac?" he repeated, like she was slow or something.

Oh, right. "Mac is what Dominic likes to be called around here. Didn't you know that?"

Now *why* had her mouth insisted on adding that last line? Now he'd think she was rude when she wasn't trying to be. Although apparently some people had a gift in bringing it out of her.

"No."

She needed to make up for this latest misstep. "May I ask if he knows if you're coming?" And that probably wasn't the way. She tried to infuse as much warmth as possible into her smile to make up for the harsh-sounding words.

Again there came that moment of indecision. "No."

"Would you like me to make sure he is fully dressed and ready?" That was more like it. See? She could do nice and welcoming.

"It's already past ten o'clock in the morning."

"That's right, but some of our residents don't see many visitors, so don't feel the need to change from their pajamas. But if you're happy to wait a moment, I'll just go check, okay?"

"Uh, sure."

She pointed to the sanitizing station. "You might want to sanitize your hands while you wait."

She didn't leave him a moment to argue, instead hurrying to Mac's room, and after his call of enter at her knock she obeyed to find him seated at the table, head bent over another crossword. "Mac! Good morning. And I think it *will* be an extra good one because you have a visitor outside."

He glanced up, his eyes wide. "I do?"

"Uh huh. And I think you'll be very pleased to see him."

"Is my son here?" Hope sparkled in the faded blue depths.

Poor man. To tell the truth or not? Oh, how heart wrenching was this? "You'll see soon enough. Now, would you like to wear a different shirt? That one seems to have a stain."

The next minutes passed in a rapid exchange of attire, and she took a moment to put away dirty dishes and mugs in the sink, and do the quickest tidy-up, all the while conscious of the man who was standing in the hallway outside. No doubt he could entertain himself on his phone for a little longer as seemed to be the way of most people these days. Finally Mac was sitting in a chair, the sunshine was streaming in, and he was ready for his guest.

"I hope you'll enjoy. I'll be at the nurse's station in case you need anything. Don't forget if you want to have a nice coffee you can visit the café. You could even go out on the deck seeing it's such a nice day."

He patted her hand. "You're a good lass."

She smiled, and fought the temptation to kiss the man's head. Displays of physical affection weren't overly encouraged between residents and staff, after some inappropriate behavior between residents several years ago. Apparently the need for boundaries for physical affection was supposed to set a good example, but judging from some of the gossip that floated around the building from time to time she wasn't entirely sure it was successful. "I'll let him know you're ready."

She clasped her hands in a praying motion and offered another grin then went outside. Sure enough, Mr. Tall, Dark and Brooding was frowning at his phone.

She cleared her throat. "Mac is ready for you now."

He glanced at her, his eyes still holding that predatory look that made her skin prickle.

"You may find that at this time of day, the aide soon comes around with tea and coffee. You're welcome to have one too, but if you want something fancier, I know Mac always enjoys going to the café we have onsite. There's a deck that overlooks the lake that would be really pretty at this time of day, too."

"Sure," he muttered, his tone giving the impression he was actually saying 'thanks, but no way.'

Whatever. "Here. Let me get the door for you."

He paused, glancing down at her from his superior height. "Do you know who I am?"

Whoa. Okay. Way to go with the arrogance. "Am I supposed to?"

His eyes flared. Wait, *was* she supposed to?

"You're Mac's grandson, right?"

His chin dipped.

She frowned. Now she remembered, she would normally have checked with the front desk to make sure any visitors were on the approved list. She should've done that before, but something about this man made her forget things. "What *is* your name?" At his narrowing eyes she added, "We have a protocol about visitors here. You did sign in at the front desk, didn't you?"

"Yes," he growled.

"Easy." She held up her hands. "How about telling me who you are so I can make sure?"

"How about I don't?" He shouldered past her and grasped the door-handle.

"Excuse me!" she said. "I really don't think—"

"I don't care what you think, lady," he muttered, and opened the door.

Wow. She was half-inclined to barge in and make sure Mac was safe. Why all the rudeness and the mystery? She settled for standing in the doorway—just to be sure—as the pushy grandson removed his baseball cap and turned his grouchy expression into a megawatt smile. She blinked. Okay, so obviously he knew how to put on the charm. Which only made her more uneasy. Who was he and what did he really want?

"Hey, Pop."

She tensed. Would Dominic recognize him? One beat passed. Two...

"You're not Peter."

That's it. She was going to go in—

"That's right. I'm Peter's nephew, Mary's son. I'm Lincoln."

Lincoln? Where had she heard that name before?

"Little Lincoln?" Mac said.

The gruff man chuckled, the sound squeezing her heart like honey. "Not so little anymore."

"That's certainly true," Mac said.

So Mac did recognize him. That was good. A relief, actually. She normally wasn't so lax with protocols, and hated how the man had gotten under her skin and made her forget. There was something about this man that unsettled her. She'd best leave.

But before she could move, Lincoln spotted her still hovering in the doorway, muttered something, then in a swift move got up and with a sneer shut the door in her face. Leaving her with a last impression of his utter rudeness, and shaking limbs, and the need to go to the front desk in order to regain her composure.

Only to discover no man had signed in under Lincoln at all.

NOT HIS FINEST HOUR. Okay, so the little brunette was annoying, but she hadn't deserved that. He might be a Hollywood star, but even he knew better than to treat people like that. His mother would be ashamed of him. And if his grandfather knew that the nurse had been standing in the doorway he probably would've invited her in. So it was good he hadn't seen. But seriously—she hadn't recognized him?

He didn't know whether to be pleased or offended—although that last suggested he was more egotistical than even he wished to admit. It was probably a good thing, he supposed. He was fairly sure one of the front desk staff had recognized him, but if most people hadn't then maybe he had half a chance of hiding up here a little longer.

Having braced for a session of meaningless chit-chat, he was set to dive into his realm of excuses for his lack of a visit when a knock came at the door. His gut tensed. Was the nurse back? But at Granddad's call of "Enter" the door opened to reveal an aide with a coffee and tea cart and an array of unappealing biscuits.

"Thanks, Marvin." Granddad gestured to the tray. "Want something?"

No, thanks. He'd rather save his calories for something he actually wanted. He refused the offer, keeping his head low, waiting until the man left.

"I can't blame you," Granddad said. "The food at this place is good, but the hot drinks are never hot enough."

Linc's heart panged. Maybe he should see about taking him to that café after all. But the thought of his identity being discovered put paid to that.

Granddad gestured to a kitchenette area behind him. "You can make yourself a tea from the kettle there. Jackie keeps it filled up."

Jackie. "Was that the nurse who came in before?"

"She's a sweet thing."

For a barracuda, maybe.

"Always manages to bring some sunshine wherever she goes," Granddad continued.

"Uh huh." Yeah, right.

Maybe his tone was too flat because his grandfather peered at him over his wire-framed glasses. "You disagree?"

"I don't know the woman, so I can't judge."

"Exactly. So don't."

Whoa. Lincoln sat straighter in his chair. Okay, what was spiking his grandfather's tea? Chili powder? Looked like this visit was going to go well. Not.

He glanced at the table, saw a half-finished crossword puzzle. "You like crosswords?"

His grandfather tapped the side of his forehead. "Gotta keep the brain ticking."

Lincoln pulled the puzzle book closer. "What's a six-letter word for irritable?"

His grandfather frowned. "I've already tried these," he complained.

"What about sullen?" Like the nurse outside. The one Pop insisted was all sunshine and rainbows. Hardly. He tried to fill it in. Nope.

"Grumpy?"

"The U fits. And the Y."

"Grouchy?" Pop offered. "No, that's seven."

"What about touchy?" Lincoln touched each square with the pen. "I think we have a winner."

"Fill it in, then," his grandfather said.

Linc did, then pushed it back.

"So, you like crosswords, eh?"

"It's a good way to fill in time while waiting on set." He tapped his brow. "Gotta keep the brain active."

His grandfather snorted. "And what brings you here after all this time?"

"Does there need to be a reason?" he asked. Heaven forbid his grandfather learned Linc's visit here was just the precursor to hiding out.

"You tell me. Considering I haven't seen hide nor hair or any of my family since Nancy passed."

Really? "Nobody has been? Not even Uncle Peter?"

"Nope. I figured you at least were probably busy, with all them movies you're off doing. And I understand your mother can't leave her job, but nobody else has been either."

Guilt gnawed at him. What must it have been like to be stuck here, pretty as the view might be, and not feel any connection from family? "I'm real sorry, Pop. I didn't know. I don't think Mom knows that either." And he was going to tell her as soon as he got a chance. Maybe she and Dad could visit once they got back from Hawaii.

At his grandfather's look of resignation his heart grew soft. Linc might bemoan the interest of a million movie fans, and he knew that while they didn't know him at least there was a semblance of caring. But for Granddad to be here, all alone... "I wish I'd known that you were here."

"You knew. What else were those Christmas video calls about?"

Oh, yeah. Those. "I guess I didn't really think about that."

"No."

Okay, the guilt card was getting pretty heavy about now. "I just hate the thought of you being here without anyone who cares."

His grandfather bristled. "I have people who care. Jackie, she's like a daughter to me."

Huh. Jackie, again, eh? His fingers clenched as he tried not to bristle himself about the implication that this nurse was as important to Granddad as his own daughter—Linc's mother—was. "She's not exactly Mom's vintage," he pointed out. This

Jackie nursing character had to be around Linc's own age. Probably younger.

"I mean, she treats me well. She cares about me. You should meet her."

"We've already met," he muttered.

"Mm." His grandfather's head tipped to one side. "So, are you going to tell me what you've been doing lately?"

"Sure." But he wouldn't share about everything.

The next hour passed as Linc shared about some of his travels, some of his movies, and his grandfather asked questions. It proved a surprisingly enjoyable back-and-forth until a knock came at the door again.

"It's probably Marvin again, here to take me to lunch."

"I can take you to lunch," Linc offered, the words surprising him as much as they seemed to his grandfather.

"You don't want to do that," his grandfather protested.

"Sure I do." How hard could it be to take the man a few yards to wherever the lunch room was? Then Linc could leave, mission accomplished, and get ready for the next part of his secret stay in Muskoka.

"I'll need to get permission to leave the premises."

"Huh?" Oh. He schooled his features as it became apparent exactly what his grandfather meant: lunch, away from the facility, in the nearest town of Muskoka Shores, maybe. Still, he couldn't disappoint him now, not when most of the conversation for the past hour and a bit had proved just how out of touch Linc had been with his family, and especially his grandfather. Who knew the man had suffered a stroke? Linc felt like this was something he probably had known but it had slipped into his subconscious, as Linc's focus had always been on his work. Which made him sound utterly selfish—which he wasn't. He cared about things beyond his movie career and reputation. But as the last hour had proved, maybe he hadn't cared enough about some of the most important things.

"So, uh, where's the best place to eat around here these days?" He had vague memories of a diner on Muskoka Shores's main street, back when he'd visited his grandparents when he was small. Two decades ago.

"I don't know. I haven't left the place much these past years. Not since Nancy passed. She was always the one who liked to try new things."

Linc nodded. He remembered that about his grandmother, too. She always had a quick smile and laugh and said things like "life is for living." A pang of grief rose, forcing him to swallow. "Well, it's about time you did try something new then, isn't it?" He glanced at the wheelchair, waiting in the corner like a chariot. "Do we use this?"

"Yes."

He followed his grandfather's instructions and helped him get into the chair. He'd done some work on a TV medical drama, so had some idea of what to do. "You ready for an adventure?"

His grandfather's chuckle was raspy. "I tell you they won't like it. Not when there is no warning."

The knock at the door came again, and his grandfather called out "It's open."

"Well, they'll have to figure it out, won't they?" He grinned, catching the look of conspiracy in his grandfather's eye. "Don't worry. We're going to bust you out of here."

"You're going to do what?"

His gaze swung to the door which had opened, and sure enough, Ms. Jackie was there. The good vibes instantly left the building. "It's you."

"And it's you." Her smile looked as artificial as his felt before it slipped away. "John Cash?"

Linc coughed. "Yeah, about that."

Her left eyebrow rose, and he was almost tempted to admire the move—he'd long wished he could do a single brow lift, and had practiced it many times in the mirror—when he realized she'd crossed her arms, her expression forbidding further speculation.

"It's my name. My real name." The one used on his driver's license that he'd showed at the front desk. And the name his parents had used after their favorite singer. Which was exactly why he hadn't used the name growing up, instead using his middle name so much so it was all he went by now. Except for certain official documents that sometimes proved helpful at flying under the radar. But hey, which kid ever wanted to be known as a famous country singer? He should at least be grateful they hadn't named him Johnny. His agent had agreed, saying Lincoln had a strong sound, therefore Lincoln he was to all and sundry.

"So Lincoln is your alias, is it? Are you a spy? Or an author with a nom de plume?"

Had she seriously just said *nom de plume*? He bit back a smile. "Actually," while he might have played both of those kinds of roles in movies, in real life he was a solid "no."

"He's an actor, remember?" Granddad said.

Wait—what? He frowned. What else had his grandfather told her? "I thought you said you don't know who I am?" he accused her.

Her brown eyes widened. "Excuse me while I battle the giant ego in the room."

Wow. Feisty, much? "Don't hold back, then," he muttered.

"Mac said you were an actor, not that you were famous."

He swung a look at his grandfather, hunched in the wheelchair, who just shrugged. Then, conscious that move had probably made him look like an arrogant tool, like he was expecting his grandfather to agree, Linc sighed, shoving his hands in his back pockets. Okay, so the woman still didn't know who he was. That was a good thing, right?

"Look, I don't want to cause any problems," he said, using his best to sound conciliatory. "I'm here to visit my grandfather and I'm planning on taking him out for lunch, and—"

"I'm sorry, but that's impossible."

"What? No. Granddad told me he wants to go out for lunch, so I'm taking him."

"No, you're not." She planted her other foot firmly, like she thought herself a giant redwood he'd have to get past. Like he couldn't pick her up and use her for lifting weights.

Linc sucked in a calming breath. Offered his grandfather a smile, then gestured for the bulldog nurse to move into the hallway and out of Granddad's hearing. "All I want to do is to take him to the local diner in Muskoka Shores and have a simple meal," he explained. "I can't believe you're being so unreasonable about this."

"You're not taking him anywhere."

"No?"

"No," she said resolutely.

"I didn't realize you kept people here against their will." Sarcasm might be the lowest form of wit but it was all he had now.

"We don't. We also don't let our residents just leave willy-nilly because some random guy shows up for the first time ever and says he's going to go do something with him."

He didn't know whether to pounce on the 'random guy' comment or be amused at the willy-nilly. He crossed his own arms. "Willy-nilly?"

Her chin lifted. "I can appreciate you wanting to make up for lost time, but it's not a simple matter of let's get out of here and go eat. You can't just leave."

"Oh, yes we can. Watch us."

She didn't shift. "Not without following the usual procedures and protocols you're not."

He swore under his breath. "Why the heck are you being so

difficult about this?" he demanded. "Don't you want him to enjoy time with his family?"

"Of course I do," she snapped. "But I also want Mac to stay alive, and if he goes off to the diner with you and eats and drinks food he's not used to, then there's every chance that won't end well. Are you going to be the one who cleans up his vomit and cleans up any accident he might have because he's eaten foods his system isn't used to?"

Huh? He swung another look at his grandfather, sitting in his chair.

"What about making sure he doesn't choke?" she hissed. "How good are you at helping an elderly man not choke on his food? Have you ever played the role of a doctor in your *acting*?"

She said the last word with so much venom he wondered what her problem was. Maybe she *had* heard of him before. Maybe she thought him the drunken druggie who said inappropriate things and couldn't be trusted. And of those four sins, he'd only put his hand up for occasionally saying inappropriate things.

"Look, I didn't know he had issues with eating. I just wanted to give him a treat. And I thought..." He'd obviously thought wrong again. Gone off in his own imagination without thinking things through. Now she'd pointed out all the potential pitfalls it was obvious he should have thought things through a little more. It wasn't the first time impulsiveness had got the better of him. It was just as well she'd called him out before they'd left. Imagine if his actions had caused Granddad to get sick—or worse?

His shoulders slumped. "I'm sorry, okay?"

The tightness in her expression melted away as her lips curved up slightly, her small smile seeming more genuine now. "I'm sorry, too. I don't normally allow myself to get so riled up at work."

"How riled up do you allow yourself to be?" Okay, judging

from the narrowed eyes it was too soon for tease. "Consider that unsaid," he mumbled.

"Look, I really do appreciate the fact that you want to do something nice for Mac. To be honest he's one of the sweetest residents we have here, and I know he's thrilled to have some family come and visit. Perhaps you could have lunch with him in the dining room today, or if baked salmon or chicken doesn't take your fancy, then you could take him to the café."

"Aren't you worried he might choke there?"

"All of our staff are trained to deal with such matters, so he'd be safe here."

"But what if I want to take him somewhere else?"

Surprise lit her features. "You mean this isn't just a one-and-done visit?"

"I beg your pardon?"

She had the grace to look embarrassed. "Sorry. I shouldn't have put it like that. It's just that we get a number of visitors who haven't seen their relatives for such a long time that they go to great lengths to make up for a guilty conscience by taking them out for all kinds of treats and activities, only to not see them again for years."

"And you thought I was one of them?" Well, obviously she had, otherwise why make that statement? Although why he kept hammering her about something which up until a few minutes ago was actually true was something he didn't want to admit.

"It's apparent you are not, which is wonderful."

She smiled warmly at him, and he suddenly wanted to be the man who lived up to the ideals of her imagination.

"To answer your question, if you want to take Mac out for a visit you need to book it in the appointments diary to make sure we have a staff member who can accompany you, unless you are trained in first aid and CPR."

"I am, actually."

"Really?" Her grin lit up her face. "Well, we just need to see certificates of proof, then we can make those arrangements."

Like he carried such documents with him always. Although the certificate might be on one of the thousands of emails he'd never bothered to open...

"Truly, I am pleased to hear that," she continued. "I know that you visiting is just what Mac has needed. Mac is wonderful, and he never complains, but I know he's been lonely, and rather desperate for family to come."

Did she mean to cut him with every word? "I didn't know."

"Well, now you do, and the fact you're here and staying—"

Whoa. That wasn't exactly the case.

"—and able to spend more time getting to know the wonderful man that he is, well, that really is..."

"Wonderful?" he suggested, his lips tweaking to a wry smile.

She blinked. "Yes."

A moment passed, thick with... something, before a cleared throat drew attention to his grandfather, still sitting in the wheelchair, still watching them. "Well, Pop," he said in a louder voice. "It looks like we might need to change our plans and visit the café here, after all."

Granddad shrugged. "I don't mind. It'd just be good to spend some time with you, son."

Linc nodded, flashing a smile that faded a little as he faced the nurse again. "Uh, thanks."

"You're welcome."

She said that with a slight inflection on the last syllable, making it sound like a question. And sure, he could understand why she might have her doubts. He hadn't exactly been his most engaging-self earlier. "And yeah, sorry about before."

"Which part?"

Now it was his turn to blink. Okay, one: he rarely apologized, and two: just how rude had his tired and head-achy unfiltered self been for her to call him out on multiple infractions? "All of it, I guess."

Her lips twisted to one side, and he suddenly knew a desire to have her smile at himself like she had before. To hear her laughter. To know her approval. Which was dumb. Like, call him arrogant, but he had a whole world of people who approved of him. How many more did he need, anyway? Surely one little nurse and her opinion shouldn't matter.

Except it kinda felt like it did. Her approval felt like it might be worth winning. And as he followed her instructions in helping wheel Granddad's chair and her directions to where the café was, he thought he might try a little harder to connect with his grandfather. And maybe he might hang around a little longer and see if Nurse Jackie might finally find another man of McKinnon lineage to approve of after all.

# CHAPTER 4

"Oh my gosh! Do you know who that is?"

Jackie glanced at the trainee nurse beside her. "Who are you talking about?"

Téa fanned herself. "I didn't pick it at first, but I just did a quick Google search and it's him!"

Jackie swallowed a smile. "Who is *him?*"

"Lincoln Cash," Téa hissed.

"Yeah," Jackie said slowly. "That is his name. So?"

"Oh my gosh! I can't believe you're so calm about this." She scowled at Jackie like Jackie was personally responsible for Téa's unmet expectations. "He's only the hottest guy on the planet."

"Is he?" He'd just looked scruffy to her.

Téa looked at Jackie like she'd suddenly sprouted horns.

"It's just he didn't look that way to me. But then, I'm not a fan of too much facial hair. It always looks like a guy has something to hide." She flashed a smile. "Like maybe his breakfast."

"Oh, you're unbelievable! Have you seriously no clue who Lincoln Cash is?"

Something about that name was familiar. Wait—was he the

man that Anna had been carrying on about the other day? "He's an actor, right?"

"Are you kidding me?"

Okay, judging from the way she was clenching her fists, Téa was in real pain. "Are you okay? Can I get you some pain relief? Do you need a Tums?"

"Ugh!"

Without further ado Téa grasped a clipboard and hurtled down the corridor in the direction of Mac's room. "He's not there," Jackie called, but Téa didn't stop.

Weird. There was no accounting for attractiveness. She wrinkled her nose at herself. Actually, there was no accounting for that moment of weirdness she had felt with him before. Maybe the man held a certain kind of appeal, but she wasn't about to lose her head over him. It seemed there were enough other people willing to do just that.

A little later, as she completed her rounds she couldn't help but wonder how things were going, so she took a break in the direction of Golden Elms' café.

Sure enough, Téa was hovering over Lincoln who had reverted to his baseball cap and sunglasses crossed-arms stoic self, while Mac seemed to be enjoying the attention from a young woman who'd never noticed him much before. For some reason this propelled her closer to the table.

Lincoln glanced up and at once it seemed his body language relaxed. He gave the slightest dip of his chin in acknowledgement.

"Well, hello again," Jackie said. "I hope I'm not interrupting." She shot Téa a raised-eyebrows look then refocused on Mac. "I just wanted to see how you were doing, Mac."

"I'm good. Lincoln here is having fun."

"So I see."

Her dry tone seemed to propel his shaded gaze at her, and

her lips twitched, before she turned to Téa. "I think you'll find your patients are waiting."

"Oh, but I just wanted an autograph."

"Mr. Cash is here in a private capacity, and I don't think that it's fair for him to have to do such things when he clearly just wants to spend time with family. I'm sure you can understand that."

"But—"

"Here." Lincoln sighed and snatched a paper napkin. "Got a pen?"

"Yes, Mr. Cash." Téa pushed her clipboard and pen at him and watched him sign his name. "Oh, thank you so much. Can I get a selfie with you?"

Lincoln glanced in Jackie's direction, but she couldn't read his expression so she shrugged. "Téa, if Mr. Cash is okay with that then you can, but you cannot put this on social media as we do not want his time in Muskoka to be interrupted by fans. If I discover that you've done this, then I will be forced to take action, do you understand?"

Téa's face fell. "Yes."

She positioned her phone and took a picture before thanking him once again and scuttling away.

"You'll take action?" Lincoln removed his sunglasses, his expression now holding a mix of resignation and amusement.

"I'll see she gets an official reprimand," she explained. Which might be hard, seeing Téa was the niece of Jackie's supervisor, Dana, but she'd try at least. "We do have protocols about such things."

"Protocols. I should've known." She was fairly sure that sigh equated with a roll of his eyes. "You get a few celebrities visiting, huh?"

"No. But the staff here do have to sign confidentiality agreements that we won't talk about our residents, and implied in that is that we won't talk about their visitors or families either.

She's a trainee, so she's new, and I'm hoping she'll want to keep her job by remembering these things."

"Remind me not to get on your bad side." Lincoln straightened in his seat. "So how likely is it that she won't post anything?"

"I don't know her too well, but I'd guess it's fifty-fifty."

"Awesome," he grumbled.

"Sorry."

"You've got nothing to apologize for." He glanced at Mac. "It's just a shame it might make it difficult to return."

"You shouldn't let one little fan keep you away from what you intended to do," she said, placing a hand on Mac's shoulder. "I'm sure Mac would love to see you again."

Mac patted her hand. "It's okay. I know the lad is busy."

She fought a smile at the 'lad' comment, amusement Lincoln seemed to share as his gaze met hers in a moment of shared understanding.

Her chest tightened, forcing her to exhale to relax. This man disconcerted her. Was not good for her peace of mind. "Okay, then. I'll leave you two to enjoy the rest of your meal." She managed a small smile for the big man who looked too large for the table, and yet still managed to look like he was poised to flee. "Good day."

Mac coughed, and she knew a moment's concern before it became clear it was a simple clearing of the throat rather than anything more threatening. "Before you go, lass, mebbe you can help us."

"Yes?"

"Do you think you can persuade young Lincoln here to attend the Canada Day festivities tomorrow?"

She pivoted on her heel. "You know about the local Canada Day celebration?"

He shrugged. "Not much. But I'm not sure if it'd be wise. I

mean, I would like to spend more time with my grandfather, but that's problematic now."

"Because of the potential of being known. I see." And while she could understand his desire for anonymity, and that Téa's actions hardly built confidence, she couldn't quite comprehend why he'd choose a small-town celebration over something more in keeping with a celebrity lifestyle. "Well, if you change your mind, you'll find we have a small celebration here in Muskoka Shores. It's not as large as some of the other towns in Muskoka, but we have a band play, and there's food stalls, although some people like to take picnics. And it would be unCanadian to not have fireworks at the end." She shrugged. "It's fun, but probably not your scene if you're used to big parties."

His lips thinned, then he shrugged. "I suppose it could be something to do."

She blinked. "There's nothing else you'd rather be doing?" No fabulous rich-and-famous parties to hang out at? Where were all his glamorous friends?

"But Pop here was saying he was going into town with some of the others from here, so I don't quite know how that would work."

Oh. Right. Because Golden Elms was taking a bus into Muskoka Shores for the daytime festivities there, and Mac had been one of the first to sign up.

"I'm not sure if what we offer here is really up to the speed of those who are used to Oscars parties and the like," she said kindly.

"Believe it or not I don't need constant cameras and people in my face," he said.

Hmm. Judging from the serious look on his face, she'd choose to believe it. "You'd really want to come?"

"It could be fun."

"Unless you get spotted."

"I know how to act a part."

"So I've heard."

He stared at her funnily, like he wasn't sure whether to believe her, then slowly nodded.

"I suppose if you dressed down, you could meet us there at the park." She lifted a shoulder. "It's a free country."

"Or maybe I could meet you here. Take Granddad there myself."

"How good are you at folding up wheelchairs?"

"I'm okay." At her lifted brow he continued. "I had to learn it for a role."

Of course he did. "I still don't think it's sensible. Especially if you're wanting to stay out of the spotlight."

"I can't stay locked away in my cottage forever. And I do want to spend time with Pop, here." He gripped his grandfather's arm.

She studied him, as a daring thought teased then spilled from her mouth. "I suppose it could be fun to see just how good of an actor you are."

"Is that a challenge?" he asked, his lips twitching.

"Look, it's your show. But you might want to dress down a little."

"I am dressed down."

"Yeah, no, not really. Lose the leather, get some flannel, find cheap jeans. I can recommend the local charity store run by our church."

"You're funny."

And he was handsome when he smiled. She told her heart to stop fluttering. "I wasn't joking. And I don't know what vehicle you're driving, but you may need to consider changing that as well if that's too expensive looking."

"What's your number?" he asked abruptly.

"I beg your pardon?"

"Your phone number. What is it?"

"I don't give out my phone number to random strangers," she said indignantly.

"I'm not random. I'm famous." His lips curved up lazily.

"You're arrogant, that's for sure." She was torn between horror at her rudeness and a maniacal desire to high-five herself for making him smile.

"Is it arrogance to tell the truth?"

She frowned. She supposed it was true.

"You shouldn't do that."

"Do what?"

"Frown all the time. You'll get lines."

"Thanks, but I don't frown all the time."

"Uh huh."

His tone said he didn't believe her. "Anyway, that is not the way to get my phone number."

"What is the way?" he asked.

"We have protocols here, and—" She broke off at the sound of his laughter. "What?"

"You and your protocols. You know, you really should just learn to relax and have fun."

"I do have fun!" Why was everyone telling her to have fun? Why was this man who she barely knew telling her the same? Did she really look so frowny and serious all the time? And why, oh why, was she still engaging in this ridiculous banter?

"Sure you do." He smiled, and her heart skipped a beat or three.

Okay, so now she was prepared to agree with Anna, Rachel and Téa and half the world's population apparently, that the man was very nice-looking. A sweat droplet trickled down her back. And maybe even hot.

"I have work to do," she snapped, glancing at Mac. "I'll see you later."

"Looking forward to it," he said.

She nodded to Lincoln then spun and walked away. The man

was beyond smug, and she really didn't need to be wasting her time on someone who clearly had issues. What was it that Anna had said? He'd gotten drunk at a movie premiere in New York? See, she had no time for someone like that.

Except... had he really? Or was that just more of the myth and speculation surrounding Lincoln Cash? How much of celebrity gossip was true?

Such questions kept her company through the remainder of her shift, chasing her as she drove to the small apartment she called home. And while she wasn't proud of herself, she wasn't above Googling Lincoln Cash to find out more about the man, the myth, the legend.

Legend in his own mind, she grumbled. Although Téa seemed enamored, and now she thought about it, Anna and Rachel had seemed rather in love with this man they'd never met.

But she had.

She had even talked with him, smiled at him, bantered with him like he was a long-time friend. Which was crazy. She might've had her fifteen minutes of fame, but she knew she was nobody special. Even if this man had a way of paying attention that made her feel like he really saw her.

Please. She rolled her eyes at her pathetic deluded self. If only Rachel could see her now, studying her computer screen at the man who even had his own Wikipedia page. Rachel would likely laugh or call her a hypocrite for reading movie gossip sites and learning about the man whose list of girlfriends read as long as Jackie's own arm.

She shoved in another mouthful of cereal, crunching her dinner noisily as she flicked through various articles that showed Lincoln Cash emerging from vehicles, kissing women, waving at crowds, lying on famous beaches, falling off a stage in New York, proving the bigness of his life meant he in no way would ever pay attention to a non-entity from Muskoka

Shores. The fact she had moved into his orbit seemed so strange.

One article listed several of his movies, and she vaguely recalled what the girls had said last week. *Incitement*, wasn't it?

An email pinged. She glanced at the subject line then let it slide to join the others demanding she put her computer skills to use in creating websites for people all around the world. Nope. It was now officially clock-off o'clock, and a long weekend to boot, and they could wait a bit longer. She had something more important to do.

She settled back on the couch and flicked on her smart TV, scrolling through the reams of vacuous-sounding titles until she found a movie that matched one on the list she'd pulled up from IMDB. Then exhaled. Was she really going to do this? She winced. She really was.

So she pressed play on the most recent of Lincoln Cash's films.

LINCOLN LAUGHED at himself as he pulled into the staff parking lot of Golden Elms. He smoothed his mustache and smiled at himself in the rear vision mirror. Nice. He might look like he was from the 1970s, especially with these awesome sideburns, but there was no way anyone would link him to Lincoln. He hoped, anyway.

He exited the hired Mercedes—it would've been much better if he could've swapped cars with Jackie like he'd wanted to, but obviously he'd gone about that the wrong way. But seriously, when was the last time he'd had to ask a woman for a phone number? Usually they couldn't wait to give it to him, like that trainee nurse who'd been busy batting her eyelashes before Jackie batted her away.

He chuckled to himself. Okay, so maybe he was a tiny bit

intrigued by the little nurse with fire in her belly, and a small part of him had wanted to see if he could pull this off today just to impress her. Yes, he knew it didn't make sense, but the past two nights had been lonely, and there was only so many movies he could watch before he got bored.

Maybe the inner restlessness of the past few days—or was it years?—had accounted for the desire to do this, too. He didn't know how people could work in the same job all the time. One of the things that had attracted him to acting was the chance to inhabit somebody else's skin, to live a different life to what he'd known, to experience different things to the usual. It was fulfilling, it was often challenging, but man, it was fun. Mostly, anyway. To be expected to show up day after day in a regular work environment was something he hadn't had to experience since he was a teenager stacking grocery shelves two decades ago. Thank God for his lucky break, and the break away from routine and monotony.

He shrugged into the oversize flannel—Jackie's tip about the thrift store had proved it to be a goldmine—and drew into character, inhabiting the space of a man here to visit a relative. Which wasn't hard, as it was true.

Another baseball cap shaded his face as he leaned against the car, waiting for the others to show, and took a moment to look around and breathe in his surrounds.

Lake Muskoka sparkled under a morning sky, the light breeze rippling across the blue in steady, small waves. It looked perfect for boating, which he'd do if he had a boat. Or friends. Tall pines and aspens shaded the pine-needle covered ground from a sun that already felt like it could sear. How the old folk would cope outside he didn't know, but apart from Granddad, they weren't really his concern. Although seeing they were the concern of Jackie, maybe he should let her know that things were liable to get hot today.

Movement at the front door saw an elderly person exit

followed by a staff member dressed in blue. Jackie? He straightened, but no, this was another woman, older, thicker around the middle. Definitely not Jackie.

The nurse glanced in his direction and he ducked his head. So maybe this was a dumb idea, putting himself out here like this. Not that he figured anyone would recognize him in a hurry, but you never knew what people might—

"Lincoln?"

His head snapped up. "Hey, um, Miss Jackie." Man, he sounded like a kindergartener. "You recognized me."

"Uh huh."

Well, of course she had, Captain Obvious. He mentally slapped himself. "All set for the big adventure?"

"What are you doing here?"

"I'm coming with. But hey, did you really know it was me? What gave it away?"

"Your muscles," she said, before blushing.

Aww. His heart softened. How long had it been since he'd seen a woman blush? This one wore no makeup, so it was an easy tell.

"And your car," she hurried to say, as if conscious of her faux pas. "Someone mentioned they saw you driving a Mercedes yesterday, so I figured…"

"Jackie!" the other nurse called.

"I have to get back. Did you, um, want to see your grandfather?"

"You know that's why I'm here."

Her gaze traveled his face, her expression melding to pain.

"What is it?"

"Sorry. But seriously, did you even look in the mirror before you left the house today?"

"Yeah."

"And you thought this"—she waved a hand at his attire—"was a good look?"

"I thought I'd not be recognized straight away, no. Obviously that didn't work out," he muttered.

"I'm sorry to be blunt, but you look kind of ridiculous—"

"Ridiculous?"

"And I can't help but wonder if you'll scare some of the older ladies."

"Excuse me?"

She gestured to his neck. "You look like you need a gold chain or two then you're set as a seventies Casanova."

Who used words like Casanova?

"I mean, if you wanted to stand out today you certainly chose the right look. People will probably think you're dressing up for a role, although I don't know if it's something that you want to have on your social media."

"What do you know about my social media?"

He didn't mean to sound like an arrogant you-know-what, but honestly, for a woman who hadn't recognized him yesterday, and had basically said she had never watched one of his movies, what the heck would she know about his social media? Would she even know he hadn't dared post anything since New York?

"Jackie!" The other nurse was sounding upset.

"You better go."

"And you should change. You'll stick out like a sore thumb, and not in a good way." She shifted to return to the elderly people, and he hurried to catch up. She glanced at him. "What now?"

The note of irritation in her voice plucked a sympathetic chord within, turning his smart-aleck comeback into a genuine, "I just wanted to see Pop."

"Well, he's right there." She pointed to an elderly gentleman sitting slumped in a wheelchair. "Excuse me. I have work to do."

He didn't turn to look at her go, although he was sorely

tempted. Instead he made his way to his grandfather. "Morning, Pop."

His grandfather glanced up at him and blinked. "Do I know you?"

Oh. He had completely forgotten about the facial hair artistry that Jackie had instantly seen through. "Hey, it's me, Granddad. It's Linc."

"Who?"

He crouched down beside the chair. "Lincoln? Little Linc?"

"You're not little." His grandfather's face pushed into an expression of distaste. "And I don't like that mustache."

Linc rubbed a hand over his jaw. Okay, that made two fails in five minutes. This facial fuzz was definitely gonna go.

He became aware of other older men and women around him, and the precarious nature of their balance as they shuffled to the waiting bus. A couple of others were in wheelchairs like Granddad, and he wondered whether the bus had a special ramp to get them on board.

"Here you go, Bernard, lean on me."

It was like his eyes couldn't help it. At the sound of the voice his gaze snapped to where Jackie had her arm around the shoulders of an elderly black man as she helped him to the steps of the bus. The man swayed to the left, almost toppling and squashing her, and before he knew what was happening, Lincoln was by his side, arm around the man as he helped Jackie to steady him.

"Whoa, there. We can't have any accidents until after people have seen the celebrations today, okay?" Linc glanced at Jackie. "Are you okay?"

"I'm fine."

Sure she was. She looked flustered. But whether that was because of the near-toppling incident or something Lincoln's personal brand of charm brought out he didn't know.

"Thank you, but you can go now," she said, her voice tight.

"Hey, just trying to be helpful."

"It'd help if you let us do our job and stopped distracting me."

"Do you find me distracting?" he asked, and was unsurprised by her rolled eyes as she encouraged the man—Bernard, she called him—up the steps and into where the other nurse took his arm and helped him to his seat.

Okay, so he wasn't needed, nor, it seemed, was he wanted. He shoved his hands in his back pockets of his newly acquired jeans—he'd washed them twice, because who knew who had last worn them?—and stood near his grandfather until it was his turn.

Jackie glanced at him. "Are you able to help Mac inside?"

"Yes." Maybe playing meek might make her trust him. She obviously wasn't a fan of over-confidence.

She studied him a moment then nodded, and he helped his grandfather to his feet. "Let's get you ready for the party."

"Are we having a party?" Granddad asked her.

"It's a national party. A party for the country. There might even be cake."

"I like cake."

A memory flashed of Linc's grandmother cooking his eighth birthday cake. He'd wanted one with cars on it—apparently he'd never grown out of a love for fast vehicles—and his mom had been too busy with school reports so it had fallen on his grandparents to hold a party. The cake—complete with Hot Wheels cars—had been the highlight. Yeah, once upon a time Linc had liked eating cake, too.

"Come on, Mac," Jackie's voice intruded. "Let's get you inside."

Linc helped his grandfather up the stairs, catching a glimpse of the wide eyes and moue of distaste twisting the older carer's lips as she glimpsed Linc's get-up. That made three for three.

He exited, almost running over Jackie who was helping a

cantankerous-looking woman with a beak for a nose. "Oops, sorry."

"Watch where you're going, young man," the old woman snapped.

"Yes, ma'am."

He mouthed a "sorry" at Jackie who offered a wry smile in return, before he caught the older woman's comment about "men dressed like seventies adult film stars."

Whoa, hold on. He glanced at Jackie, pointing to the older woman who'd just ascended the steps. "Did she mean me?"

She winced. "I'm afraid so."

"I should go deal with this mustache, shouldn't I?"

"You really should."

He waited a few minutes longer as the rest of the residents entered the bus just in case they needed his muscles—he still couldn't quite believe Jackie had noticed them, let alone said anything—but when it was apparent they could manage just fine without him, he stepped back. Jackie glanced at him, before entering the bus.

"See you there, then," he said.

"You're still coming?"

"Once I deal with this." He pointed to his mouth and jaw. "Where will you be?"

"Probably near the bandstand. That's in the park near the lake where most of the activities will be. But we usually have a spot claimed near the big oak where there's a number of wooden seats. You might see us there."

"Okay. Keep an eye out for me, okay?"

Her lips lifted on the right. "I can keep an eye out, but it doesn't mean I'll recognize you, depending on what awesome disguise you come in next time."

"I obviously need to try harder."

"Obviously."

They stared at each other, and for a moment he wondered if

she meant try harder at his disguise or if she meant something else. But then, a cough from inside the bus drew attention there was a bank of windows filled with aged faces staring avidly at them, which reminded him that he needed to go. "See you soon, then."

"Not if I see you first." She smirked before stepping inside and closing the doors before the bus finally rumbled away.

His mouth hitched. Yeah? Game on.

# CHAPTER 5

This was insane. She was officially insane. She was here, at the Canada Day celebrations at Muskoka Shores, surrounded by people she knew, people she worked with, people she cared for, and all she could do was keep searching the crowds for a handsome celebrity in hiding.

Which was wrong. She *had* to pay attention to the residents. Bad things happened when carers didn't. She'd heard about some truly awful things that had happened—runaway wheelchairs and lakes—when people got distracted, but she couldn't tamp the stupid strain of excitement at the thought that Lincoln Cash, *the* Lincoln Cash—yes, she was so sad she was starting to think in italics like a teenager—was out there, or soon would be, and would be looking for her.

Which had a hurricane reading of maximum five for utter dumbness and potential for catastrophic devastation. He wanted to spend time with his grandfather, she *knew* that. But there'd been something in those moments when he'd studied her and she suddenly wished she wasn't so plain and flat-chested and boring, and she'd wished he wasn't so famous or handsome or such a non-Christian.

A silent sigh escaped, and she glanced at the red-and-blue plaid picnic blanket, covered with a variety of safe and elderly-appropriate foods. That last one was the marker she'd always clung to. There was no point in being interested in a man if he wasn't a Christian. Hence her long, lonely existence, as the few guys she knew who were Christians had soon been snapped up by other, more interesting women, that she'd barely had a chance to have her interest piqued, let alone try to do anything about piquing theirs. Not that she could. She seemed to have a faulty gene which meant flirting was impossible. She wasn't an Anna, or a Rachel, or a Serena. She lacked basic boy-awareness or something. Maybe she just had really low hormone levels. Which meant this... thing... whatever it was between her and Lincoln was completely weird. As well as wrong. For even if she was living in the real world, and Lincoln wasn't a huge movie star, how could anything work out when they didn't share basic beliefs?

Besides, hadn't she found contentment in God? She'd said as much to Toni, Serena, Anna, and the others at the Galentine event back in February. And it had been true. It still was true. She *had* found contentment. She didn't need a man to 'complete' her. That was God's job. She knew that. So any thoughts of dissatisfaction or discontent meant she wasn't leaning hard enough on God. Which meant maybe she needed to lean a little harder, to refocus her thoughts heavenward, to pray a little more. And take every thought captive that wasn't thankful, or God-honoring, or led to fruitless daydreams. Which all meant it would be best for her to shove thoughts about Lincoln Cash away, and to focus on what was real instead of playing with make-believe.

The conversation among the older folk had slowed, the warm weather and band playing jazz tunes dulling conversation to only what was necessary. She forced herself to ask Mavis how she was doing, and sure enough, the response was tetchy.

She bit back another sigh, her gaze lifting to where Bernard sat. He winked at her, and she smiled, as she always did. It was funny how some people could infect others with their mood, and others could break through that with a simple gesture like a wink or smile. In the past two days she wasn't sure what kind of mood she was projecting.

"What's a nine-letter word for celebration?" Mac asked nobody in particular, slouched over his crossword.

"Party?" Mavis offered.

"I said nine letters, not five," he said.

"Well, excuse me," she sniffed, folding her arms, petulance settling on her face like a crumpled tissue.

Fabulous.

"Carnival?" Maureen, the other nurse on duty, suggested.

"That's only got eight."

"Merriment?" someone else offered.

"Nope. The E fits, but that's all. Come on," Mac grumbled.

"You might need to give us some more clues," Jackie said. "So the second letter is an E. Are there any other letters?"

"Third letter is an S."

Es... "Festivals?" Jackie offered, after thinking through the letters.

Mac frowned. "The first part fits. The last bit not so much."

She moved over to where he sat, his crab-like handwriting scrawled in the tiny boxes. "Ooh, look, it ends in a Y. So what about Festiv..." She lingered, waiting for him to find the right word.

"Festy?" asked Mavis.

Mac rolled his eyes. "Festivi...Festivity!"

"Well done!" Jackie clapped her hands as he filled it in.

He grinned at her, and her heart was soft as she returned it. Forget men whose smile held caramel-like charm. This was what she was called to do, how God wanted her to spend her time. Those silly daydreams were just that. Silly.

"Perdón."

She glanced up.

A man in a red baseball cap, wearing long shorts, a loose t-shirt, and sunglasses atop a red-and-white paint-streaked face grinned at them. "Hola."

She struggled to follow the long stream of Spanish that followed, her gaze falling to his shoulders, his biceps, his forearms—good grief, what was wrong with her that she was noticing such things? It didn't matter what a man looked like. It shouldn't matter. It *wouldn't* matter. Not for her, anyway. God was enough. Really.

When he kept talking she pushed herself upright from her seated position. "I'm sorry, sir. I don't think we can help you."

He bowed his head. "Si, senora," he said, shuffling away.

She saw no reason to correct him—senora she would never be—until she recalled the look of mischief in his blue—blue!—eyes. "Hey!"

She hurried after him, grabbing his arm and forcing him to face her.

"Gotcha." He smirked.

She slapped his arm. "Are you crazy? Or should I say loco?"

Lincoln laughed. "You're funny when you're all fired up."

"Yeah? Well, you're just…"

She couldn't finish her sentence, conscious of his nearness, conscious he must've had a shower or something as well as a shave because he smelled really good. Like sea-salt and pine.

"I'm just what?"

His voice held a husky tenor that made her stomach swoop like a seagull after a French fry. Then her gaze fell to the red mark on his arm as she realized she'd just hit him. She winced. "Sorry for hitting you."

He rubbed his arm. "It really hurts, too."

"Really?"

"No, Jackie. It felt like a moth's wings."

A what? "You think I'm like a moth?" Wow. Secret, stupid delusions crashed to the ground with an almighty clatter. She rated as nothing more than a boring, tiny moth?

"Actually," his head tilted as he studied her, "I think you're more like a sparrow. Little and brown and always busy."

"Wow. That's like one thousand percent better."

Amusement crossed his features. "You care about what I think of you?"

"Don't be ridiculous. Although it's obvious you care what others think of you."

"Well, I couldn't have people think you're associating with a star from a certain type of film." He waggled his eyebrows.

"Please don't say that—or do that—ever again. I'm trying to get the memory of what you looked like before out of my mind."

He chuckled again. "You're funny."

"You're weird."

"Yeah, but you're the one still talking to me. Hey," he leaned closer, "is it just me or are all the old folks looking at you?"

She glanced behind her. Oh, how embarrassing. She gave a little wave. Hitched her lips up in a grimace-like smile. "I think they're all looking at you," she countered.

"Yeah, they're probably wondering how you suddenly got so good at Spanish."

Ugh. How was she going to explain this? Did she even need to? Maybe she could just say she was trying to help him find his way to wherever he needed to go. She personally knew that place should be anywhere as long as it was far, far away from her. "I need to get back." She waved a hand at his patriotic get-up. "Good effort, by the way. You fooled us. Well done."

His lips twitched in the world's quickest grin as he sidled a fraction closer. "Hey, do you think maybe later we could—"

"Jackie?"

She glanced across at the new voice. Serena, holding hands with Joel, followed by Toni and Matt who was pushing baby

Ethan in a stroller. A savage pang to be in a couple like them tweaked her chest. She pushed it down. Pasted on a smile. "Hi there!" So apparently she needed to start leaning on God a *lot* more than she'd previously believed.

Serena glanced at the man beside Jackie, then back at Jackie, before saying, "Are you going to introduce us?"

"Uh." Jackie glanced at Lincoln.

"Are these friends of yours?" he asked in a soft voice.

"Yes." He studied her, then nodded, and held out his hand. "My name's John."

Huh. John, not Lincoln. Okay. It was his legal name, but for a minute she'd thought that he trusted her enough to trust her taste in friends, to know they were never the type to leak a confidence. Clearly, she was being completely delusional today.

There was a round of handshakes as she explained he was one of the family members of one of the residents, which was how they had met.

"I see." Serena didn't do subtle, her raised brows and smirk making it plain exactly what she thought she saw. Toni's expression held a similar measure of doubt.

Which wasn't true. Which begged to be explained away. Except she had a horrible suspicion that the more she tried to explain the more guilty she would look and that it would be another case of protesting too much. Best to just get back to the residents and leave Lincoln or John or whoever-he-wanted-to-be-known-as to his own devices. "I better get back. I'm working today."

"Don't work too hard," Matt said.

She nodded, knowing he knew it to be true, after he'd nearly burned out earlier this year. "I won't." She hugged Serena and Toni, ignoring their whispers of "we need details, please" and pressed a kiss to Ethan's head, then lifting a hand in farewell for the three men. "See you later."

"I thought—" Lincoln began.

"I need to get back. Excuse me." And before she could succumb to his charm or the blueness of his eyes or whatever this crazy connection between them was, she turned on her heel and moved away. Back to the residents of Golden Elms. Back to duty and responsibility. And away from the big, handsome temptation that was Lincoln Cash.

∼

"What's a seven-letter word for boring?" Pop asked.

Lincoln shifted from his position on the ground. He'd had to confess his non-Spanish status to the older people, mostly because he'd realized that his disguise had meant he'd not be able to hang out with his grandfather as he'd wanted if he didn't own up. And they'd been cool. Well, all except that Mavis woman, who looked like she hadn't been happy about anything since about 1963. And Jackie, whose open-mouthed surprise when he'd followed her had reverted to frowning speculative looks when she thought he wasn't looking. He knew because he'd kept looking.

"Dreary," someone said.

"Seven letters," Lincoln mumbled.

"Tedious," Jackie said, eyes narrowed at him.

"It fits!"

As his grandfather scribbled in the words Linc shot his own raised-eyebrows look back at her. "What?"

She shrugged and glanced away. Okay, whatever he'd done he was sorry. Well, not that sorry. Maybe it was grade-school-like but he kind of enjoyed stirring Miss Jackie. He wasn't used to people who didn't treat him like some kind of king. And the fact she was blunt—and sometimes outright rude—made him pay attention. She wasn't afraid to call him out on some of his obnoxious behavior, which he wasn't so arrogant to not recognize.

Yeah, Linc could be a jerk sometimes. There were countless articles online about just what a jerk he could be, but he put that down to a quick tongue and not thinking about how his words might be received. He regretted it. Just like he'd started noticing how some of the things he said actually did sound arrogant to other people's ears. Which made him want to be different.

He glanced at her again, noticed her face turn away. Had she been looking at him? Man, how big-headed could one man be? She clearly didn't like him, even if her brown eyes held a mysterious ability to hold his, like a magnet.

"It's so hot," Mavis grouched again. Her first name really should be Oscar. What was the female version? Oscarina? Oscette?

"We'll be leaving soon," Jackie promised.

They were? And he'd barely had a chance to talk to her. Or his grandfather.

Lincoln rolled to his side and propped himself up on one elbow. "Want to go for a walk, Pop? Or maybe a wheel?"

His grandfather nodded. "Sure. It'd be nice to see the lake a little closer."

"Okay." Lincoln scrambled to his feet. Dared to look at Nurse Protocol. "Do I have your permission to take my grandfather to the lake?"

Her lips flattened and she nodded.

"Thank you." His tone sounded haughty even to his own ears.

So much for showing her a different side to him.

"We will be returning in half an hour, so if you can be back by then that would be good," she said.

"Sure." He glanced at his Apple watch, taking note of the time, then crouching next to his grandfather. "Point me where you want to go."

He followed his grandfather's suggestion and steered him over uneven ground then down near the sand where little kids were building sandcastles. The air was filled with the scent of barbecue and hot dogs, and the synthetic scent of sunscreen. The water was filled with youngsters and a few older people—man, how old did that make him sound?—and he smiled at how people were having fun. As he steered the chair past a group of people around his age he heard his name.

"John?"

He turned, and recognized Jackie's friends from before. Huh. So they hadn't put two and two together. He lifted a hand, then bent to his grandfather. "Do you mind if we go and say hello?"

"You know people here?"

"They're Jackie's friends."

"Ah." His grandfather smiled.

"What's that look for?"

"Nothing. Take me over. I think I recognize one of them now. He comes to the home and does a church service."

That made sense. Now he remembered hearing Jackie say something about church. *Our church*, she'd said. That probably explained the slight look of judgement he'd seen in her eyes. Maybe she hadn't known who he was to begin with but he got the impression she sure as heck knew who he was now, and had a pretty thorough understanding of just how much of a sinner he was. Well, he'd say hello then get out of there.

He steered his grandfather to a more shaded spot and introduced him.

"I've seen you at Golden Elms," Joel said to Pop.

"I've seen you too," Pop rasped.

The curvy woman—Serena, he thought her name was—chuckled. "It must be nice to have your family visit today."

"It's been a while."

Guilt stole across Lincoln's chest. "Work gets a little busy sometimes."

"And what do you do?" the other man—Linc thought his name was Matt—asked.

"A bit of this, a bit of that. I'm usually in California, so visits here are rare." *Redirect, redirect.* "What do you do?"

Matt mentioned something about investment funds, which made Lincoln shrivel a little inside. Anytime anyone talked math and figures he internally glazed over, conscious that while he could remember his lines after one glance, he'd always felt a little less-than when it came to math and his IQ. He'd never been good at sums. Hence his deep appreciation for his agent and manager.

"Are you having fun?" the brunette with the baby asked.

"It's been nice," he said. He couldn't quite figure out the dynamics here. Clearly the brunette and the blond money man were an item, but he only saw a ring on her finger, and not a wedding ring, either. So who did the baby belong to?

"And you know Jackie?" Serena asked.

Ah, the real reason for why they'd called him over. "Not as well as some," he said, offering a smile. She grinned back, and he could almost feel the prickles of hostility from her husband, so he dimmed back the smile to neutral. "Not at all, really."

"You didn't recognize her name?"

"Jackie?" What, was she some kind of celebrity? He bit back amusement. "Sorry, I don't even know her last name."

"Ah." The two women exchanged glances.

"What?"

His grandfather brushed a hand through the air. "It's not surprising he doesn't know. He lives in a world of his own and probably never heard."

"Heard what?"

"About our local hero," the Serena woman said.

The brunette nodded. "You should look her up online. She's pretty amazing."

"I get that impression from what my grandfather has said." But why they felt like he needed to know he couldn't quite figure out.

"She's pretty special," Serena said.

"Okay," he said politely.

Joel laughed. "I think you're freaking the man out, honey." He held out a hand. "It's good to see you, John."

"John?" His grandfather said. "I thought you were going by Lincoln these days."

Ah. Now there were five faces staring at him curiously. "Lincoln is my middle name," was his lame explanation. Looked like it was about time to go before his grandfather said anything—

"He's an actor," Pop said.

"Really?" The brunette looked skeptical, like his get-up suggested he acted on TV commercials or something.

Which was actually perfect to go with. "Yeah. Nothing too major." Not compared to Tom Cruise, anyway. He made a show of looking at his watch. "Sorry, better go. Someone here has a bus he needs to catch."

"Nice to meet you," they chorused.

"Maybe I'll catch you at the chapel service tomorrow," Joel said to Pop.

"Maybe." Pop nodded. "I remember my Nancy used to love going."

Lincoln remembered that too. Part of his visits to his grandparents had always involved a visit to church. He vaguely remembered going out the front after making a prayer one time, something that had made his grandmother very happy. Huh. He hadn't thought about that in years. "We better leave before someone gets antsy."

"Speaking of," Joel said.

"Here you are."

At the sound of Jackie's voice he spun around. "We were just coming, weren't we Pop?"

She didn't look impressed. "We've been waiting."

"Sorry," Serena said. "It was our fault. We got talking and

distracted him. Oh, but that reminds me. You should bring him to the fireworks tonight."

Jackie's head swiveled to meet his gaze then back again. "I don't think so."

"Come on," he said, knowing it would annoy her, but unable to stop his tease. "That sounds like fun, hanging with your friends here, getting to know you more. Like, I didn't know you were a celebrity."

Her mouth sagged then snapped closed as she shook her head.

"What? Don't be shy. As soon as I get a moment I'm apparently going to need to Google you."

Her shoulders sank. "It's nothing, really."

"Please," Toni interrupted. "She saved our lives! That's hardly nothing."

He blinked, fascination making him see Nurse Jackie in a new way. "You saved people?"

Jackie turned to her friends and huffed, "I can't believe you told him."

"But we haven't told him," Serena protested. "Not anything specific. But you can find out all you need to know when you Google Jackie O'Halloran and Muskoka Shores." She said this last to Lincoln with a wink.

He chuckled, and held up his hands when Jackie glared at him. "Sorry, but I didn't know my grandfather was in the care of a superhero."

She sighed, shook her head, and grasped hold of his grandfather's wheelchair handles. "We're going to be late."

"Let me." He gently pushed her away, catching her low-voiced comment to her friends.

"I don't know if I'll be here tonight now."

"Aw, come on," Serena wheedled. "Bring your friend if he's not busy."

"He's not my friend," she hissed.

Her words stung. He sucked in a breath and turned. "Actually, I'd love to come. Where and when?"

"Here and whenever you can make it."

"I'll see you then, then."

"You wouldn't dare," Jackie said.

"I think I just did." He smirked.

He was pretty sure that sound was the gnashing of teeth.

"Just wheel Mac to the bus, please. And don't say another word."

"Sure."

Okay, so that last one he really hadn't meant to slip out. But it was too easy for him to banter with her. She was like a fire he wanted to keep poking, to keep the sparks alight, and every poke caused him to warm and feel more alive than he had in years. He liked her, the fact she could see through his bull and call him out on it. And he liked how she had deep compassion for his grandfather and the other residents at Golden Elms. And then to learn that others considered that she actually was a hero? He'd only ever played the role of one, and now his finger itched to pull out his phone and discover all he could. All in all, that made her intriguing. He couldn't wait to return and find out more tonight.

## CHAPTER 6

The sky was getting darker by the time he returned to the same spot on the beach. Sure enough, Joel, Matt, Serena, and the other woman whose name he couldn't remember were there with someone he was fast thinking he might never forget.

Jackie.

She whose exploits at a wedding back in February had apparently saved three lives from a madman. Little, quiet, unassuming Jackie. He'd Googled her and found hundreds of articles and interviews that mentioned her, that had reported on the remarkable presence of mind then near superhuman strength that had seen her lift a heavy Muskoka chair and throw it at the man as he tried to attack Matt and Toni and Toni's baby. The cottage Linc was staying at had a Muskoka chair. They were heavy, and he could barely lift one, let alone imagine throwing it. Her insistence that it was a miracle put him in mind of those people who lifted cars to save trapped people. Miracle or not, sometimes humans could do extraordinary things. And the fact this woman was so humble about it made him all the more intrigued.

"Hey."

"John! Welcome." Joel motioned to a blanket on a patch of sand. "Pull up a pew."

That's right. The man was a pastor or something. He'd always thought they had to be old. The ones in the church Gran had taken him to years ago always had been. He nodded to the others then found a spot near Jackie.

A million questions begged to burst from his lips, about how she had done what she'd done, about her courage, humility, and strength. He settled for, "Hi."

She fiddled with her hem of her pink t-shirt—she looked more relaxed in casual clothes—as she glanced at him. "I'm surprised you came."

He shrugged. "I figured it had to be better than just staying home."

"Good to know where we rate."

"Hey, I didn't mean it like that—oh." He caught the glimpse of her smile in the dark, and realized her wry comment was humor.

She glanced at the others then shifted slightly nearer. His heartbeat increased. Maybe she was less standoffish in the dark. "Aren't you worried about being spotted?" she asked in a lower voice.

Way to go with the misread. He shrugged, hoping to appear nonchalant and not like her nearness bothered him. "I figure it's dark enough so it shouldn't be a problem."

"Hmm."

"What's with the hmm?"

"I don't get it."

"What?"

"Why you're insisting on being here with us. When you could be anywhere, doing anything with anyone, and yet you're here."

"Maybe I'm patriotic."

"Uh huh."

"Or maybe I like small town celebrations."

"Right." Her tone held skepticism.

"Or maybe I like your company," he dared.

"Please. We both know that isn't it." His protest was cut off as her head tilted. "Are you studying for a role about a small-town guy? Is that it?"

"No. Hey, why is it so hard to believe I just want to relax here in Muskoka?"

She stared at him through the darkness and finally nodded. "Okay, I'm still not buying, but just so you know I have some friends who are returning to join us soon and they may know who you are."

His chest tensed. "I'm simply John here."

"You're simply flirting with danger by staying," she countered.

"Flirting, huh?"

She rolled her eyes and eased back. "Don't complain to me when you're busted. I'm happy to keep your secret, as these guys would be too," she said, gesturing around her. "But I can't promise the same about Anna and Rachel. They're getting food now, but I'm warning you to be ready for when they return as they're both huge fans."

"Yeah?"

She huffed out a breath. "You don't need to sound so conceited."

"Sorry, I can't help it."

She shook her head and shifted away, going to the little baby crawling on the picnic blanket shared by Toni and Matt.

He watched as Jackie picked him up and started talking to him in a soft voice he couldn't quite hear, and his stomach tensed with new emotion. She wanted to be a mom. That was as apparent as the brown hair trickling down her back. She looked prettier with it flowing loose, less tightly bound. He got the impression that she was pretty tightly wound most of the time. And wondered when the last time was that she'd actually relaxed.

"Hey, John, have a chip." Joel passed a packet of artificially-enhanced excessive calories his direction, and he was sorely tempted to say no when he realized that he needed to make friends and a pass on the chips might mean a pass from them in other ways too.

"Thanks." He took a couple and shoved one in his mouth, and then discreetly crushed the other in his hand and sprinkled the crumbs on the sand. Gross. He didn't like the artificial flavor, but he appreciated the gesture. He didn't know what it was about this group, but in Jackie he'd sensed a genuineness, something authentic he didn't see too often in his industry where everyone wanted something from him and would fake their way to getting it. It was clear Jackie wanted nothing, nothing except for him to care about Mac, which he was more than happy to do. This quality of caring made him want to know her more, to know more about these people she counted as friends. Even if some of them might have a crush.

"So John, where are you from?"

Okay, so here was some of that tight rope Jackie had been hinting at when she talked about the challenge of walking between fiction and the truth. How much should he reveal that was real? "I grew up not too far from here," he admitted, "and my grandparents lived in Muskoka Shores for as long as I can remember."

Serena nodded. "I remember your grandmother, Nancy, was her name, wasn't it?"

He nodded.

"I remember she used to come to church. She always made these ginger cookies for morning tea that were so delicious."

Huh. "I remember them." Afternoons on vacation, sitting on their porch, gazing out at the sparkling lake after a big day swimming or fishing. Grandma had loved to fill him up on milk and ginger cookies.

He grew aware that Jackie still held the baby but was listening. He tried not to make it look like he'd noticed.

"Then you moved away," Joel prompted.

"Yeah. My mom got a job in BC so we moved there, and I've lived and worked on the west coast since."

"And what did you say you do?" Serena asked.

Okay, here went nothing. "I um, do some work in the entertainment industry."

"Really? Like writing or something?"

She didn't recognize him either?

Serena's smile held apology. "We have an author friend, so it'd be fun to know if you two knew each other."

"What's her name?"

"Staci Everton."

"Sorry. I don't know her."

"That's okay. She's been on a book tour in New York and…"

The rest of her words were lost as his heartbeat hammered at that city's name. Okay, so this was nice pretending he could be normal, that he could fly under the radar, but it didn't stop the juggernaut of reality that was his life. He hadn't switched on his phone since he'd arrived, and he'd muted all notifications to carve out a degree of peace. But the list of missed phone calls and emails had to be piling up. His publicist would be getting worried. His fans on social media were likely panicking because he hadn't even sent out a tweet. They probably thought he'd gone into rehab or was dead or something…

"John?"

The name took a second to register. "Sorry. I was a million miles away." Or nearer a thousand kilometers, anyway.

"So, where are the others?" Jackie's voice brought him back to himself. "It's taken a long time for them to get food. I don't know about you all, but I'm getting hungry."

Food. Right. Yeah. He joined the chorus of murmurs, even though he wasn't that hungry, and he was pretty sure any food on sale here wouldn't be trainer-approved. Not that his trainer was around to see him eat. Not that he had any appointments with Bernie scheduled soon. Or maybe he did, and the phone silence meant he didn't know.

But living in this part of the world, on the go-slow, so it seemed, felt like a different version of reality, like what his life could've been if he hadn't been scouted on a Vancouver street and left a life packing shelves to have a short-lived modeling career before he'd fallen into acting. Well, hadn't actually fallen. More like had an opportunity in a small indie-film open up that saw him selected in a new dystopian TV show that became an instant hit. Those drama classes in school had paid off.

Here, it felt like he could maybe breathe again, without the crushing weight of other people's expectations. He felt like he could almost go back in time and find the John Lincoln Cash he'd once been before fame. Someone who cared, was connected, had roots. And that here, maybe, that it was even possible to be that man again.

"I'm back!" A woman appeared, using a Jack Nicholson voice a-là *The Shining*. "Here you go. Hot dogs for all, plus a few extra." She gestured to a man holding out a flat box. "Dr. James saw our plight and stepped in like a caped crusader."

The man set the box down between the picnic blankets as a smell of ketchup and mustard tickled Lincoln's nose.

"I can't believe the queues tonight," the woman said, seating herself next to Serena.

"Where's Damian?" Serena asked.

"Oh, he's taken the kids down to the water, so I'm off duty for a few minutes at least. After dealing with the kids all day I think I've earned a break. Oh, hello." She peered through the darkness at him. "Who are you?"

"Jackie's friend," Serena said, her voice holding a smirk.

"Well, hello Jackie's friend," she purred.

He didn't need a Matt-sized IQ to figure this was one of the fans Jackie had warned him about. "John."

"Rachel," she said, hand on chest. "Nice to meet you."

"This looks good," Jackie said, distracting him as she held a hot dog. "You want one?" she asked Lincoln.

"Thanks, but I'm okay."

"There's enough," she assured. "Our friend Anna just texted to say she's on her way and bringing more food so there'll be plenty."

"Okay, then, thanks." He grabbed one that looked less sauce and mustard-attacked. If he couldn't eat clean food, then he'd do his best to avoid too many extra preservatives.

"Thanks, Rachel. Thanks, James," Jackie said, holding up her fully loaded dog before taking a bite.

"No problem," the other man said. He glanced at Lincoln. "Hey. I'm James."

"John."

Rachel laughed. "We just need a Mark and we've got our four gospels." She pointed to Matt. "Matthew, James, John. See what I did there, Joel? You should be proud of me. I made a Bible joke."

There was a round of chuckles. "Except it's Matthew, Mark, *Luke* and John," Joel pointed out kindly.

Yeah, Lincoln had thought it sounded slightly wrong.

"Never mind, James. You're still okay in our eyes," Rachel said. "Hey, you should tell them what you told me about Staci."

"Yeah, where is she?" Toni asked. "I thought she'd be back by now."

James swallowed his mouthful and put his hotdog down. "She got talking to her agent in New York, and she told me it was okay to tell you all, because she'd like your prayers, but it seems she has some movie people interested in optioning her books, so she'd stayed to talk to them this weekend."

Lincoln tensed amid the round of "That's awesome!" and "Congratulations."

Yeah, there were a lot of movie people out there, it didn't mean he would be in their circles. But still, he'd need to be careful.

"Did she say which book?" Matt's girlfriend—Toni, that's right, he remembered her name now—asked.

"I think it's the first one."

"Oh my gosh, that's so exciting," Rachel said around a mouthful of hotdog. "I hope they get someone hot to play the lead."

Uh oh.

"Mmm. Do you think Lincoln Cash would do it?"

He choked, then as faces turned to stare he tried to swallow, but it was like a boulder was in his throat. It only eased when Jackie handed him a bottle of water and he could finally gulp it down.

"You okay there, buddy?" James asked.

"James is a doctor, so if you're choking he's the man you need," Serena said.

"I'm fine," he rasped. "Bit of food went down the wrong way."

He passed the bottle back to Jackie, but she murmured, "Keep it."

"So, John, tell me more about how you and Jackie met," Rachel said.

"There's nothing to tell." Jackie's voice was flat. "He's the grandson of a resident and joined us on our outing here today where we met everyone, and Serena invited him back tonight."

"Oh." Rachel's voice held disappointment. "I thought Jackie had a man-friend at long last."

He caught the way that Jackie's shoulders slumped, and he got the impression that this wasn't the first time that she'd been teased about a boyfriend—or lack thereof. But he didn't know what to say, or what could ease this situation without making things ten times worse.

"He's not, and I don't need one, so there's nothing to see here," Jackie finally said.

Wow. He'd worked with a number of voice coaches over the years and he was pretty sure he identified that tone as defeated.

And it stirred the strangest desire to show her she was more valuable than that.

IT WAS QUITE possible she was going to die tonight. Between the land mines of conversation with Rachel and the heart pangs that constituted her interactions with Lincoln, she wasn't sure she was gonna make it to the fireworks. What on earth had possessed him to want to come tonight? Loneliness she understood, but when a man explicitly said he didn't want to be recognized, and that he wanted to fly under the radar, what was he doing among hundreds, if not thousands, of people, pretending to be just like them?

And then, when Rachel, one of his superfans, mentioned his name he'd almost given himself away with a choking fit. What would happen when Anna finally made her appearance?

She peeked at him now, and had to stifle a spurt of hysterical amusement. What would Rachel say if she knew her crush was sitting a meter away?

"Are you okay?" Serena asked Jackie.

"I'm fine."

"He seems nice," she murmured.

Jackie shook her head. "It's not like that."

"What *is* it like?"

"You're embarrassing yourself," Jackie hissed.

"I think I'm embarrassing you, and I have to say, that is kind of a good thing."

"Who's embarrassing?" Rachel asked, as if she wasn't the queen of embarrassment herself.

"Nothing," Jackie quickly said.

"Are you two talking about Jackie's new man?" she said, in a voice that Jackie wasn't convinced could not be heard by the man in question.

"Keep your voice down," she whispered.

"He seems nice," Rachel said. "It's a bit dark to tell what he looks like, but if his voice is anything to go by then he's plenty fine."

Way to go with not being shallow. "He's not anything to do with me," she said firmly. "And I'd really appreciate it if you stopped assuming otherwise."

"Oh, come on," Rachel said. "You finally show up somewhere with a guy and you don't expect us to notice?"

"I didn't show up with him. You know that I came here alone. He just showed up."

"But you obviously know him enough to hand him your water bottle."

How had she forgotten that Rachel possessed eagle eyes? "That was an act of charity," she insisted. "I wasn't about to crush Mac's spirits by letting his grandson die."

"Hmm. I'm not convinced."

Jackie shrugged. "Don't be." Honestly, why was she the one having to deflect when he was the person who had got her into this mess? "Go talk to him if you don't believe me."

"Is it just me or does Pastor Jackie sound just a little defensive?" Rachel asked Serena.

"Come on, Rachel, leave her be. It's nice she has someone to talk to."

Jackie's heart stung. She knew that Serena didn't mean to sound condescending, but she still felt patronized all the same.

"What will Anna say?" Rachel asked. "Look, here she comes."

Serena's sigh echoed the one in Jackie's heart. She really

didn't want to have to deal with the fallout guaranteed to eventuate when Anna's disappointment was made known. She knew Anna desperately wanted a boyfriend, and the sight of a man associated with Jackie—even though there was nothing romantic there—was sure to be difficult to cope with.

Anna was carrying a cardboard box of her own. "Hi, everyone. Sorry I'm so late. The party went on forever, but I managed to grab some leftovers."

Joel stood. "Let me take that for you."

"Sure, thanks." Anna sank into the spot where he'd been next to Serena. "Whew. I didn't realize how far it was from the parking lot to here." She rubbed her arms. "Good workout, though."

Joel lowered the box to reveal a selection of doughnuts and cream-filled delicacies.

"Got any healthy treats in there?" Serena asked.

"I made sure they put aside an apple tart for you." Anna pointed to a small pastry, before taking a doughnut.

Serena scooped it out. "Thanks."

"Jackie?" Joel asked. "Gonna be tempted?"

"Only because it's unpatriotic to say no." She snatched a chocolate doughnut. "Thanks."

"John?" Joel asked.

"John?" Anna asked, peering behind Jackie. "Who's he?" she added in a whisper.

Oh dear. She braced. Here goes…

"Someone Jackie met at work," Rachel murmured.

No, that made it sound like—

"Jackie has a boyfriend?" Anna's voice was way too loud.

"No," Jackie hissed. Bits of doughnut flew from her mouth. How uncouth. She bet Lincoln didn't see too many women spraying people with their food. Good thing it was dark.

"When did this happen?" Anna's voice now held a tremulous wobble.

"It's new," Serena whispered.

"It's not," Jackie insisted. "I mean, it's not anything. Oh my gosh, I can't do this. There is nothing to see." Frustration made her turn to the man behind her. "John," his name sounded foreign on her tongue when in all her thoughts she called him Lincoln. "Do you mind telling my friends why you're here?"

She caught the glint of his smile through the darkness. "You invited me, didn't you?"

"No!"

Serena chuckled behind them. "I invited him."

"See?" Jackie knew she sounded petulant, but she still felt boxed in a corner of his making. And now her friends were making all kinds of wrong assumptions.

"So you're not going out?" Anna asked him.

"Anna," she hissed.

John—Lincoln!—laughed. "I'm only here for a while visiting family before heading back west. So no."

Why did her heart sink a little at his words? "See?"

"Okay. Sorry for jumping to conclusions." Anna leaned back on her hands. "It's just hard feeling like I'm the only one without a boyfriend."

"I know." Jackie squeezed her hand. "But you're not alone, remember? God is always with you."

"Yeah, but it's just sometimes I wish He had skin on, and could give me a hug, and let me know I'm loved."

"You *are* loved," Jackie reassured her. "You just need to remind yourself of that. Our feelings don't need to dictate how we see ourselves. You know God loves you."

Anna's sigh and murmured yes wasn't especially convincing. But it was the best she could offer right now.

Rachel dusted off her hands and rose unsteadily from the sand. "I suppose I should go and be a good mother and find that husband and those children of mine. I'll see you good people later." She winked at Lincoln. "And I hope that means we'll be seeing you too, John."

"Nice to meet you," he offered.

"Thanks for lining up to get the food," Joel said to Rachel.

"No problem. We were already there, so it meant we got it quicker than if you'd had to line up half a mile behind us." She flashed a smile. "Enjoy the fireworks." She pointed a finger at Jackie. "Especially you."

Jackie bit back a groan, then another, as she heard the muffled chuckle behind her. How could Lincoln think this was funny? She dusted her own hands, half inclined to leave.

"Don't go," Serena whispered. "Stay for the fireworks at least."

"I hate that everyone is misunderstanding this," she murmured.

"If it doesn't matter, then don't let it matter." Serena eyed her seriously. "Unless it does matter?"

She shook her head.

"Then stop making a big deal about it, otherwise people will start thinking there really is something to it all."

Jackie flattened her lips and nodded.

"Hey, it looks like they're getting ready," James said, pointing to some barges on the lake.

"You might want to cover Ethan's ears," Serena said to Toni. "It gets pretty loud."

"That's why we brought these." Toni drew from her baby bag a set of cute blue headphones and carefully placed them over Ethan's ears. He tried to push them off, but his mother wrapped him in her arms and held him.

There was a boom, and the night sky exploded with a splatter of red and gold sprinkles. The crowd all "oohed" and "ahhed" as the fireworks display continued.

Jackie grew aware that Lincoln had moved closer to her, his long legs stretched out on the blanket as his head tipped back to watch the display. She snuck a peek at him, tracing the outline of his nose, his strong jaw, his neck, his chest before snatching her gaze away. Just because she so happened to be sitting next to one of the most handsome men in the world didn't mean she had to gaze at him like he was dessert.

"It's so pretty," Anna murmured.

"It's so good it's a clear night," Matt said, placing an arm around Toni who leaned into him.

From her position she could see the fireworks reflected in the lake, and the light showed Joel holding Serena in a similar embrace.

Her heart grew tight. Imagine if she was in a relationship, if there was a man in this world who loved her, who cared for her, who noticed her, that she could watch fireworks with. For all her attempts to comfort Anna, she understood what loneliness felt like. A sudden tug of longing made her catch her breath.

"Are you okay?" Lincoln's husky voice wafted past her ear.

She nodded, drawing her knees up and wrapping her arms around them. She didn't want to draw attention to how near he sat to her. It wasn't wise to harbor thoughts about him. He might be nice—much nicer than she'd first assumed—but as he'd said before, he'd be leaving soon, so that was that. And besides, as far as she knew, he wasn't a Christian, so that really *was* that. She had no desire to allow her emotions to get the better of her mind and soul. God didn't want her to be yoked with an unbeliever, and she knew that meant a non-Christian man was out of bounds for her. But oh, oh, she wanted to know love.

Suddenly she understood Anna's pique, the way she sighed and carried on about feeling alone, about not wanting to be single all her days. Truth be told neither did she. But she wouldn't admit that. Her friends might tease her and call her Pastor Jackie, but she had worked hard to cling to faith and trust God's ways for her life. And that meant trusting Him to open the right doors and close the wrong ones. And if that meant He never opened the right door for a man to walk through, then she had long ago settled in her heart that would be okay.

And it *would* be okay.

No matter how handsome the temptation. No matter how nice a guy could be. If he wasn't a Christian, then she had no right thinking on him in that way.

As if that man would be thinking about her in that way, anyway.

# CHAPTER 7

*L*incoln studied the small building. The stone and timber church was the same one he used to visit decades ago, but now it was like a forcefield did not permit him to enter. He was already late. He should just turn around. Joel hadn't really meant his invitation last night after the fireworks. Inviting people to church was probably something he did all the time anyway. And he could bet his next movie contract that Jackie had no expectations of seeing him there. She had barely said goodbye, let alone offered a smile that he could take with him to his dreams.

But when he'd woken this morning, and the long day stretched out before him with nothing to do except visit Pop again, he had felt a desire to check out this place. Of course, there was every chance a heathen like him entering a service might mean the walls and roof caved in. But Joel had assured him he'd be welcome. And now, with the music and singing indicating that the service had actually started, maybe he could sneak in and find a spot at the back…

"Morning."

He peered over his shoulder as a young family hurried their way toward him.

The woman flashed a smile. "Are you coming in? We don't bite."

"Rachel." He recognized her now.

Her expression lit. "John, from last night!" She paused, clutching the arm of the man beside her. "Damian, this is the man I was telling you about. Jackie's *friend*."

The man shook his head slightly, as if used to his wife's antics, and stretched out a hand and Linc gripped it. "Damian Taylor. These are our kids. You're welcome to come sit with us."

"Thanks. But, um…" It was too much, too overwhelming. "I was just passing."

"Oh." Rachel's face fell. "Well, you're always welcome in our church if you change your mind."

"Thanks." He pulled his baseball cap lower and took a step back. "Enjoy."

Damian nodded, and hurried his kids up the steps and inside, Rachel pausing to look back at him curiously.

He ducked his head and moved away, annoyance tightening his gut as he strode away. So coming into town had been a dumb idea. And it felt even dumber because now he wouldn't be able to hide in the back row of the church. Instead, he was prowling the streets of Muskoka Shores looking for something to do. And while there were stores aplenty—with everything from a bookstore and an in-demand ice-creamery to a place selling vintage toys and another selling nuts—the place was buzzing with tourists, and he was running the risk of recognition with every step he took. Maybe he should just get back in his car and go see his grandfather after all.

But there had been something in the conversation last night, something in the easy camaraderie between Jackie and her friends even despite the teasing, something that made him long to feel a part of things. To not feel like he often did where his 'friends' wanted something from him. To not feel the undercurrents of tension and competition that made him second-guess their motives. These people didn't know him, so wanted nothing from him. He liked that. He wanted that for himself. He wanted to feel like he was accepted just for being himself.

And more than that, even with the tease, he'd felt among these friends a sense of peace. It was so long since he'd felt any degree of peace that it had a sense of a siren call to him. His life was one of striving, of comparison, of wanting to be seen to be the best. He didn't know how to rest, to let it go. He sensed here in Muskoka that was possible, but he couldn't stay forever.

"Lincoln?"

He turned, eyes widening with surprise. "Jackie."

"What are you doing here?"

"What are you doing? I thought for sure you'd be in church."

"I'm running late." Her mouth twisted. "Obviously."

In the bright sunlight he could see the shadows under her eyes. "You didn't sleep well, either?"

"I had some things on my mind," she admitted. "You?"

"Same."

Like how long he could keep his phone switched off for before being an adult and reconnecting with the real world. Like how long he could hide out here without being given away or giving himself away.

"Well, I'm going in." She gestured to the church. "You're welcome to come too."

His heart thudded, as that same something that insisted he get to town this morning insisted that he agree to go inside the church now. But whether it was because of this woman or something more he didn't really know. "Are you sure? I don't want to cause you any problems."

"You don't have to sit with me. But if you want to come, you'd be welcome."

"Could I sit with you?" he asked. How had those words fallen from his mouth?

Her eyes widened. "Why?"

He shoved his hands in his pockets. "I was just thinking if the roof caves in because I'm there, I might have half a hope if I'm seated near you."

Her lips pressed together. He noticed those lips today. She'd worn lipstick for the first time, and they showcased perfectly shaped lips. Perfectly natural lips, without a hint of filler. Lips that were currently pulling into wryness and suggesting he needed to say something else, fast. So, he settled for the truth.

"And it'd be nice to sit with a friend."

"A friend?"

He nodded, hoping she'd agree.

"You've got plenty of those," she scoffed. "I've seen pictures of your groupies."

"They're fans, not friends. I… I don't have many real friends."

Her lashes lowered, and he could almost see the battle inside as she struggled with what to say. Finally she looked up at him. "Okay then."

She moved up the path, and he hurried to open the door. By now the singing had stopped and an older man—not Joel—was standing at the front. A few curious faces turned to see them, and he followed her to a seat in the back row.

The pews were like he remembered, but the rest seemed the same. Quilted verses hanging on the walls, a stained-glass picture of Jesus and a dove, although the front area held music instruments, and not the organ he recalled.

The man was talking about something and the sensory overload—sights and sounds and scents, like a subtle fragrance of jasmine drifting from Jackie's hair or perfume—meant it took a while before he settled enough to start to pay attention. But soon he had stilled enough to listen, even though some of the words the man spoke did not make sense. Why was he talking about atonement? Lincoln had seen the movie—he liked Joe Wright, the director—but he had never quite understood the concept. And what did that have to do with a runaway child?

"We cannot atone for our sins," the man said. "We can never be good enough. We can never do enough good things to earn God's favor. But that is what Jesus came for. To make a way for us to have a relationship with God."

He could never be good enough? What kind of stupid talk was this? What was the point of people trying to do good in the world if it didn't mean anything?

That same thing that had caused him to hesitate outside the church now fell on him again. He wanted—needed—to leave. He glanced at the door, caught Jackie's glance at him.

"Are you okay?" she asked softly.

He nodded, not trusting himself to speak. He gripped his knees, forcing himself to remain seated as the man talked on.

The rest of the service passed in a fog, and he was glad for the song leader's tip that the next song would be the last. It meant he could murmur to Jackie, "I need to go," and she glanced at him with wise eyes and nodded.

So when everyone rose he did too and eased out of his row then out the door, where sunshine and freedom met him again. He had to get out of here. He didn't belong. Whatever that... that *presence* was before, was something he didn't want to experience again.

"Lincoln, wait."

He glanced behind him. Jackie stood on the steps. "What is it?"

She hurried to him. "What's wrong?"

He threw a hand through his hair. He must look like a mess. "I don't know, but I couldn't stay." He looked past her. Others were making early exits. "I need to go."

"Of course."

He nodded, then pushed his sunglasses on and drew his cap

from his pocket and shoved it on. It made a flimsy disguise but it was better than nothing.

"Are you going to see Mac today?" she asked.

"I don't know. Probably. Maybe."

"Okay."

The way she said that, looking all small and forbearing, spurted words to his mouth. "You could come with me."

"To see Mac?"

"To hang out. I—" He glanced back at the church. There were more escapees now. "I don't want to be alone, but I can't do people right now."

Her lips curved. "So I'm not a person?"

"You're different." She was safe. Someone he could relax with.

Her head tilted, and she studied him gravely, and again he sensed the battle within. Come on. What was so wrong with her spending time with him?

"I'm supposed to have lunch with Anna and Toni today," she said slowly.

"Blow them off and have lunch with me."

"I hate breaking my word to people."

"I'm sure they won't mind. Just tell them an emergency came up to do with one of the retirement home people."

"You're an emergency, are you?"

Right now he felt like one. "Please?"

"Why?"

"Because," he swallowed then admitted the truth, "you're easy to be with, and I think I can trust you. I want to hang out with someone who is starting to feel more like a friend than most people I've known for years."

"Because I call you out on things?"

"That, and because you're different. I get the feeling you care. And… and I like that. But hey, if you'd rather not, I understand. I'm not everyone's taste, I get that."

A beat passed. Another. Then she said, "Okay."

"Okay what?"

"I'll have lunch with you."

"Thank you." His heart eased and he gestured her to where he'd parked his car.

"But on one condition."

"Name it."

Her smile appeared then was gone so quickly if he'd blinked he might've missed it. "We're having lunch strictly as friends. No falling in love with me, okay?"

He swallowed amusement. "Fine. But just so you know, you have my permission to fall in love with me."

She suddenly veered away, and he had to run to catch up with her. "Hey, where are you going?"

"To my car," she said.

"I thought we could go together."

"I thought that too, until your ego just inflated and I realized there would be no room for me as well."

He chuckled. "You're funny."

Her face was serious. "You say that like you think I was joking."

Shoot. She wasn't?

Then she cracked a smile and he realized that she was. "You're way too good at messing with me," he complained.

"Some people bring it out of me, apparently." She tilted her head. "Are you sure you want to have lunch?"

He'd never been so sure of anything. "Let's do this."

She stared at him a long moment and then nodded. "But I'll follow you in my car."

"You don't trust my ego?"

Her lips twitched. "I don't trust the gossips around here."

Hmm. Good point. He didn't want to do anything to damage Nurse Jackie's reputation. So he gestured to the parking lot, and together they walked to their cars and the great unknown.

WHAT ON EARTH was she doing?

Jackie glanced out the huge picture window to where Lake Muskoka sparkled in the sun. Eating here, alone with a man who she was still pretty sure wasn't a Christian, blowing off her friends, what in heaven's name was she doing?

But it was precisely that, the fact she had felt this compunction to go, even when she hadn't wanted to. It was like heaven was compelling her to say yes to his invitation, even though everything else screamed that this was a bad idea.

She had read the articles. She knew he had been—probably still was—a player, that he'd squired dozens of actresses around. More. When she'd made that flippant comment about him not falling in love with her she'd said it more for her own benefit than for him, like her ears needed to get the memo and transmit it to her heart. And his "fine" had only reiterated that, that she was foolish to wonder if he might think of her in any way beyond the merest friend. But even that felt like an honor, that she was one of the privileged few to see beyond the glossy veneer to the man inside. To see someone who thought antipasto platters made for a great lunch, who'd paid attention to what she had said she liked to eat and made it happen, ducking into the gourmet food store to pick up a hamper of the most expensive treats.

Someone who had seemed torn at church, firstly about going in, then about John MacPherson's message about the prodigal son. And it was that moment, when she had sensed he wanted to leave, that had made her start to pray for him in a deep and real way. That same sense had made her chase him outside, and she wondered if he'd find it annoying, but had been relieved when he seemed glad to see her. He seemed to be struggling with God, and while she hated to blow off her friends she couldn't leave a drowning man adrift, not when she knew Someone who could give him peace.

Her phone buzzed again. She glanced at the text. Anna. *Are you okay?*

*Yes,* she typed back, then switched off her phone.

"Okay, here's a coffee." Lincoln placed it on the coffee table in front of her, then took a seat on the leather couch beside her. Not too close, she noticed with relief. She had no intention of stirring up feelings that could go nowhere. And there was something about the man's aftershave that went a long way to stirring feelings she hadn't experienced before.

"Tell me if it's not okay. I'm still figuring out how this coffee machine works."

She took a cautious sip. "It's good." Not quite as good as at The Coffee Blend in town, but the man's ego didn't need to know that. For all his bravado, he seemed a little fragile at times, as witnessed by his raw vulnerability when he'd admitted to having few friends. That had been the final push she needed.

Okay, so she didn't really know any famous people—she'd met a few, like hockey star Dan Walton and his wife Sarah, but didn't really know them—but she sensed it was rare for celebrity types to admit to having millions of social media followers but few friends. And while part of her wondered if this was all some kind of elaborate plot of his to do something with her, but for what she didn't know—research for an upcoming role? She doubted he had anything more nefarious in mind—another part of her hurt for him. She sensed his loneliness, that he'd actually enjoyed yesterday's times with others when he could relax and just be. He didn't have to be the showman. He didn't have to be 'on' or 'Lincoln Cash'. And in those moments she had seen behind the at-times egotistical talk, and seen someone who was kind and thoughtful, who cared about his grandfather and the other elderly people, someone who was trying. Why else would he have chosen to spend last night with her friends?

She glanced at him now over the rim of her coffee cup. He'd been looking at her. Again. "What?"

"Thanks for coming."

"Thanks for inviting me." She gestured to the living room with its huge bank of arched windows that overlooked the lake. "I've never been inside a place like this."

"My agent was able to negotiate it last minute. It's way too big for one person, but it had privacy, which was important."

And a private dock. And a hot tub. And million dollar views she bet were even nicer at sunset. "Are you feeling okay now?"

"Okay compared to what?"

She shrugged. "I meant earlier today at church, but I suppose compared to New York would work, too."

"It's weird, but sometimes I can almost forget about that." His head angled. "How much do you know about that, anyway?"

"I heard you'd fallen off a stage because you were supposed to be drunk."

"I wasn't. And I wasn't on drugs, either."

She nodded, catching the way he looked at her like he wanted her to trust him. "I believe you."

He exhaled slowly. "Thanks. Just for the record I've never done drugs. I've never even smoked one cigarette." Another sigh. "I get migraines occasionally, and I took some pain meds and I had one glass of champagne—one glass, Jackie—and they took pics of that and assumed I was drunk." He rubbed a hand over his face. "I barely drink, so why they leapt to that conclusion I don't know."

"You're an easy target."

"Maybe." He groaned. "And then Natasha said that stupid thing about Chlolinda, and suddenly I'm the bad guy. Like, I might've thought it was true, but I didn't actually say it."

"What did she say?"

"Something about how Chlolinda wasn't high on the IQ scale, that she was searching for a braincell or something like that."

Jackie winced.

"I know." He held up his hands. "It was unkind, and believe me, I'm not claiming to be an intellectual here, but it's like we have to be so politically correct these days that we can't actually speak the truth. And some of the stuff Chlolinda has done is just dumb."

"She probably doesn't appreciate it being pointed out though," she said.

"I know, and it was mean, and didn't need to be said. But still, I wasn't the one who actually said it." His face screwed up. "Now I think on it, I did say something dumb, sorta mocked her when she talked about being in a real movie."

Jackie wasn't about to tell him she'd seen that interview too. Or that she could understand the temptation to mock someone making silly comments.

"I guess it's understandable they have a go at me, especially when linked to my fall from the stage." He rubbed his face again. "Man, I looked like an ass."

She bit back her smile. She had a feeling he was actually referencing a donkey, and not… anything else. "At least you had nice hair."

He laughed. "Nice hair? So you did see some pictures then?"

"I felt it wise to do a background check, to make sure Mac was in capable hands."

"Yeah, you won't find much about my background on any of the sites. My agent and publicist and I have worked hard to make my career about my career, and not other things."

Other things. Like relationships? His family? These mysterious migraines she'd never read about in any article? Tempted as she was to ask, she'd respect him by not going there. Heaven forbid she seem like a groupie.

"Do you enjoy acting?" she asked.

"Sometimes. Most of the time, actually. Sometimes we get stuck with scripts that aren't exactly what we originally signed up to do, or directors who don't seem to really know what they're doing. The acting part is fun, but I don't like some of the marketing, even though it's obviously a necessary part of the job."

"I can't imagine doing what you do." She sipped her coffee, glancing at him. How bizarre. Yep, the man was still there. Looking at her. This wasn't a dream.

"Well, I can't imagine doing what you do. How do you manage to have patience for all of those people?"

"I think I was born with more than my fair share."

"You're so good at your job. I don't know how you can keep smiling when Mavis keeps being such a…" He squinted. "A witch."

"She's got her own issues. The hardest thing is for me to remember that."

"Well, I think you're amazing."

Her heart leapt, but she tamped down the emotion. No falling in love, remember? It was probably best to get this conversation headed to where she wanted it. "So, tell me about church today."

He instantly looked uncomfortable, and she rued having pushed the topic so bluntly.

"I mean, I was surprised to see you there."

"Joel invited me."

"Joel invites plenty of people, but they don't all come." Which made the fact he did… impressive. And made her more curious. "Did you ever used to go to church with your grandmother?"

"Yeah. When I was a kid."

She studied him. She'd attended the same church in Muskoka Shores since she was small, but couldn't picture him.

"Just on vacations." He shrugged. "My parents didn't really

do church otherwise. They were always too busy, or I had sports, or work, or theatre group, or whatever."

She nodded, giving space for him to talk. She sensed this conversation could either naturally flow and release some of his experiences, or her careless words could dam him up forever.

Through the windows she could see the glimmer of lake, and the two Muskoka chairs positioned near the water. What a perfect place that'd be to see sunsets. The afternoon sky held a blue that made her heart soar as she prayed for him, prayed for wisdom to know what to say—and what not to.

"I haven't thought much about church since I came here, to be honest," he admitted. "I remember though…"

"Remember what?" she prompted gently.

"Remember when I was here one time there was some visiting minister who invited us out the front. I can't even really remember what happened, but I think I prayed a prayer. My grandmother was really happy about it."

She blinked, as her heartbeat grew rapid. "Did you pray to become a Christian?"

"Maybe. Probably. I don't remember."

She stared at him. "Do you believe in God?"

His lips turned wry. "I wouldn't have gone to church today if I didn't."

"Do you believe that Jesus died on a cross and took the punishment for all of our sins?"

He exhaled. "Want me to be honest?"

"Please be honest," she whispered.

He studied her a moment then glanced away. "I don't know if I do anymore."

Her heart felt like a piece of paper someone was crumpling in their hand.

"I mean, it's all a lot, isn't it?"

"What do you mean?"

"I mean, Jesus, dying on the cross and coming back to life

again. I can see why as a kid I might've believed that, but as an adult, I don't know."

"I believe it's true," she said quietly.

"I get that, and I don't mean to knock your beliefs or anything, but I just don't know if it's true."

She had no words. For all that her friends might mock her as Pastor Jackie, right now she couldn't think of a word to say that might convince him. *Lord, help.*

The silence now held a tension, something she couldn't quite explain. He seemed to feel it too, his foot jiggling, like agitation begged to leave his body.

"You could talk to Joel, or I have some books you could read," she began.

"Thanks, but I don't really want to talk about it." His blue eyes held a warning. "Some things are private, aren't they?"

Yes. "But when they are good things, things that bring peace and joy and contentment, should that be locked away?"

His scrutiny held an intensity she didn't know what to do with. "Leave it, Jackie."

Emotion pricked the back of her eyes as a swooping sense of loss and sadness for him drew tension within. Still, she nodded and glanced away.

"Hey, I want to know about you and the Muskoka chair."

"How did—oh."

"Yeah, oh." His expression held slight amusement now. "Come on. Talk me through what that was about."

"Haven't you Googled me?" she said, taking a leaf out of his own book.

"I did," he said bluntly. "And I couldn't believe it when I read about the fact that a little bitty woman could pick up a chair and throw it."

Little bitty? "I'm not that little."

"You're not that tall. Which made it all the more amazing."

She pushed back in her seat. "Well, in that case you probably saw the articles and maybe an interview where I described it as a miracle." She turned to face him. "You know that I'm a Christian, and when I was at Joel and Serena's wedding I 'just so happened,'" she rabbit-eared the words, "to feel this need to check on Toni, Joel's sister, because she'd been being harassed by an ex. So I went outside and 'just so happened' to be there when the ex came along and started making threats. I got my phone out and filmed it, because I knew that Toni needed proof that the ex was making threats like that. And then I realized he had a knife, so I did what anyone would do and looked around for some sort of weapon—"

His eyes had widened, his lips tweaked to one side.

"—something I could use to stop him, but I didn't have anything except my phone, and then I just felt this... I can't describe it as anything but a righteous anger fell on me. Like, how *dare* this man spoil their special day because of his selfishness. And I think it was in that moment of sheer anger that I picked up a chair and 'just so happened' to manage to throw it."

His mouth parted.

She hurried on. "Fortunately, it got the ex and not Toni or Matt or, heaven forbid, little Ethan. It was only later that I realized that Rachel was there and had somehow recorded that bit, too." Before uploading it to Facebook, where it had taken on a life of its own, going viral. Then the interviews had started, and her meager fifteen minutes of fame. Fame? No, thank you. "The police used that as evidence to convict him and he's now behind bars."

It was funny how that she had shared the same story so many times but hadn't really felt it be absorbed so intensely as right now. Lincoln was looking at her with what looked like respect in his eyes, shaking his head a little. "A real-life superhero."

"Please. Don't be ridiculous."

"I'm not being ridiculous," he said. "I've played the role, but never had a real life and death situation where my actions mattered. You're amazing."

"No. Like I said, I think it was a miracle, that God gave me the presence of mind and the strength to lift and throw that thing. I think most people would've tried to help."

"Yeah, I don't know. I think most people would've tried to save themselves rather than put themselves in harm's way."

"I wasn't in harm's way," she pointed out. "That was Toni and Matt and little Ethan."

"Is Ethan the ex's?"

She nodded.

"Now it makes sense," he murmured, as if to himself. "You care for Ethan, huh?"

"Yes." Why, was something wrong with that?

"I noticed it the other day," he said. "You looked like you should be working in a preschool, not with old folk."

"I'm happy doing what I do."

"I know. I mean, I can see that. Anyone can tell you like your job. But you looked like you enjoy little kids too."

She did, but she wasn't about to confess that she longed to be a mother. What was the point of that? Especially to a man who was obviously not a Christian. He might be someone she was prepared to call a friend, but that was about as far as it could go. It wasn't like he was about to start praying for her or anything. "I enjoy hamburgers too, but it doesn't mean I want to work at McDonald's."

He chuckled, and she couldn't help but notice the little laugh lines around his eyes. "You're funny."

"You keep saying that. It'd be enough to make an insecure girl feel like you're calling her weird."

"Good thing you're not insecure, eh?"

"Yeah."

It was weird how easy he was to talk to. Even if he clearly did not want to go back to the meaty conversation of before.

And while it was tempting to stay and gaze at the perfection of his features she knew that would not be helpful in the long run. "I need to go."

"Do you?"

Aw. He actually looked disappointed. But then, he was an actor, so he knew how to put on an act. In fact, he probably barely knew when he wasn't acting.

Emotion clawed at her chest, and she picked up her coffee cup and moved to the rose gold accessorized kitchen, which was five times the size of hers. "You'll still have time to go visit Mac at Golden Elms if you go now." She glanced at the oversized wall clock. "You will have missed the chapel service by now too."

"What a shame."

She didn't smile back. She couldn't. The emotions stirred by this visit made her want to run away. She collected her handbag. "Thank you for the nice lunch. I haven't eaten venison prosciutto before so that was interesting."

"It's good with the figs and cheese, right?"

"Yep." She ducked her head and moved through the foyer to the front door. Thankfulness filled her that she insisted on driving her own car. Leaving like this would've been impossible if she had followed his inclination in driving her here. But every twenty-first century woman knew a woman had to rely on herself and not to trust a man they'd only met a few days ago.

"Is everything okay?" he asked, following her.

"Yep, everything is fine." Everything was not fine. She might've felt like God wanted her to come here, but she couldn't help but feel like it was a big mistake. "I just need to go."

"Are you working tomorrow?" he asked.

"Why?"

"I dunno." The toe of his sneaker stabbed the dirt. "I wondered if maybe we could do something."

"Like what?" A tiny, foolish trickle of hope dared to wonder…

"Maybe hang out. Apart from seeing Pop, there's not much to do here."

So she was only an antidote to his boredom? Offense at his words—and his obliviousness to the beauty of this area—heated her chest. She folded her arms. "I'm sorry, but I really don't know what you want from me. Was it to find out about my Muskoka chair throwing incident? Well, you've heard about that now."

He frowned, his hands in his pockets. "I just want to be your friend."

She knew it was wrong for her to blame him for her own frustrations, for the stupid hope that had led her here and teased that he might actually see her as more than just a little bitty woman. She'd been wrong, and while her anger wasn't at righteous proportions yet, she still felt like smacking something hard. Like his handsome face, maybe. Which wasn't fair, but she knew the longer she stayed in his company the more the tendrils of hope curled around her heart. And she couldn't, she *wouldn't*, let herself fall for a man of charm but no conviction. Even now she felt herself teetering on the precipice of attraction.

Which was dangerous.

Which was wrong.

Which meant 'Pastor' Jackie had to fake a smile and explain that she was busy then to thank him once again, and get in her car and drive away. And not look in the rear vision mirror, knowing that temptation that way lay.

## CHAPTER 8

He'd been right. He didn't really know how to do a quiet life. The highlight of his past few days in Muskoka had been visiting his grandfather and spending time with Jackie. But since Sunday's lunch she'd blown him off, which left him wondering what he had done to mess up.

She wasn't rostered on when he'd visited Golden Elms today. He did learn from Pop however that she'd been working here for eight years, and it was her birthday soon. That information was enough for his imagination to wonder what she might like as a present, to wonder what she might not have been given before, what would make her pay attention.

He didn't really know why he wanted her attention, only that she was different, and even the fact that she was obviously not going out of her way to chase him made him appreciate her more. It felt almost like she could be a sister, although his conflicting emotions suggested something more. Which was in itself dumb. He liked her, but she so wasn't his type, so to think of anything in a romantic sense was stupid. And doubly stupid because it was obvious she felt nothing for him. Maybe she would if he was as holy as her friend Serena's husband. Or if he had a baby like Ethan. Man. What was he doing thinking like this?

He had to stop thinking dumb thoughts. He sighed, eyeing his phone, and finally switched it back on. At once it started buzzing with a million missed messages and calls. He groaned, rubbing his forehead, tension riding high as the musical ringtone he'd not heard this past week danced past his ears. Richard's name displayed on the screen. He didn't have to wonder why his agent was calling. It was obvious the way he had gone off-grid this past week and hadn't touched his social media or emails. Richard probably was desperate, so Linc had better adult up and answer.

He pressed accept call. "Hey, Richard."

"Finally! Man, I was almost ready to send in a search party," his agent joked.

"No need. I'm alive. It's all good."

"It is now. Did you hear what Kimmie K just did?"

What followed was a long spiel about the latest in celebrity gossip land which held little appeal. It almost seemed unreal, like these were people he'd never met, never air-kissed at parties or sat next to at events. That life felt light-years away.

"Sorry, hadn't heard a thing. I've been bunkered down here in Nowhere, Muskoka, and haven't touched my phone until now."

"Well, you haven't missed much, although you have been missed. Jolene's been losing her mind—"

Lincoln heard Richard's satisfaction. There was no love lost between agent and publicist.

"—and freaking out, calling me every day or two. Gotta say this was a good move of yours, disappearing without a trace. You've got your fans so worried they are starting to wonder if you've died."

"And that's a good thing?"

"That's a great thing," his agent confirmed. "If they're so

worried about you, they're going to be overjoyed when you return all rested and tanned from your little jaunt north."

Except Lincoln didn't feel overly rested. Coming here had made him question things, like whether he really did want to throw himself back into the fray of celebrity and moviemaking again.

"Linc? You still there?"

"Yeah."

"What's going on, bud? You're being a little quiet."

"It's pretty quiet here," he joked, hoping for a bit of the old Lincoln magic again.

"Which makes it the perfect time to come back," Richard said firmly. "You've had a week, people are now forgetting your little stumble in New York, and—"

"Little stumble?" Linc interrupted. "Do you mean that people aren't begging for me to be going to a drug rehab now?"

"People can be dumb, can't they? Jumpin' to conclusions, not wanting to believe facts. Anyway, doesn't matter now, especially as Jolene and I have the perfect pitch for you."

"What do you mean?" Trepidation lined his stomach. He didn't always trust Richard's 'perfect pitches' – some of them had proved more glitter and less gold.

"You, the reason for your absence, and hey, if we spin it right, this could be the reason why you had your little mishap in New York."

"What could be?"

"You visited your grandfather, didn't you?"

"Yeah," he said slowly.

"Then we tell the truth. You had to leave in a hurry because your poor Grandpappy was dying and you had to rush to see him."

"Except he wasn't dying."

"They don't need to know that."

"But I know it. And everyone here knows it." And he

suspected Jackie would never let him live it down if it became known he'd lied about his reasons for coming north.

"Come on. It's all about getting the sympathy vote."

"I don't want the sympathy vote, not if it means I'm lying. I'm prepared to say he's been sick, and he had a stroke not too long ago, but I don't want anything being said about him dying. Because he's not." Just the thought of that made him scared. And made him want to stay. "I can't leave now anyway."

"Why not?" Richard's voice had hardened. "We agreed for a week's hibernation, and that's done. It's time to get back out there and be seen. Jolene's right. You have commitments you're committed to, and you need to be seen by the masses."

"I can be seen, but I'm not going back to California just yet. I've still got things to do here."

"Like what?" A beat passed. "You haven't fallen for a girl, have you?"

Lincoln stared as the hand on the giant clock made another rotation. Had he fallen for Jackie? No. But he didn't want to leave without getting to know her more. And he knew that getting to know her would be a hundred times easier here than if he was in a different country and two and a half thousand miles away.

"You have!" Richard's voice in his ear reminded Linc he hadn't denied the question.

"Nope," he said firmly. It wasn't like it could work, anyway. They were from completely different worlds. And besides, a girl had to be interested, and this one sure wasn't. But he needed another reason. Fast. Otherwise Richard would start thinking Linc was finally settling down or something stupid like that. "I just want a chance to be with my grandfather some more before work gets so busy again."

"You know you're supposed to be in rehearsals for *Space Man*."

He grimaced. "Send me the script and I'll practice here."

"They're on your laptop already, bud. I emailed them a few days ago."

"Ah. I haven't turned that on, either."

"Well, as much as I hate to admit it, Jolene's right, and it's probably time you started rejoining us in the real world, Linc. Your fans want you, and you ain't gonna get a higher profile if you can't be found."

"I don't want to be found," Linc protested. "I'm actually enjoying feeling anonymous for once."

Richard made a dismissive noise. "Anonymous? You? That'll be the day. No, get back to posting on social media, give your fans an explanation about why you've been silent, and make sure it's a good one, and get rehearsing."

"I'm gonna rehearse here," he said firmly. It felt like one way to own his life again.

"Fine." Richard huffed out a breath. "One more week. And then I expect to hear you're going back to LA. You have an important interview with Variety coming up, or did you forget that too?"

"I haven't forgotten," he lied. Shoot. Another thing on the rapidly-filling plate. Once upon a time he might've liked projects galore like he was a teenager at a smorgasbord. Now it all felt too much.

"You better not. Jolene tells me you're supposed to be meeting Jennifer Jones on Thursday, and you need to be there at five."

"And the cottage here?"

Richard sighed. "I'll see if I can negotiate it until Wednesday next week."

"Thanks, Richard. I appreciate it."

"You better. These people don't mind playing hardball when it comes to cold hard cash."

"I don't care what it costs, if you can make it happen."

"I expect an extra nice Christmas present this year, then."

"You got it. Thanks, Richard."

"Five, Thursday, LA. You better be there."

"I will be."

He hung up, and sat looking out at the lake. Inhaled a deep breath, then released it. Okay, so here went nothing.

He took a pic of the clock then one of the view, wrote a few lines and posted it to Instagram, before getting up and moving outside. From here he caught sight of the two Muskoka chairs waiting before the view, two chairs just waiting for someone to come sit there with him. A face flashed to mind. He dismissed it. She didn't want to see him. She'd made that clear. Although how he was supposed to hear from her if a miracle happened and she decided she wanted to contact him she had no way of doing it, not without his number. He wished he'd insisted on getting hers before.

But no. He might have a dozen anonymous texts on his phone—clearly he needed better spam filters—but none that might possibly be a message from her. How else might he find her?

He tapped on Facebook, ignoring the hundreds of notifications as he moved to the names. Was Jackie O'Halloran here? He found a photo, then dismissed it. This Jackie lived in Australia. Found another. Nope. This one had red hair.

A third. Settings set to private, but the tiny profile pic could be a match. She lived in Canada and had studied health science, anyway. It could be her...

He tapped on the Message tab and thought about what to write. Something innocuous in case it just happened to be the wrong Jackie, but still personal enough that it would make her curious enough to open it and want to reply.

*Hey Jackie, I can't stop wishing I could see you again. I hope you'll be at Mac's soon. Let me know if you are. Maybe I can finally book in a time when we can all have coffee.*

Before sending, he changed his own profile pic to something

less obvious, then went back to Messenger. And with a breath that might've held a tinge of a prayer, he pressed send.

~

Was he for real?

Jackie's heartbeat stuttered as she glanced at the message.

Lincoln Cash had messaged her.

Oh my goodness.

She couldn't respond. Wouldn't respond. *Should* not respond.

Not now, anyway, when she was supposed to be leading Bible study, and half a dozen young women really wanted to know all that could be known about Jael, Sisera and a hammer, and—

"What's wrong?" Toni asked.

Jackie shook her head. No way was she going to get distracted. No way was she going to spill the beans. It had been hard enough skirting around the truth when she'd apologized for leaving Toni and Anna to have lunch without her on Sunday. "Let's just focus on the Bible story now, okay?"

"No," Anna said, pointing to the phone. "Something clearly has you rattled. What's going on? Is it something to do with Golden Elms again?"

Was it a lie to have said that was the reason for her Sunday no-show? As Lincoln had said, he was connected to a retirement home resident, which meant technically he was 'something to do with Golden Elms.' "It's nothing," she said, pushing the phone away. "Okay, back to Jael—"

"Nope, we're not going back there," Anna said. "We all know that story, she was a tough chick, killed a man with a hammer, just like Thor—"

"Well, not exactly," Jackie objected.

"And look, it's almost time to finish, anyway. I think it's definitely time to pray then go home." She pointed a finger at Jackie that suggested she knew exactly what she'd be praying about, then glanced at the others. The other women nodded, they prayed, then soon left Jackie's apartment.

Leaving Jackie to face Toni and Anna alone.

"Okay, so what's really going on?" Toni asked.

Jackie sighed.

"Are you unwell? Is it your parents? Your grandparents?" Anna guessed.

"No, it's nothing like that. It's just… Ugh." She shoved her face in her hands.

"Is it John?" Toni asked.

"Who?"

"John? That handsome man who was at New Year's? A birdie named Rachel told me he was sitting up the back at church, too." Toni's eyes widened. "Is that what your Golden Elms 'something' was about?"

"No. Well, maybe. Yes," she added in a small voice.

"You blew us off for a man?" Anna cried. "I can't believe it!"

"And neither can Ethan. He's going to think you're two-timing him," Toni joked.

Jackie stretched out a hand and stroked his plump cheek. "I'm not two-timing. I'm just… confused."

"About?"

"About whether this is a good thing or not. Honestly, sometimes I feel like this is what God wants me to do and then other times I just want to run away and have nothing more to do with him."

"With John, you mean?"

"With Linc—I mean, John, yeah."

"Linc? Who—?" Anna's mouth fell, and she snatched Jackie's phone and tapped the screen a few times. "Oh my gosh. Oh my gosh! Are you *kidding* me? Tell me you're kidding and he's a lookalike. I can't believe this. At all!"

"What is she going on about?" Toni asked.

Jackie sighed.

"I cannot believe it. Are you seriously dating Lincoln Cash?"

"What? No." Not exactly. Not at *all*. Meeting a man for lunch didn't count as a date, did it? Except, when put like that, it kinda did.

Toni's eyes rounded. "We're not talking about the movie star, are we?"

"Yes," Anna said. "Yes, we are. And she," she pointed a finger dramatically at Jackie, "has been keeping this from us."

"Because there's been nothing to tell!"

Ethan's face screwed into displeasure, his eyes following the loud voices.

Jackie dropped her voice. "All that happened is that he came to Golden Elms to visit his grandfather and we had a few incidents—"

"Incidents?" Anna interrupted. "What do you mean?"

"A few run-ins."

Toni's mouth gaped.

"No, nothing too serious, but enough for him to talk with me a bit, and then, I don't know, he kept wanting to hang around. Then Joel invited him to church, and I saw him outside and encouraged him to go in, then he seemed a little lost after."

Anna shook her head. "No. No, you can't just tell us this. We need the other girls now."

"What? No…"

But it was too late. Anna was already getting out her phone and messaging the other girls and within two minutes Serena, Rachel and Staci were all on the phone, albeit in small boxes as part of a video call.

"What's the emergency?" Rachel said, pushing a clump of hair from her eyes.

Anna placed the phone where they could all be seen. "This one," she pointed to Jackie, "has been holding out on us."

"I haven't—"

"You kind of have," Toni said with a half-smile.

"I didn't mean to," Jackie murmured. "It's just a little messy." And she'd wanted to avoid all this drama and fuss. It wasn't any wonder Lincoln wanted to avoid the same if this was a taste of his daily experience.

"Can someone please get to the point?" Staci asked. "Sorry, I've had a huge day, and my brain isn't tracking with all the subtext."

Anna shot Jackie a look. "Are you going to tell them or am I?"

"There's nothing to—"

"Jackie is going out with Lincoln Cash," Anna rushed to say.

There was a moment of silence, then, smirks and muffled laughter.

"Uh huh," Rachel said, with a roll of her eyes. "Sure she is."

"She is!" Anna insisted. "That guy John from the other day is really Lincoln Cash. I don't know why we didn't figure it out before."

Serena's eyes widened. "Okay, I need to go to the living room to discuss this." Her picture blurred as she moved location.

"You can't be serious. Tell me you're not serious?" Rachel asked.

"Who's John?" Staci asked, a crease in her brow.

"John is a sweet guy we met at the fireworks on Saturday night. James met him," Toni said.

"But he's actually Lincoln Cash," Anna added.

"The actor?" Staci frowned.

"Yes! The actor. And Jackie here has been going on secret dates with him, and—"

"I have not," Jackie mumbled. "It was only lunch. One time."

"Are you for real?" Rachel asked, blinking. "Like, I was half asleep and Damian woke me up, so I'm not really sure if this is real or just a dream."

Serena laughed. "Have you been dreaming about Jackie and Lincoln Cash?"

"I might've been dreaming about me and Lincoln, so it's probably good I woke up. But come on. Tell us the truth, Pastor Jackie. You're just pulling our legs, aren't you?"

Should she be offended that everyone was so shocked? "Actually, it is true that John is Lincoln Cash. The actor, yes."

She braced for the hail of squeals and interrogations, but even knowing what was coming wasn't enough to deal with the sudden overwhelm.

"Oh my gosh! Oh my gosh!" That was Rachel.

"Isn't this completely insane?" asked Anna.

"He sure had us all fooled," Serena observed. "He fit in so well, too."

"He's an actor," Rachel said. "And a really good one to fool all of us."

Misgiving stretched tight across her stomach. And that was the thing. Lincoln was trained in the art of pretense. So how much of what he said and did was true?

"He's a babe," Staci said. "The movie people I spoke to in New York mentioned his name as a potential for the pirate, but they weren't sure about his reliability. But if he's hanging out with Jackie that's sure to change."

"Is he a Christian?" Serena asked.

Jackie sighed. And that was the crux of the matter.

Before she could answer, Rachel jumped in. "Don't be silly. He's off drinking all the time, and sleeping with all kinds of beautiful women, and—"

"You know those things don't mean you're not a Christian," Serena said. "Jesus drank wine. And we know others of us here don't mind the occasional cocktail, don't we, Rachel?"

"Well, no. But that's different. Anyway, how about—?"

"How is it different?" Jackie asked. "How can we judge someone else for their drinking and make assumptions about them? We don't know what God has done in their life. We don't know if God is working on their heart right now."

"Is God working on his heart?" Anna asked.

"Maybe? I think so," Jackie said. "Which is why I went to lunch with him after church. I just felt like God wanted me to."

"Even though he's not a Christian, and has a reputation a mile-wide? If this was Jane Austen's time he'd be considered a rake."

"You don't honestly think all of what you read about him is true, do you?" Jackie said. "For what it's worth, he told me he only drinks very occasionally when he's at functions."

"Right, and a guy has never lied about anything ever in all the history of mankind." Anna rolled her eyes. "What about all the women? Did you ask him about that too?"

Jackie's lips pressed together. She had no desire to. She might feel attracted to him, but it was obvious many other women had felt attracted too. Anyway, "I barely know the man, so no. I haven't asked him about that, and I have no intention to, as it's none of my business. It really doesn't matter anyway because we're only sort-of friends. Which is exactly—"

"You're friends with a movie star!" Rachel squealed. "Oh my goodness, I can't believe this."

"Which is exactly," Jackie continued more loudly, "why I didn't say anything, because there is literally nothing to say. We're not going out, we're bare minimum friends because his grandfather is at Golden Elms. And this," she pointed to the others, "is why I didn't feel like I needed to tell you. I don't want a fuss, and I really don't want anyone saying anything. You know I love you, so please don't say anything to anyone. He's here to try and recover from the New York thing—"

"Wasn't he drunk there?" Anna asked. "You need to be careful, Jackie. Especially if he's not walking with the Lord."

"I *am* being careful," she insisted. "And no, he wasn't drunk. He gets migraines, and—"

"Oh, poor thing," Staci said. "I hate it when that happens."

"And it was a mix of champagne and pain meds, and that's all that happened," Jackie finally finished.

"Can we meet him?" Rachel asked.

"No," she blurted. "I don't think it would be a good idea."

"Why not?" Anna and Rachel said in unison.

"Because then he'd know that I'd told you, and he doesn't want people knowing. Please, I beg you, can we just leave this? It's getting late."

"It's getting interesting," Staci said with a grin.

"And no, I don't think it's fair for you to just shut us down like this," Rachel complained. "Not when he's my secret love."

"Rachel." Serena rolled her eyes.

"No. I insist on meeting him, Jackie. I mean it. I'm a huge fan, and I promise not to tell anyone, but I really, *really* want to meet him. Please. Pretty please. With cherries and chocolate and all the good stuff on top."

Jackie drew in a breath. How could she get out of this?

Anna gasped. "That's who the message is from! Oh my goodness. I can't believe I didn't figure this out until now."

"What message?" Serena asked.

"The message on your phone?" Toni asked. "Was that from him?"

She'd give anything to be able to deny it. "Yes."

Anna squealed and grabbed Jackie's phone, waving it in front of Jackie's face to enable Face ID while Jackie tried to snatch it from her without success. Finally the facial recognition software kicked in and Anna unlocked the phone. "Where—?"

"Give it back," Jackie commanded, agitation rising.

"It's not on messages—oh, Messenger! Oh!"

"What does it say?" Rachel asked, even as Serena protested.

"You know that's an invasion of privacy."

Jackie wrestled the phone from her. "Thank you!"

"Must be a good one if she's prepared to wrestle Anna." Rachel rubbed her hands. "Come on. Share."

"Stop," Toni said. "This is crazy. Jackie is our friend. You can't invade another person's privacy like this. It's wrong. She can tell us if she wants to, but if you say you love her, then give her the respect she deserves and trust her to tell us if there's anything we need to know. But otherwise, stop hassling her, okay?"

Anna's mouth fell open, and she glanced between Jackie and Toni. "I just wanted—"

"There's nothing to say," Jackie said. "How many times do I need to say this? I thought we might be becoming friends, but now I don't know that I would even dare to."

"I'm sorry," Anna said. "I didn't mean to be nosy. It's just that if you have a boyfriend too, then that means I'm—"

"All alone, yes, we know," Jackie interrupted. "You let us know all the time. So you can be relieved to know it's not like that at all. I'm just as alone as you are, so I hope you're happy."

"I'm not happy," Anna said in a small voice.

"Oh, I know that," Jackie snapped, deliberately misunderstanding her. "You act like you'll never be happy until you have a boyfriend, and I hate to break it to you, but having a boyfriend won't make you happy either. Sooner or later, Anna, you have to decide to find happiness yourself, to let God be the one who gives you joy. Until you find that you're always gonna be dissatisfied."

Anna's mouth fell open. But Jackie couldn't deal with it.

"Thanks, ladies, for a great night. I'm going to bed."

She snatched her phone, gave Toni a tight smile and ignored Anna as she marched to her room and locked it, adrenaline still pumping. What on earth had just happened? She didn't act like that. She had more patience than that. That had escalated so quickly into a horrible place of discord.

Beyond the door she could hear the others saying goodbyes

and the murmur between Anna and Toni before furniture moved and the front door opened and closed.

And she huddled on the bed, eyes wide open, wondering how on earth she was going to face John Lincoln Cash at Golden Elms tomorrow.

## CHAPTER 9

Lincoln didn't want to be nervous. Nerves only added to the tension that forever lined his forehead, tension that seem to have eased in recent days since he'd been here in Muskoka. Until he'd sent that message. Or maybe since he'd gone to church. The two seemed entwined somehow: Jackie, church, or maybe Jackie and God. For so long he'd shut down any thought of God, but now…

It was like he'd started noticing, like his ears had a radar-like way of tuning into mentions of God, just as his eyes now paid attention to the perfection of nature. Nature couldn't have just happened like that. It didn't make sense that the beautiful order of things just happened out of the random chaos of a big bang. But it made sense if it was designed by a Creator.

His life made more sense if designed by a Creator, too. Who was he otherwise? What was the point of a brief passage of time called life without heaven on the other side? And more than that, he felt this inner urging to respond, to make things right, a feeling that in coming to Muskoka he was actually finding his way home. Which was kind of dumb. He'd last lived here over two decades ago. His visits to his grandparents he could count on one hand. But it was more than that. It was like the preacher had said the other day about that lost son. Lincoln felt like that. Lost, but with the strangest sense that he could possibly soon be found.

"Morning." He nodded to the Golden Elms staff on the front desk, sliding his ID so they could check his name.

The trainee nurse from the other day beamed at him. "Good morning. Mr. McKinnon is looking forward to seeing you, sir."

Sir? It made him sound like an old man but he'd take it. Better that than her dropping his name and all and sundry knowing who was here.

He nodded, pivoted to leave, then spun back. "Is Ms. O'Halloran in today?"

Some of the pleasure in her smile dialed back a notch. "She's on duty, yes."

"Thanks." He turned away before any more of her disappointment could touch him.

This. This was what he was nervous about. He'd sent the message, but Jackie hadn't responded. He knew she'd seen it, had read it, but she hadn't answered. And all of that begged the question why?

Hadn't he been subtle enough? Or had he been too subtle? He wanted to see her, but dreaded that she might say no, that she might cut him loose, that she might want nothing more to do with him. He'd thought lunch had gone well, and had applauded himself for not instantly following it with an offer for a date. She was a funny mix of openness and reserve, and she'd seemed a little distant after the discussion about God and church. But then, he'd figured that all of this was probably overwhelming, so he'd let it slide. But had at least thought she'd be open to seeing him again. But what if she wasn't?

Hence the need to keep things cool, casual, like if they ran into each other today then that was a bonus, but if they didn't that was okay, too. Except he knew it wouldn't really be. The longer he went without seeing her, the longer it felt like he didn't see the sun, and now his skin, his pores, his mental health was crying out for vitamin D. More like vitamin J.

He hurried down the passageway, keeping an eye out in case she walked past, but no. Did this need to see her make him pathetic? Maybe. But he didn't really care. The only ones who knew how he felt were himself and Jackie, and even then he wasn't sure just what she thought about him.

He reached his grandfather's door and knocked, heard his grandfather's voice say, "Come in."

Lincoln did, then pulled up short. Jackie was here too. "Hey."

She nodded, offered a quick smile without meeting his gaze then turned to his grandfather. "Well, now you have company I'll leave you be."

"You can't go," Lincoln said. "I need to talk to you."

"And I have work to do."

She still refused to look at him, but now in the morning light he could see the way her skin was pale, and there were shadows under her eyes. Was she unwell? "Are you okay?" he asked softly. "I messaged you and you didn't reply."

"I'm fine, thanks for asking," his grandfather said loudly.

Lincoln shifted closer to the bed, offering his Pop a strained smile. "Hey, Pop. Good to see you."

"But not as good as seeing a certain someone else, huh?" His grandfather's head tipped to Jackie, standing near the door.

"I just wanted to ask her something."

"Go ahead. Ignore me. I'm just the man lying in bed here. I got nowhere else to be."

Way to go with the guilt. "Look, Pop, you know I love you, but I just wanted—"

The door clicked closed. She'd gone.

Lincoln blew out a breath. "Pop, I'll be back in a moment. Don't go anywhere, okay?"

"Where am I gonna go?" His grandfather's complaint chased Lincoln out the door.

He caught sight of her striding quickly to another room, and he ran to catch her. "Jackie, please. Just give me a moment."

Her head bowed. "I can't. I have rounds, residents to see."

"Please?" He gently grasped her arm.

She stilled, as if she felt the electricity passing between them too. Then she eased her arm away. "Please don't touch me."

"Jackie, what is it? What have I done wrong?"

"Nothing."

"Then why won't you talk to me? Why don't you even want to look at me?"

As if by a great effort her chin slowly lifted until her dark eyes gazed at him. His breath caught. Dark circles underscored her eyes, as if she hadn't slept well for weeks. "Are you okay?"

"I'm fine. I didn't sleep well last night."

"That makes two of us."

She stepped back. "What do you want, Lincoln? Yes, I got your message, but it wasn't very clear."

"I want to spend time with you. I want to—"

His words broke off as he realized the trainee nurse was standing at the end of the corridor gazing at them. This couldn't look good for Jackie. And she was right. She was supposed to be working, and he was getting in her way.

"I'm sorry for bailing you up at work. Please, can you visit me after your shift ends? I don't know what I've done wrong, but I want to apologize and have the chance to make it up to you." When she started to shake her head, he pressed. "Please? Just one visit. Come for dinner, and I promise I'll never bother you again."

"Never?"

"Never," he declared, before adding more honestly, "Only if you want me to."

Her sigh was audible, as was her wrinkled nose when the

scurry of footsteps drew attention they were going to have another witness to their conversation very soon.

"Fine. I'll be there at six."

"You will?"

"I said I would, and I always keep my word." She said that like it was a personal challenge to him.

"Thank you. I promise, it'll be worth your while."

Her tweaked lips drew awareness that he'd just reverted to sounding like the arrogant man of those first encounters. He hadn't meant it. Well, he had, but not like that.

As the footsteps drew closer he took another step back. "See you tonight then."

She nodded, lips curved at the corner but with no eye contact or genuine pleasure in her face. Which only fed his insecurity, and fueled the weirdest desire to pray for her.

THE HOURS PASSED in time with his grandfather, when he kept hoping that Jackie would return and the ease between them would quickly follow. She didn't. He returned to the rented cottage via a quick stop at the grocery store where he'd managed to rush past a few gawking teens—and an overly curious checkout attendant named Rochelle—and grab supplies for tonight's meal. He wasn't any great chef, but cooking did relax him, and he couldn't really mess up steak, salad, and baked potatoes, right? Followed by a pie of local apples and cranberries and ice cream, he didn't care if it was trainer-approved as long as Jackie might enjoy it.

Once home he put the groceries away, managed a swim, then killed more time lying on the sofa as he scrolled through some of the comments on his Instagram feed. Great. Looked like the hunt to find his location was well and truly on. Amid the relieved comments about him being 'back from the dead' were those guessing where he might be. Upper New York? Michigan?

Thousand Islands? His pic out the window had led to all kinds of speculation.

His phone buzzed with a message. His heart leapt, then he glanced at the number. Richard. He should probably take this. "Yo."

"Since when do you do public service announcements for the Ontario police?" Richard asked.

"Huh?"

"You. Ontario highway patrol. Jolene just sent me a link to a Facebook post where you're mentioned in a hashtag. Any second now and the internet will be in a furor, with every woman between the age of ten and eighty hunting for you in that state."

"Province," Lincoln corrected.

"Whatever. Is this your idea of staying low?"

Lincoln explained how it had come about, adding, "It was the better alternative than being fined or being arrested. That sure wouldn't be fun."

Richard sighed. "I thought you were trying to do better."

"I am doing better," he insisted. "I even went to church the other day. How's that for turning over a new leaf and looking squeaky clean?"

"You went to church?" Incredulity filled Richard's voice.

"I went to church." And it had messed with him ever since. "I can't see myself going back," he admitted—hello, he was due to fly to California before too long.

"Good."

"Good? Why good?"

"Because if you were known as a God-botherer, your roles would dry up. People want a hero, not some wet goody two-shoes."

"Wow. Why don't you tell me what you really think?"

"I really think you need to be looking over that script and getting ready to head back to California. You've left the New

York incident behind, people are now curious about where you are, so that's great. We like intrigue, we want people to wonder. We don't want you killing half your audience because you've got religion or a girlfriend."

"I haven't found religion or got a girlfriend, so you don't need to worry." Although he wouldn't mind exploring the possibility of changing one of those statuses tonight.

He glanced at the clock. Almost six. "I need to go."

"Don't go off script any more, got it?"

"Yes, Richard." Lincoln rolled his eyes, glad this wasn't a video call. "Bye."

He didn't wait to hear Richard's response, stabbing the red button on his phone as a knock came at the door. He pushed to his feet and hurried to answer it.

"Hey, Jackie." He smiled.

She shouldn't have come. This was a mistake. Hadn't she just heard him announce that he had no interest in God or in her? Yet how could a man say that, then look at her with that deep look of interest? How could he look that pleased to see her if he didn't really care?

"Please, come in." He gestured her inside, like she hadn't been here just a few days ago. "Can I take your jacket?"

"No, thanks." She needed it. Not because it was cold but because she needed every layer of defense against this man. Not that she thought he would do anything, but because she didn't trust herself when she was around him. Which made her visit tonight all the more reckless and foolhardy. But she knew she couldn't stay at home either. Not when staying home would mean a certain visit from her friends who seemed to have decided she and Anna needed an intervention. And without recourse to go home or anywhere else she might normally go, there seemed no safe place in Muskoka Shores apart from coming here and perhaps finally clearing up whatever this weirdness was between them.

Of course, a little voice whispered, she needed to clear up the strain that had sprung up between herself and Anna. Yes, she needed to apologize, but she didn't have it in her today. After last night's lack of sleep, she barely had it in her to work today, so tonight's visit was probably as much born of surprised capitulation as it was her desire to avoid her friends.

"Can I get you a drink?" He pointed to a bar where a number of Rachel-approved bottles stood waiting.

"A peach tea and soda would be great, thanks."

See? Not boring.

He poured her drink, added some ice cubes, and gestured to outside. "I thought it might be nice to sit and watch the water, if that's okay. Unless you're starving and want to eat now."

Truth be told she was a little peckish. "I can wait a little bit, but only a little bit." And if she waited too long she might not wish to leave, and after his comments she'd overheard earlier, that could get problematic.

"Ah, I should've realized. Okay, we can go watch the sunset later, and I'll get cooking now. But we can't have you fainting, so here's something you can eat now. Ta-da!" He drew an antipasto platter from the fridge and she smiled. He'd remembered her favorite things from the other day.

She helped herself to a green olive. "Thank you."

He paused and smiled at her, and her heart kicked a corresponding throb. "What?"

"You're pretty when you smile."

"Gee, thanks."

"I mean—" He winced. "Man, this is not going how I thought it would."

He could say that again. She shifted to look out the window, blinking to hide a rush of emotion. Her emotions felt so pointy and sharp, with as much ability to pierce her self-control as it might harm him. This was a bad idea coming here when she felt so tired and confused about so many things.

"I meant to give you a compliment," he said, his words soft. "I like your smile, Jackie."

And she wasn't pretty without it. She got it. She knew she wasn't attractive. Which meant her foolish fantasies in coming here today were exactly that. Foolish.

"So, what did you want to talk about?" she asked, glad her voice was holding steady.

His sigh finally dared her to glance at him. His gaze was on her, and she shivered.

"You."

She sipped her drink, unable to ignore the spine-length rush of tingling at his deep look. "What about me?"

"What's wrong?"

Her throat grew tight, and for a moment she couldn't answer, could only shake her head.

"Don't tell me nothing. I know it's not polite to say, but you look tired, and I get the impression you're burdened by something."

"You're observant." She'd give him that.

"I have to be. It's part of my job."

That's right. And his job was as an actor. Which meant specializing in make-believe. See? None of this was real.

"So, what's wrong?"

What wasn't? She'd single-handedly blown his cover and destroyed her friendship group through one silly overreaction and misunderstanding. All because a man she was reluctantly attracted to had sent her a message. A man who clearly didn't think of her in any capacity beyond a distraction from his own boredom, and for whom she didn't want to have these silly feelings anyway! But how to explain any of that without sounding like an idiot? It was best to deny it all and say, "Noth—"

"And don't tell me nothing. That'd be a lie, and I might not know you too well, but I know you're someone who doesn't tell lies."

He wanted the truth? Fine. "I had an argument with my friends last night about you."

Boom. Watch the truth bomb explode.

He simply raised his eyebrows. "Yeah?"

"I hate arguing with my friends, and I might've over-shared about who you really are."

"Is that so?"

Why was he being so calm about this? "Look, I'm sorry for spilling the beans. I didn't mean to, but they were hassling me about your message and I accidentally dropped your name."

He picked up a cube of cheese. "So how did that turn into an argument?"

"Anna."

His face screwed as if trying to place her. "The superfan?"

"One of. Rachel is the other one." She grimaced.

His lips twitched. "Let me guess: she was part of the conversation too."

"Oh my gosh." She climbed onto a kitchen stool, while he drew out salad ingredients. Normally she'd offer to help, but she just felt too tired. She watched as he started cutting cucumbers. "It was insane. I was at Bible study when your message came through and I was so surprised that I got distracted, and—"

"Sorry about that."

She shrugged. "Anna couldn't believe it was you. Rachel couldn't believe you actually wanted to be a kind-of friend."

"Kind-of friend?" He paused in the cucumber dissection. "I thought we were—we are friends."

The intensity of his blue gaze drew a fluttery sensation inside, followed by the heavy practical internal voice that said, "See? Friends. Only friends. Nothing more."

"I like you, Jackie," he said simply. "I sent that message because I wanted to know if there was possibility for more."

She choked on a caper. A sip of iced tea cleared the burn. "More?"

"More."

How was it that men could simply state what they wanted while it seemed women danced around the subject and wondered to the nth degree? Maybe it was time to take a leaf from his book. "What do you mean by more?"

He cleared his throat, hands flat on the counter as he studied her. "I want to know if the superhero nurse might ever be interested in dating me."

Good thing she was sitting down. As it was, there was every chance she was going to slide off the stool in a puddle of astonishment. "Why?"

"Because I like you. I think you're interesting. And I think you're honest and real, and that we could have fun together."

Why was he saying this when they hadn't even had the first course? "I don't know what to say."

"You could say yes."

He grinned, and the moment stretched into temptation, as she dared to consider his words. Maybe she'd fallen into one of Rachel's dreams because this did not seem real in any way, shape, or form. To go on a date with Lincoln Cash? To be Lincoln Cash's girlfriend? How amazing would that be? But where would that put her and God?

The light in his face faded. "But you don't want to, do you?"

She pressed her lips together in case she spilled the truth. Yes, part of her wanted to. But another part knew she couldn't. Shouldn't. So she shook her head.

"Hey, it's okay. I thought it worth a shot. But I hope you know what the price for saying no is."

"Leaving?"

He chuckled. "Funny. No, instead you have to explain your reasons over steak."

She knew he hadn't said that because of arrogance, but couldn't resist the tease. "Couldn't it just be because a girl doesn't find you attractive?"

"Wow." He placed a hand on his heart. "That cut deep, Jackie. You wounded me."

"You'll recover. I'm sure there are plenty of ladies out there who will help heal your heart."

"I don't want them." His demeanor grew serious. "I want a girl who doesn't see all that, but can see the guy I really am."

"And who is that?" she whispered.

"Someone who wants to be honest, who is loyal, who gets things wrong sometimes but is trying to be better. You don't want that?" His voice held apprehension.

"I do." But she wanted him to follow Jesus, too. And the fact that if she said that, and he said he did, or eventually said he did, would leave her wondering if his commitment to God was because of her or because it was really real. *Lord, what do I say?*

"But you're not attracted to me. I get it."

He returned to fixing the salad, as if she hadn't just shut him down. "Do you want me to leave?"

"No. Why would I want you to do that? If you won't go on a date with me I'm going to make the most of any time we have together now."

"Why?"

"I told you. I like you." His smile was crooked. "I like that you prefer honesty and openness and you're committed to your friends and family. And I gotta say I like the fact you stand up to me and give me sass and call me out on my bull. I think your confidence is sexy."

Had she died? Because this dream was better than anything even Rachel could've imagined. "Are you feeling well?"

"I was feeling better before you gave me the straight out no, but like you said, I'll recover. A man's gotta have hope, right?"

"Right." But the thought of him finding another girl made her want to cry. So she swallowed the rest of her drink and hopped off the stool. "I think you need to point me in the direction of your knives and forks so I can set the table." Doing something had to be better than nothing.

After such intensity, the conversation flowed surprisingly easily as she set the table and he cooked the steaks. He retrieved the potatoes from the oven and they ate their meal with a side of humor and repartee. Her heart ached, knowing this could be hers for the taking. Finally, she could be like the others and have someone to share jokes and laughter, to exchange banter like she heard between Staci and James, and Serena and Joel. But what was the point if he didn't share the most important part of her life, if he didn't share her heart for God? She didn't believe in relationship evangelism. Friendship evangelism, yes, but anything more was asking for trouble.

Dessert followed, a delicious apple and cranberry pie, then he gestured to the windows which the sunset was streaking in rose, dark blue and gold. "Want to go watch the sunset?"

"Sure."

She followed him out onto the deck then onto the wooden path to the little beach and the chairs placed beside the water. He'd brought down a blanket, but she didn't need it, the night was still warm, and there was enough breeze to chase away mosquitoes.

The air held a heavy kind of peace, the golden edges of the day slipping into dusk.

"This reminds me of you," he murmured.

"What does?"

He pointed to the sky. "You have this same kind of peace, too."

Was this her moment to share? Her escalating heartbeat

suggested so. "You know it's God who offers that peace." She glanced across and saw his forehead had creased. "You can have that peace, too."

He sighed. "Can't we just enjoy the moment?"

His rebuttal felt like a slap. She wasn't trying to be pushy.

"Sorry." His voice was soft.

Tears pricked. Rare was the time she heard a man apologize. Even her grandfather, Christian though he was, had never been big on acknowledging his mistakes.

His hand touched hers where it lay resting on the arm of the Muskoka chair. "I know you want me to get right with God, and maybe one day I will. But right now, I just want to enjoy this moment with you."

Heart dancing which had started at his words of "maybe one day I will" slowed. Her prayers grew, doubling and redoubling in intensity as she prayed for God to touch his heart.

"Jackie?"

Oh, right. She probably should speak. "It's good to be still." And know that God was God. "Especially when it means we can appreciate the majesty of heaven," she added with a smirk.

"You're as subtle as a sledgehammer, but yeah. It's good to stop and pay attention."

Her nerve endings stood up to pay attention as his hand slid over hers. As his fingers tangled with hers. As her skin tingled at his touch. She didn't sit holding hands like this with her friends. But her protest died as he said, "Tell me something about you that nobody else knows."

She gazed out at the glorious skies and shared another fragment of fear from last night. "I think I was too blunt with Anna last night," she confessed.

"How so?"

She sighed, keeping her gaze fixed heavenward, even as she sensed his attention on her. "I told her she needed to stop looking for a man to make her happy, to find that happiness by trusting in God, and she got pretty offended." Even if everyone else had been understanding, and dare she say it, even appreciative for Jackie's bluntness. Although all of them were in relationships, so that might've contributed to their feeling.

"You don't think a man can make you happy?" His thumb gently caressed the back of her hand, robbing her of breath.

"I think a man could contribute to my happiness, but I shouldn't rely on it." She wished he'd stop doing that. It was very distracting. She drew her hand away, pulling up her knees and wrapping her arms around them.

"See?"

"See what?"

"That's that confidence I like about you."

She needed to leave. Any more of his compliments and she might well yearn to stay. "So how about you?" she said instead. "What's something about the famous Lincoln Cash that nobody else knows?"

He groaned, and for a moment she thought she'd pressed too hard. But surely such a question was only fair?

"Something that nobody else knows? Okay." A long exhale. "Sometimes it feels like I am juggling all these balls, trying to keep everyone happy. My agent, my fans, directors, my publicist, everyone wants a piece of me and I'm so tired of all the juggling. Sometimes it's like I don't even know who I really am anymore. Coming here felt like I dropped one of the balls, but my agent and publicist reckon it will bounce back. But to be really honest?"

"Please," she whispered.

His hand lay open, as if waiting for her to slide her fingers through his again. She swallowed, then followed that impulse, hearing the hitch of his breath as she did so before he gently squeezed her fingers again.

"Sometimes I don't know if I want it to bounce back. Sure, I like being an actor, but I don't like all the obligations or the never-ending nature of it. Coming here, seeing Pop, meeting you, reminded me there's a whole other world outside of my bubble and I actually want to live in that world more."

Her heart thudded. What was he really saying? That he wanted to spend more time with her? Maybe this could have half a hope if—

But no. That was ridiculous. He might like her company, and she might enjoy his, but they remained too different. And as long as his faith wasn't the same as hers then there was no way they could be together. She glanced at their entwined hands and her heart physically hurt.

"I don't know what to do, Jackie. I want more of what's real, less of the fake, but I can't say no too often, otherwise I won't get jobs."

"Can you take more time off? Give yourself a year's break?"

His sigh seemed to come from his toes. "I wish it was that simple, but I'm committed to projects. I've signed contracts so if I back out now then I'm gonna have to pay back quite a few dollars."

"That's the price of mental health, huh?"

He groaned again. "See? This is why I need you in my life. Nobody speaks truth to me the way you do."

"Maybe you need some more truth-tellers in your world."

"I thought I found a few here in Muskoka," he admitted.

Her lips curved. "You can probably find a few in some of the churches in California."

He chuckled. "And she's persistent, too."

"Of course I am. Why would you ignore something that is obviously what you want and need? You want the peace and assurance God gives, you want people who will keep you grounded and will be honest. I'm not about to stop telling my friends about the hope that only God can bring. That'd be so selfish of me."

Another gentle press. "And you're anything but selfish."

The moments passed as the sky deepened into violet and coolness drifted from the lake to settle across them. She shivered, and drew the blanket he offered around her. "Thanks."

"You're welcome." A beat passed. Two. "I'll need to return to California soon."

Emotion wrenched her chest. "I know."

"I wish I could stay."

Maybe if he stayed he'd finally find God. But then, the question remained whether he would find God for himself or because she wanted him to. It was probably best she deflect with a reply that didn't show her heart anguish. "Muskoka tends to have that effect on people."

"I know I said I wouldn't ask for more than tonight, but do you think you'd mind if I messaged you occasionally?"

*Lord?* She sensed peace. "Only if you promise to stay as friends, and not ask for anything more."

"You're really sure you don't want more?"

Her heart ached as she whispered, "Yes."

His sigh held resignation. "Fine then. Friends, it is."

"We can all do with more friends, can't we?"

"People say that. I have to wonder if it's true."

She heard what he wasn't saying. But it didn't matter what he wanted. Until he got his heart right with God and started following Jesus, they could only ever be friends.

Friends. Not anything more. Just friends.

She could do that.

*Lord, help me.*

# CHAPTER 10

As he waited for his grandfather to complete his latest crossword—and okay, maybe for the entrance of a certain brunette—Lincoln scrolled through his Instagram feed, and felt a frown form between his eyebrows. How much of what he posted didn't really matter? There were so many photos of glitzy premiers and movie roles, including—he winced—an unfortunate amount of shirtless ones, but few of what really mattered. He switched to his photo collection on his phone and realized just how few pictures he took of real things. That was going to be rectified today.

"Hey, Pop," he said, turning to the man in the bed. "Can I take your photo?"

"You wanna break the camera?" his grandfather said with a wry grin.

"No. I want a photo of you. I'm heading back to California soon, and want to remember my visit here."

His grandfather snorted. "You need a photo to remember that, do you?"

"No." But maybe, if the past pace of his life was anything to go by. Life had a way of making him forget some of the more important things, and a photo—hey, he could make it his phone and laptop screensaver—would help ground him in what really was important. "I wondered if maybe I could post a pic of us on Instagram, too."

Pop guffawed. "I've seen your pictures on Instagram—"

He had? How?

"—and I don't think that'd fit with the rest of what you post there."

Pictures that showed someone laughing and grinning and dressed to the nines, but it was all fake. Actually, if he didn't know it was himself in those pictures, he'd say it kind of made him look like a tool. Huh. Jolene said it was best for his image to appear this way, and as she was his publicist he guessed she knew best. But was it any wonder he only got the beefcake himbo roles when this was what was projected? Maybe doing something different would help people take him more seriously as an actor.

"It's time that changed," Lincoln finally said. "So, if you don't mind, I'd love to share a photo of someone who's really important to me. As long as you'll cope with all the messages about to slide into your DMs," he teased.

His grandfather gave a raspy chuckle. "I don't need DMs to be propositioned by women."

Lincoln choked. "Excuse me?"

"Some of the ladies here—but a gentleman names no names."

Nor did a movie star wanting to avoid litigious claims. "How do you know about Instagram and DMs anyway?"

He waved a hand. "Someone here showed me. I don't post much, but—"

"You're on Instagram?" Lincoln snatched his phone and opened the app. "What's your handle? What's your name? I should follow you."

He paused. Except if he did, then all his followers would see, and they might try to harass his grandfather, and Pop might know some basic things about social media, but Linc doubted he'd know how to deal with trolls. The main reason Jolene approved Linc's posts was to stop the trolls, and to separate his public persona with his private life after a troll attack too many had shown him just how vulnerable he could be to stalkers. But then, never posting anything he really cared about made Linc as fake as the next Tom Cruise wannabe. Social media was a minefield.

The door opened, and his heart leapt as sunshine walked in the room. "Hi, Jackie."

Her smile didn't look as big as his—he was pretty sure he looked like a kindergarten kid at Christmas—but the warmth in her eyes before she focused on Pop made his heart glow.

After their dinner he'd been desperate to see her again, but knowing she had work, and he really needed to take time to look over his script meant he practiced self-control for once and only messaged her, for which she'd given the briefest reply. He got the impression that they never really cleared up her 'don't contact me after this' comment. She obviously wasn't abiding by it, given she'd replied.

Once she completed her check on his grandfather she turned to him. "And how are you this morning, Mr. Cash?"

"All the better for seeing you."

She rolled her eyes.

"He is, y'know," Pop said. "He brightened up like a shiny silver button when you walked through the door."

Her twisted smile said she didn't quite believe him, even though it was true—although a little humiliating to have his grandfather point it out.

Her gaze fell to Linc's t-shirt, and her lips tweaked higher. "I see."

He glanced down, and realized he wore the shirt that said, "Actually, I am a big deal."

"Way to go with the humility." Her eyebrows arched. "Does this mean you need to be dealt with?"

Oh, her burns were good. "It depends. Are you offering?"

"Offering what?"

"To deal with me?"

His grandfather's cough drew awareness that they weren't alone, and judging from the expression on his face it probably wasn't a conversation he wanted to be party to.

"Sorry, Mac," Jackie said. "I was taken aback that the movie star who keeps disguising himself because he wanted to remain incognito is now going around boasting about how amazing he is."

"I wasn't—"

"He's always been a little big-headed."

"Pop! I haven't," Linc said to Jackie. "I'm not—man," he complained as Jackie and his grandfather started laughing. "Why do you two always pick on me?"

"You make it so easy," his grandfather said.

"And you probably need to throw that shirt away," Jackie said. "It's not exactly screaming humility."

"Yeah, but I bet you'd have a problem with someone who screams about their humility too, am I right?"

"You're funny."

"Finally, she finds something nice to say," Linc grumbled, even as his heart danced at the humor in her eyes.

He loved this sweet sass about her, the way she could pin him with a glance and take his measure, how a word from her could crush him or make his heart soar and believe anything was possible.

Pop jerked a thumb at her as he turned to Linc. "You should get a picture of Jackie, too."

"A picture? Oh, I don't think—"

"Excellent idea, Pop. Hey, it can be of my two favorite people in Muskoka."

He caught the way her face softened, even as she protested, "But I don't have any makeup on today."

"Some people need it," Linc said softly. "Not you." Her beautiful heart shone straight through, animating her features with a glow he'd never grow tired of seeing.

"I really don't—"

"Please? You don't want to disappoint one of your favorite residents now, do you?" Linc stage-whispered.

"You're incorrigible."

"Yes, I am."

She groaned, but agreed and leaned near Pop as Linc took a photo of the two of them, then took a selfie of the three of them. "Happy now?"

She smoothed back her ponytail as he studied the picture. For a candid shot, the morning light streaming through the window seemed to have showcased the best of each of them: Jackie's smile and eyes held joy and peace, his grandfather's languid humor, and whatever it was fans liked about Linc. "It's perfect." Unstaged. Genuine. Real.

"Good. Well, I need to go check on the other residents now, so I'll leave you two to compare notes about your handsomeness."

"You think I'm handsome?" Linc asked, wincing as he heard the echo of those words. No wonder she thought him arrogant. "Forget that."

"Oh, she does," Pop said with a side-grin.

"On that note, I'm leaving. Goodbye."

"Why do you think her cheeks are pink?" Pop teased loudly, which only seemed to hurry her exit as she closed the door with a gentle thud.

And drew defensiveness on her behalf. "Pop. Don't."

"So, you two, huh?"

"There is no 'you two,'" Linc scoffed. "We've agreed to be friends, that's all."

"You mean *you* agreed after she said that was all she wanted to be," his grandfather said, with way too much accuracy.

"She wants a good man."

"A Christian man." His grandfather nodded.

"Well, I'm not exactly either of them."

"Yes, you are," his grandfather insisted.

"I'm not exactly good."

"Who is? Nobody's perfect, son. But I meant the other one."

"A Christian? Please."

"Don't argue. I may not remember as much as I used to, but I still remember how excited Nancy was when you came back from church one day and told her you'd accepted Jesus as your Lord and savior."

"I was ten. That doesn't count."

"Doesn't it?" His grandfather's eyes held intensity.

"Anyway, I haven't exactly been living like a monk ever since." There'd been too many parties. Too many women. Too many experiences he regretted and would rather now forget.

"From what Nancy used to say, being a Christian is about what you believe, not about how good you are."

"I think some people only see the actions."

"If you mean Jackie, then I think you're doing her an injustice." Pop shook his head. "She's like Nancy in that way, cares more about the heart than the outward appearance."

For some reason that comment thumped a chord within. Hadn't Gran used to say something similar? Man judged the outside, but God looked at the heart, or words to that effect. He glanced at his grandfather. For someone who'd never expressed much interest in Christianity, Pop seemed to have an awful lot to say. "So why didn't you ever make that decision?"

"What decision?"

"Becoming a Christian. Why haven't you?"

"Who says I'm not?"

Lincoln blinked. "Are you saying you are?" At his grandfather's nod he continued. "So why don't you go to church, or chapel at least?"

"And have to listen to Mavis sing off-key? No, thanks. No, I have my Bible and my devotional." He gestured to the drawer in the bedside table. "They're in there. I read them every night, then I go to sleep and pray for you, your folks, Peter, Jackie."

"But not Mavis?" Linc said slyly.

His grandfather sighed. "That's enough disrespect from you, young man. I think God has convicted me enough about her," he added in a grumble.

Linc's mind was still spinning about the earlier revelations. "You really pray for me?"

"Of course I do. Why else do you think you're here?"

Lincoln slumped back in his seat. Was all of this part of some grand masterplan? By God, no less? The spinning in his head before ramped up to tornado levels, pounding against his skull. He closed his eyes, pressing against the pain.

"You okay there, son?"

"I thought I came here because Mom wanted me to."

"She might've wanted, but you're the one who had to make it happen."

Who'd got his agent to make it happen, but whatever. "I don't know what to say."

"You don't need to say anything," his grandfather said. "But know that God wants you following Him. He's designed you to always feel like something is missing until you discover Him."

This was so not a conversation he'd ever thought he'd have with his grandfather.

His phone buzzed. Jolene. "Sorry, Pop. I need to take this."

"I'm not going anywhere."

Which meant Lincoln probably should. He gestured to the patio, his grandfather nodded, so Linc slid the door open and stepped out into sunshine and birdsong. "Jolene."

"Linc, at last you're taking my calls. How are you feeling

now?" Her voice held faux sympathy. He knew she cared more about her pay packet than her clients.

"I'm fine. Actually, I'm great." He felt the most level-headed he had in years. "What is it?" She hadn't rung him to play games. A straight-shooter was Jolene.

"It's about that police interview you did."

"What police interview?"

"The candid one, with the Ontario highway patrol? They've gone viral with the video, and judging from the traffic it's getting—"

"Funny."

She paused. "I don't get it."

Yeah, Jolene might share Jackie's directness but lacked her sense of humor. "Forget it."

"Anyway, as I was saying, it seems that you need to be prepared for some of your super fans to find you."

"Ontario is a pretty big place."

"But there are some crazy kind of people out there. And after you posted your picture of the lake there are even more people now trying to find out where you actually are."

"It's a good thing I'm leaving for LA soon, then, isn't it?"

"I hope you have enjoyed this little break, Lincoln, but it's way past time for you to be seen again. People need to know that you are here, that you're available, that you're interested, and it sure doesn't look like any of those things if you're thousands of miles away."

He tamped down the impatience he was feeling. "I'll be in LA next week."

"And if you're going to post anything, make it about the movies you're in. Give your fans some of those shots they love. Seeing you're at the lakes, maybe you could get some of you swimming, or boating, or just showing off your abs."

He rolled his eyes. Yet more of the superficial life. Sure, he appreciated having vacation time as much as the next person, but this felt a little like boasting. "I don't want to look like a poser," he said, feeling his way into an objection she might actually hear.

"You don't look like a poser; your fans all think you look hot."

"But I don't want to just be seen as hot," he complained. "I want people in the industry to take me more seriously, to offer me grittier roles, and they never will if all they see is the same kinds of beefcake shots."

"Beefcake shots? Seriously?" Her laughter sounded high and tinny. "Sounds like you've gone back in time, not just crossed the border."

"Actually, I've loved my stay here. The people are way more real and honest than anyone I've ever met in LA. It's made me question a few things, not least about how fake everything feels, and I don't want to keep playing the same tune. I want people to see a more real version of me, whether that's swimming or being at an old person's home."

Her chuckle faded. "Wait. Are you serious?"

"That's what I've been doing, Jolene. Visiting my grandfather in an old person's home. He's awesome, and so are the other people here. Way more awesome than any celebrity I've met, and—"

"But—"

"—and," he continued determinedly, "I'm wanting—I'm *going* to be posting shots that help producers and directors see I'm more than a face and some muscles. I want them to see the actor who cares about things, who's prepared to do what it takes to be taken seriously, to remember I won that award for best newcomer all those years ago because of my acting, not my looks."

"Have you talked this over with Richard?"

"Some of it," he said cautiously.

"You remember why you hired me, don't you?"

"I'm not wanting to get too personal, so there won't be room for the stalkers and crazy fans to find me, but there has to be a balance between what's contrived and what's real. I just need more real in my life."

There was silence for a moment, then, she said, "Post some more shots of your lakes then, maybe add one of your grandfather, if he's okay with that. It'd be good to be seen as the caring grandson—"

"That's not what I meant." Frustration edged his words.

"Lincoln, you've been in this industry long enough to know that intentions mean little. Fans will see what fans will see and interpret it their own way, that's just how it is." A subtle beep came through the line. "Now, I have another call. But stay in touch, okay?"

He ended the call, not bothering to say goodbye, knowing she would've already moved on. He sank into a white wicker chair, gazing out as Lake Muskoka sparkled softly. What he'd give to stay here, to somehow find a job that allowed him to stay, to get off the trajectory that his agent and publicist and all his fans seemed to want for him.

A groan escaped, then, conscious he didn't want to worry the man inside, he clawed at his face. Good thing his grandfather couldn't see Linc now. What could he do? How could he change? Richard seemed firmly set on Lincoln pushing into the big leagues with movies, probably because Linc, and therefore Richard, would earn a much bigger pay packet. But the thought of signing up for endless years of moviemaking left him cold, and he sensed Richard would fight Linc's change of heart every step of the way. What alternative did he have?

His grandfather's words from earlier wafted back into awareness. Pop said he'd prayed for Lincoln, that that was why he was here. Such a thought felt too big, but hey, it couldn't hurt to pray, could it? He had nothing to lose by giving it a go.

He propped his head in his hands and studied the tiled floor before shutting his eyes. "Hey God," he whispered. "I know it's been a long time, but do You think You could help me?"

~

"Hi, Mom."

Jackie paused the website under construction and leaned back in her chair as she answered the phone call. Some summons could be ignored, like the one sent from Lincoln earlier today, requesting if she could have dinner with him tonight, which she'd regretfully turned down due to commitments she'd ignored this past week. Other requests, however...

"Oh, how are you, honey?"

She closed her eyes as the tender note drew softness across her heart. "I'm okay."

"Just okay? What do you mean by that? Is something the matter?"

"No. Everything is good." Or it would be as soon as she stuffed these unwanted feelings about a certain superstar back in the box where they belonged. "How are you? How is Granddad and Granny Joan?"

Her mother sighed, the sound a twin for the one cascading through Jackie's own soul, as her mother explained about the latest round of medical visits, the restless nights, the unrelenting pressure of being carer to two elderly parents with complex medical needs.

"I've booked my vacation time, Mom. I'll be there in a week or two."

When Lincoln left. It wasn't because he wouldn't be here anymore; she'd booked this months ago. But it probably wouldn't hurt to be elsewhere and to forget what seeing him on a near-daily basis had meant, the way his gladness at seeing her had a way of pepping up her day.

As her mom continued sharing about her day, Jackie's

thoughts veered back to the man she had started praying to forget. Because she knew all of this emotion was a waste. He'd go back to Hollywood stardom, and would never think of her again. Except, maybe, in a kindly way as he thought fondly about his grandfather. Besides, it didn't matter what he said, he couldn't really mean any of those sweet words he'd said. It had to be more of his acting. What did they call it when someone immersed themselves in a role? That's it. Method acting. He'd probably taken on the role of a small-town boy and wanted to know what it was like to date a small-town girl. Well, too bad. She sure wasn't about to be fooled by that.

"Honey? Are you there?"

Guilt snapped her attention back to her mother. "Sorry, it's been a big day."

"How is work going?"

"It's good." Even if Téa looked at her angrily at times, as if wondering why Jackie had the temerity to tell her off from bothering Lincoln Cash, before spending time with him herself. It wasn't like Jackie could easily explain why he seemed to be around her so much. And because it often happened at work, it wasn't like she could tell him to go away. Or even that she really wanted him to leave her alone, either, if she was completely honest.

"Well, you're just full of details, aren't you?" Her mother chuckled, some of the strain from earlier having faded away. "It will be good to see you, hon. It's been too long."

"It has."

"And I feel selfish in saying this, but it will be good to have someone here who knows how to care for the elderly. My back is killing me these days."

"Surely there are respite programs available. You should investigate them."

"There are, but Mother doesn't like strange people coming into her home."

"They wouldn't be strangers if she got to know them."

"I say that to her, too, but she's set in her ways."

"I'm sorry, Mom."

"Me too." Another sigh. "But at least you coming here will provide some of the respite I need."

Jackie grimaced, as a memory of something said at Serena's soiree resurfaced. Yes, she loved her mom and her grandparents, and yes she wanted to help them, but oh, Jackie needed a break too.

As if sensing this, her mother rushed to say, "Don't worry. It won't be all toil. I know you've been working hard."

"A change of scene will be good," Jackie offered.

"Yes."

She spoke to her grandparents briefly, before the late hour saw the call end not too long after, amid a round of prayer points and goodbyes.

She pushed up from her chair and paced the room, stretching out the kinks in her shoulders and neck. As much as she hated to admit it, the thought of traveling hours just to do more of the same held little appeal. She loved her grandparents, she loved her mom and yes, she wanted to help, but everything felt like more obligation. She'd do anything to run away to a tropical island somewhere. Maybe even with some of those cocktails Rachel was always going on about…

Her phone buzzed another message. She glanced at it. Was it Lincoln again?

Her heart fell, then she rebuked herself for a lack of gladness when she saw it was Serena. *Hey, you've been in my prayers*, Serena's message read.

*Thank you*, she typed back. *I need it.*

*Have you heard from Anna?*

Anna. Yet another relationship she should be focused on fixing, rather than the mythical one with someone who had once played a god-like hero in an action blockbuster. And who had ridden a horse in *As the Heart Draws*, a western filmed near Calgary, and kissed the heroine, Ainsley Beckett. Okay, so she was sad and had watched a few more of his movies in recent times. A girl had to do something when she couldn't sleep. Not that watching him kiss beautiful women on movies made her dreams easier…

"See how distracted he makes you?" she muttered to herself. "Stop it. And focus."

*Not yet*, she typed back to Serena.

There was a whirl of swirling circles indicating Serena was typing. Then, *She's been avoiding all of us lately, and not responding to anyone's messages. I know she's been away with her family this week, but maybe she'll be up for a visit after that.*

Maybe. Except Jackie would be away with her own family, then. *It's probably better to talk in person*, she typed back.

*Amen*, came the swift reply. *You're in my prayers.*

A second later there came another text. *Any more news on John / Lincoln?* This was followed by a smiley face.

*No.* She swallowed. *We've agreed to be friends, and he's leaving next week too, so that's that.*

The interval this time stretched long enough that she wondered if she should revisit the website she was building for the Nuthouse in town. She placed the phone down, visited the bathroom, then moved back to her desk and checked her messages again.

A new one. From a different person. *How about dinner tomorrow night?*

Lincoln.

## CHAPTER 11

Lincoln scowled at the script, each word revealing just how unbelievable the plot was and how lame the dialogue. Why Richard—and okay, to be fair, why he'd—agreed to do this he had no idea. The story felt like a mash up of every space movie from the last thirty years, like a gaggle of scriptwriters had tried to pull together all the best ideas and come out with a regurgitated mess. And Lincoln would be the patsy shouldering the blame, his name as top billing for the first time in his life. Top billing was awesome... but not for a movie like this.

He grabbed his phone, checked messages—Jackie still hadn't replied to his text from yesterday—so he continued to his agent's number and waited as it rang.

"Lincoln! How are you doing, my man? Have you checked out that script yet?"

"Yep. Reading it now."

"It's a good one, huh?"

Lincoln let his loud exhale do the talking.

"Don't tell me you're not loving it?" Richard asked.

"I'm not loving it."

"Are you kidding me?"

"It's a mass of clichés, Richard. There's not an original idea here anywhere."

"People don't want original ideas. Everything is just the same type of story told over and over again. You know that."

"I don't want to do the same type of story anymore."

"Do I need to remind you just how hard I had to work to get you this part? You got top billing, my friend. They don't give that to just anyone. When I think of all the other great young actors who could've got this role—"

Who'd probably turned it down when they saw the quality of the screenplay.

"— but instead the producers gave it to you, then I think you need to think hard about what you're saying here."

"I don't want to do it."

Richard gave a bark of laughter. "I think you're forgetting that you scribbled your name on a piece of paper that's called a contract."

"I'll pay them back."

"No, no, you won't. I'm not letting you back out of this just because you've enjoyed your vacation a little too much."

"You can't make me act in a movie I don't want to do."

"Your signature says I can. Look," the hardness in Richard's voice eased to melted butter. "I know it's been a confusing time, but you'll see. Everything will start making sense once you're back in LA."

La-la land. The place that sent him crazy. "I'm moving," he said abruptly.

"I beg your pardon?"

Yeah, well Richard might. The thought had barely passed through his brain and Linc had blurted it out. But it made sense. Especially when returning to Hollyweird made him want to throw up. "I'm giving up the apartment and moving back to Canada."

An expletive dropped. "Are you serious?"

"Never more so."

"Don't tell me you're going to move to the sticks. You are, aren't you? You're going to throw it all in and move to the lake and start fishing. Have you found a girl there, is that it?"

"I found a girl," he said, simply so he could enjoy Richard's horrified gasp. "But she doesn't want me."

"What?" Another blue word filled his ear, along with a pithy assessment of the intellect of any woman who refused Lincoln Cash. "So you're staying there to try to change her mind, is that it?"

"No. But I know I need to live somewhere where I can connect more easily with nature."

"You can connect with nature in LA. The place is surrounded by nature. What do you want? You've got hills, mountains, snow, ocean, desert, you name it, California's got it. Why would you want to live anywhere else?"

"I can't breathe there, Richard. I can't just be myself."

"Hate to break this to you, Lincoln, but you can't be yourself anywhere on this planet. Everyone knows who you are, and if you think you can go live somewhere in the back of Nowheresville and pretend to be normal you're fooling yourself."

Way to go with the support.

"Plenty of famous people live in LA, and you don't see them carrying on like this."

Except… you kinda did. Or worse.

"Come on, Linc." Richard's voice had grown soft again. "You know this movie is what we've dreamed about for years. Getting top billing is what you've worked so hard for. Do the film, then if you want to reassess, do that."

"That's the thing, Richard. I feel like I have been reassessing and I know what I want and what I don't. And I don't want to do this movie."

He could hear the irritation weighting Richard's lengthy exhale.

"So you're gonna be a prima donna, is that it?"

"No. But as I've said before, I want to do serious roles, roles that demand my acting more than my muscles, and this movie won't achieve that."

"This movie will make you rich."

"I don't need more money."

"Everyone needs more money, kid."

Richard was pulling out the 'kid' card now? He must be running scared.

"I want you to find me a role in a Vancouver or Toronto-based film or TV series."

"That's where you want to live?" Richard's voice crescendoed to a squeak.

"Yeah. That's where I want to live." As he spoke he realized the truth of it. Both cities held sizeable film-making industries, and both had relatively easy access to nature. Heck, if he lived in Toronto, maybe he could even come visit Muskoka again, buy a lakeside cottage of his own.

"I think you're making a grave mistake." Richard's voice was flat. "This is something we need to talk about next week when you're here. I can't help but wonder what's got your head in such a spin that you're not thinking straight. If it is this girl then you probably need some time away from her to really figure out what's what, because if you walk away from this film, chances are you're walking away from ever making movies again."

Awesome.

"You better be there for that interview with Variety on Thursday."

He bit back a sigh. "I'll be there on Thursday."

"You better."

The phone slammed down in his ear.

Well, that went well.

He threw his phone on the sofa and lay down, eyes closed, hands clasped beneath his head. What exactly had just happened? He didn't know if that had been a masterstroke or a master class in failure. Whatever it was, things between him and Richard were going to be different now.

How he wished he had someone to talk to. But Jackie was ignoring him, and apart from her, he didn't feel like there were many other people in this world he could count on to tell him the truth. He'd already visited his grandfather today, and while he knew Pop appreciated Lincoln's company, he wasn't exactly cognizant of what all of this might mean for Lincoln's career. He needed someone. Now.

"God," he prayed aloud. "Was that You making all that happen? Half the time I didn't even really know what I was saying, but hey, if it was You, then thanks." His fingers pressed into his skull, where the beginnings of a new headache pounded away. "Do You think You could help me figure out what to do next? I've got no idea, and I really need some wisdom and direction, please."

He lay there, listening, hoping for an answer in the way of an audible voice, but… nothing. Nothing except for the slightest easing of the tension rimming his head and his heart. That was something, at least.

His phone beeped a message. He snatched it up. His heartbeat thudded.

Jackie had replied at long last.

*Sure.*

~

"I STILL DON'T KNOW why I'm doing this," Jackie whispered to Serena as they moved around Jackie's tiny kitchen.

"Because you felt like he needed to know some of us before he left," Serena whispered.

That, and she'd had the strangest compulsion that God actually wanted her to see him because Lincoln needed a friend. Tonight. But because she barely trusted herself or her feelings when around him, she'd instantly sent a message to Serena and Joel asking them to come too. She knew from Lincoln's expression when he'd arrived that having two extras was not what he'd expected, but he was good enough to hide his dismay and pretend their company was exactly what he wanted.

And now, looking at him talking with Joel seriously on the tiny apartment patio as they cooked hamburgers—yeah, she really knew how to put on a movie-star-worthy spread—maybe this was exactly what God wanted to do. From all he had said she gathered that Lincoln didn't have too many genuine friends, and from what she'd seen at the fireworks there had been a sense of camaraderie between the two men that could easily deepen into friendship. And hey, it sure wouldn't hurt for Lincoln to be friends with a solid Christian man.

"I still can't get over the fact you have a movie star in your house."

"It's insane, right?"

Serena chuckled. "What's insane is how calm you are, like you do this all the time. If it was me I would've been cleaning for months, and yet you're so cool and collected."

"I'm a duck, paddling madly underneath the surface."

"Well, duckie, keep on swimming. It looks like they're coming back inside."

"Awesome."

"What's awesome?" Lincoln asked, carrying a plate of meat as Joel placed the barbecue tools in the sink.

"It's awesome that you decided to forgo wearing the 'I'm a big deal' t-shirt tonight."

He grinned. "I'm getting the feeling that you actually like that shirt." He winked at Serena. "Probably because it shows off my muscles."

Serena laughed. Traitor.

"You're supposed to be on my side, remember?" Jackie hissed.

"Are there sides?" Joel asked mildly. "I didn't realize this was war."

"It's not a war," she mumbled.

"But it looks like it's time to eat," Serena—hostess with the mostest, even when it wasn't her house—said, before taking a seat at the little table. Joel sat next to her, which left Lincoln to take the spare seat beside Jackie.

She swallowed. To any observer they look like two couples sitting down to a meal together. Heaven forbid Anna ever see this. She glanced at Joel. "Would you mind saying grace?"

"Sure."

He held out his hands and her breath suspended as Lincoln's palm stretched to hers. She gingerly clasped his hand, closing her eyes as Joel prayed. But she barely heard his prayer, so conscious was she that this was the first time she had held Lincoln's hand since that night on the beach. What was he thinking of all this?

"Amen," Serena repeated her husband, prompting Jackie and Lincoln's echoes too.

The next minute was spent assembling their burgers—meat patties, freshly sliced tomato and cheese, lettuce, pickles, pineapple rings, bacon rounds and fried eggs. Yeah, it made for a potential mess, but it was guaranteed to be delicious.

Jackie stole a look at Lincoln, peeking past a chunk of hair. When Serena had arrived an hour ago she had taken one look at Jackie's unbrushed hair and sent her straight to the bathroom to make herself look more presentable. "I know you want to be authentic and real, but that's no reason to not look your best."

So she'd helped style Jackie's hair so it fell in soft waves instead of the usual flatness, and helped apply some subtle makeup that made her eyes look bigger and her skin seem clearer and less red. The lip-gloss had probably all been wiped away with the cheese and crackers before, but she'd seen the effect her subtle transformation had had on Lincoln before. If she was a vain woman, she might even think he'd been impressed. That's what his wide eyes had suggested, anyway. Until they had widened even further when he realized Serena and Joel were there too. "You look beautiful," he'd whispered, before offering a handshake to her friends, greeting them like seeing them was the highlight of his day.

And that was the other thing. She didn't trust herself or her emotions when she was around him. And as an actor, she wasn't sure just how much of what he did was an act or was genuine, so having friends she trusted, like Serena and Joel, meant they might be able to see what she herself was missing. Lincoln Cash might be a good actor, but surely given they had the Holy Spirit and Godly discernment, they should be able to tell whether he was faking all these compliments or not.

"Nice burger," Lincoln commented, before taking a huge bite.

She smiled. Okay, that comment she was prepared to overlook. She might not have gourmet tendencies like Serena did, but a burger a person built themselves had to be okay. And she had at least made the patty herself, using a mix of ground beef, diced onion, and sweet chili sauce.

She took another sip of iced tea and snuck another look.

Lincoln's eyes were wide as his meat patty and fresh cut tomato slipped from his bread roll bun, which itself then broke apart and slopped juice and sauce all down his front.

"Oh my goodness!" She handed him a paper napkin as Joel smothered a chuckle with a cough. "I'm so sorry. I didn't expect the bun to fall apart!"

Lincoln laughed, and refused any more napkins. "It's okay. I just look like a man who loves his food, right?"

"You certainly do," Serena said, stifling a giggle.

"Just keeping it real," Joel said, his tone and look holding a weight Jackie didn't understand, but it appeared Lincoln did as he nodded to his phone.

"Do me a favor? Take a photo?"

"Of you looking a mess?"

"Of me being real," Lincoln explained, grinning at the phone camera as Joel took his photo. "Thanks."

He wiped his hands and then tapped the screen a few times. "Sorry to be so rude, but I wanted to make sure I go with the moment here."

"What are you doing?" she asked.

He slid the phone into his back pocket and picked up the remains of his burger again. "I told my publicist I wanted to showcase more realness on my social media, and I figured you can't get much more real than this, huh?"

"You're posting that on social media?" She gestured to his stained shirt, and slightly less-stained-now face.

"Keeping it real for us mortals," Joel said with a grin.

Okay, so what was going on between these two? Clearly conversation had been had out on the patio, but she didn't know what to make of it. A raised brow glance at Serena saw her shrug too.

"So, what's next for you, Lincoln?" Serena asked. "Jackie mentioned you were heading back to LA soon."

"Next week," he admitted. "I have a big interview on Thursday which I'm unexcited about, and then I need to consider what I'm going to do about this movie I'm supposed to do, but I don't want to be in."

"Why not?" Jackie asked.

He turned to face her. "Because it's silly, and I don't want to do those kinds of roles anymore."

"What kind of role would you like to do?" Serena asked.

"Something that allows me to act and not just stand around trying to look nice and kiss a few girls."

"You do that well," Serena said.

Kiss girls? Jackie's heart tensed at the scenes she'd watched.

"Look nice, I mean. What?" she murmured as Joel nudged her. "It's true."

"Anyway, I've been looking for a way to figure out what to do next," Lincoln said. "My agent has told me that if I break the contract I'm liable for a huge amount of money, so it's a bit of a mess, and I can't really see which way to go forward. It's all just happened today, and it's all kind of fresh and my head is still spinning, so if I'm a little vague, then please forgive me."

"I'm glad you could come tonight," Jackie said to him.

"You might find this hard to believe, but I actually prayed that God would send me a friend, and then you messaged me, and here I am with three friends."

Serena placed a hand on her heart, the 'aww' in her expression likely mirroring Jackie's own. He'd prayed? Did that mean he was reopening the communication lines with God? This, plus Lincoln considered her friends as his? Were there any more wonders to be revealed tonight?

"We'll be praying for you, Linc."

Joel now called him Linc like they were best buds since preschool, and that the man she sat next to wasn't a famous movie star?

"Thanks, man. I appreciate it."

Okay, she needed caffeine to spark some sense to her brain. It was like she had fallen into some alternative universe where her dreams might just come true.

"Well, now that Lincoln has thoroughly destroyed his burger, I'm wondering if anyone wants dessert." She glanced at Lincoln. "You don't need to worry as I'm not responsible. Serena made tiramisu, and she's the best cook I know, so it'll be delicious."

Lincoln patted his flat stomach of the Instagram-worthy abs. "What my trainer doesn't know won't hurt, right?"

"Except he might if he sees what you posted on Instagram."

"She," Lincoln murmured. "My trainer is a woman."

Okay. See? Just when he appeared a dozen kinds of normal, and she was almost prepared to let her guard down, he comes out with something like that. He had a trainer. A publicist. An agent. He was surrounded by beautiful women he was paid to kiss. How on earth was she supposed to get her head around any of that? It was just as well they'd agreed to be friends because thinking about this too much would do her head in.

"You're welcome to come running with me and my girl," Joel said, wrapping an arm around Serena's shoulders.

A discussion followed about running, which saw Jackie clear the plates, waving off their offers to assist, as she explained the kitchen was only really big enough for one.

She retrieved the ice-cream from the freezer, giving it time to defrost a little, then loaded the dishwasher, thankful for the time to recalibrate, to draw in God's presence as she sucked in deep breaths. Tonight had not gone the way she'd imagined. Linc kept surprising her, and Joel and Serena as well she suspected, with his mix of honesty and self-deprecation, humor, and wit. It was like the man from two weeks ago had had a personality transplant. Or maybe he'd just had the chance to relax and finally reveal the man he'd always been.

"You need any help in here?"

She couldn't look at him. He made her too tense. Surely God didn't want her to stir up feelings for someone like this? Of course He didn't. She clenched her fingers until her nails dug into her palm. Of course not. It was clear now. The reason God had prompted her to invite Lincoln to dinner tonight was so he would have the chance to connect with Joel on a deeper level. God obviously wanted to use Joel to reach Lincoln's soul, seeing she'd been unable to.

"Jackie?"

His voice was soft, and she blinked away tears, swallowing

the egg-sized lump in her throat. "If you could get the dessert from the fridge that'd be great. It's the one with plastic wrap. Oh, and there's a bowl of berries beside it."

He obeyed, then paused. "Are you okay? You've barely spoken to me all night."

"I think you've got a new fan in Joel."

"I'm glad for the chance to get to know him and Serena some more. But they weren't who I came to see tonight."

She peeked up at him now. "Sorry for ambushing you."

"Hey, it's fine. Actually, it's been exactly what I needed. Sometimes I find it way too easy to live in my head, and it was great to have another perspective on some of the things I've been struggling with."

"I didn't know you've been struggling."

"Nobody likes to admit they don't have it all together. But sometimes I don't."

His eyes held vulnerability, chasing away a stupid impulse to tease. She didn't want to spoil this moment with a childish joke about his over-confidence. "When don't you have it together?" she asked instead.

His lips tweaked to one side. "Like when the girl I like tells me no, and I have to pretend it doesn't hurt."

Her breath caught. "Lincoln, I…" Didn't know what to say. Apologize for hurting him? She couldn't, as she wasn't sorry for having Godly standards, even though she was sorry he felt sad. She licked her lips.

His gaze fell to her mouth, like he'd found something sweeter than what he held in his hands.

"Hey, are you two bringing out dessert or do we need to come in there?" Serena called.

"I know what I'd rather be doing than eating dessert," he murmured, his gaze flicking back to her lips.

Oh my goodness. These summer temperatures had a lot to answer for. Maybe she should go hold the ice cream because she suddenly felt very hot.

"Hey—oh!" Serena skidded to a stop, her smirking gaze flicking between them. "Don't let me interrupt. Or maybe, let me. Where's that dessert? Come on, you two. A girl can't wait all day."

But she could. Jackie had waited nearly thirty years for her first kiss. And while she knew next to nothing about flirting, she was pretty sure that was what Lincoln had meant. She shivered. He wanted to kiss her?

"Hello, Jackie!" Serena found the pile of bowls and spoons Jackie had set out earlier, as she shooed Lincoln back to the table. "Come on. You know you love my dessert."

Jackie snapped from her trance. Smiled. There'd be time to think on all this later. "Yes, I do."

"You're blushing," Serena whispered.

"Am I?" She placed cool hands on hot cheeks.

"I know I'm not the romance writer, but I'm pretty sure he likes you."

Had she explained to Serena that Lincoln had said he wanted to date her? Clearly they needed a thorough catch up.

Before she could move ,her phone flashed a message. She glanced at it. Anna? "Oh!"

"What is it?"

"Anna just messaged me."

"Hallelujah, it's about time," Serena said. "I've been praying for her to do so. What did she say?"

Jackie frowned as she studied the message. What did she mean?

*Thanks for not inviting me.*

Huh? "I don't understand." She showed the phone to Serena. "Do you know what this means?"

Serena's breath hitched. "Oh no."

"What?"

She held up the phone. She hadn't noticed it before, but now

Anna had sent through a screenshotted picture. A picture of Lincoln's Instagram feed, of him grinning at the camera as he held the remains of a burger. He'd captioned it "Delicious meal with friends, even if this man can't hold his burger. #Keepingitreal."

"How'd she know it was here?"

Serena pointed to the cross-stitched picture of an English manor house and garden in the background, complete with the words 'God bless this home,' the picture that had taken Jackie months to complete.

The picture that was hanging right there on Jackie's wall.

# CHAPTER 12

*Oh my gosh! So adorable.*
*Doesn't the man know how to eat?*
*Classy, Lincoln. Real classy.*
*Who are your friends?*
*Looks like you enjoyed that.*
*Yum! Lincoln looks like a snack.*

Lincoln's lip curled at the last one—objectification, much?—then tossed the phone on the car passenger seat. So his first attempt to be more real may have backfired in the eyes of some, but he suspected they were the kind of people he wasn't out to impress anyway. But steering this ship from curated glamor and glitz to something a little less pretentious was going to take time, he knew that. Even if Jolene had been less than impressed, or so her voicemail this morning had suggested.

And now, he was here, on his last day in Muskoka before he had to catch a flight from Toronto tonight. He'd been tempted to ask Jackie if she'd drive him to the airport—that wasn't an unreasonable request to ask of a friend, was it?—before realizing that his hire car would need to be returned anyway, and if she was spotted sitting there with him, it could lead to all kinds of speculation she really didn't need. So he'd had to content himself with seeing her one last time at Golden Elms, even if it felt far, far less than what he really wanted.

He opened the car door to be greeted with the soft drift of air scented with summer. Pine trees sang in the gentle breeze, begging him to pause and soak it in. But he couldn't stay. He had a schedule to keep, obligations to meet, expectations to fulfil. Even if coming here to Muskoka had confounded every one of his own expectations.

He grabbed his phone and took a photo looking up at the blue sky from the base of the pine trees, as the branches fanned out in rhythmic grace. Another pic uploaded to the Gram and his millions of followers. #Lovethisplace #Muskoka

It wouldn't matter if people knew where he was now. He was leaving. They wouldn't find him today.

He switched his phone on mute then shoved it in his pocket and entered. Nodded to the front desk staff. The grin of the trainee nurse faded more quickly than usual, but he didn't care. He had somewhere else to be. Two important people to see. Two people he wasn't sure how he'd cope with not seeing for a long time.

How long until he could return? His footsteps echoed along the corridor as he walked to his grandfather's room. He had the Variety interview tomorrow, then production on the space flick was supposed to begin soon, requiring solid rehearsing in LA for the next few weeks. Unless he could get out of it, but from Richard's last email, complete with heavily underlined clauses included in the contract, it seemed impossible. Still, Joel's sermon on Sunday seemed to suggest God was into solving impossible situations, so maybe God could help Linc out again. Of course, the fact that the Creator of the universe would deign to help little Linc out with anything seemed wildly bizarre. But if what all his newfound friends said was true—and the fact he now had friends seemed yet another of those miracles—then maybe God's mercy didn't run out and He had more good things lined up for Lincoln, too.

"Knock, knock." He tapped on Pop's door and opened it, then wheeled away at the sight of his grandfather's bare chest. Who knew old men looked like that? "Sorry, Pop. Didn't mean to intrude."

"Doesn't matter. Now if you were your favorite nurse and mine it might, but you're not, so that's okay."

"Has she been in yet?" Linc settled into his usual seat.

His grandfather gave a wheezy sounding cough. "You and I both know that the reason you're here now is because this is when she usually does her rounds."

"Is it? I didn't know."

Pop shook his head. "What are you going to do about her?"

"What do you mean?"

"You're leaving today, aren't you? So have you told her how you feel?"

"Yeah."

"And…?"

"And she's still not interested."

"What? Are you sure?" His grandfather's eyebrows lowered. "Have you told her about being a believer yet?"

"I haven't really had the chance to talk to her privately since you told me that last week." He explained about Saturday night's dinner at her house where he'd been surprised by Joel and Serena. "And I didn't mind, as they seemed really nice, but they didn't leave until I did, so we couldn't talk afterwards. And yes, Joel invited me to church on Sunday, and I went, but left before anyone could see me." He shrugged. "Jackie had some girls' group thing on all day, then she's had meetings the last two nights. It's a good thing I'm so secure otherwise I'd wonder if she was avoiding me again."

"Should she be avoiding you?"

"Not at all. I've been a perfect gentleman." He crossed his heart. "Gran would be proud of me."

Pop studied him a long moment then nodded. "Have you talked to your mother recently?"

"Yesterday." His folks had gotten back from Hawaii, and it'd been good to touch base. He'd needed to do something to mitigate the disappointment of not seeing Jackie last night. "She said they're going to try to get here in the next few weeks."

"Good. Now if Peter could do the same we could almost play happy families again."

Linc nodded, studying the dirt smudge on his Converse, as his grandfather's words ate into his thoughts. See? Another reason to leave LA was to be near his family. Yeah, he'd had to leave in order to build his career, but maybe his career was at a stage where he could settle down rather than chase locations around the globe, leaving his apartment empty for months at a time. That was no way to build security. That was no way to settle down.

Settle down? He rubbed a hand over his face.

"You feeling okay, son?" Pop asked.

"Just dandy."

"Sure don't look it."

Lincoln shot his grandfather a fake scowl as a knock came at the door and his grandfather called, "It's open."

He straightened, smiling, even as his heart yearned for Jackie to pay him attention. "Good morning, Mac. Mr. Cash."

"Ms. O'Halloran."

She shot him a quick look then refocused on his grandfather, allowing Lincoln the luxury of watching her, unobserved. He noticed afresh her gentle movements, the little caresses, the way her features lit as she smiled. His heart wrenched. If only she would smile at him that way, instead of this weirdness where he never really knew where he stood with her.

"…and how do you feel about that?" she asked Pop.

"I'll miss him, but he's just told me his mother's planning to visit soon, so that'll be something."

"Wonderful."

Linc studied her. Something seemed a little off with her. Was she upset he was leaving? He could only hope.

"Right, well, I guess that does us here. I'll see you later, Mac." Her glance found Linc, and she nodded. "Mr. Cash."

"You can't just leave," he blurted.

"I have rounds, and—"

"I'm leaving today." He pushed to his feet. "I need to talk to you."

"I understand, but you know I have work to do, and I can't just stop because someone wants to talk to me." She moved to the door.

He glanced at his grandfather. "Sorry, Pop. I'll be back in a moment."

"Do what you gotta do. You know where to find me." He winked. "And what I'll be doing." He pressed his hands together in a praying motion.

Linc jerked a nod and followed Jackie out the door. Maybe his grandfather's prayers meant he'd have half a hope of being heard. "Jackie, wait."

Now he was close he could see the tiredness rimming her eyes. He touched her arm. "What's wrong?"

"Nothing's wrong." She shifted her weight, then gasped, glancing behind her.

"What?"

She shook her head, rubbing a hand over her eyes. "I thought I saw Téa take your photo."

"It doesn't matter now. Not when I'm leaving today."

Her lips pressed together and she glanced down.

"Jackie? Have I done something wrong? I feel like you've been avoiding me these past few days, I really needed to talk to you about some things."

"I'm sorry." She sighed. "I told you about my friend Anna, and the fact she's been struggling with you and me. She sent me a text message on Saturday night which threw me and that's why I was a bit distant." Her gaze met his. "She saw your post and recognized my house and got upset I didn't invite her to meet you."

"I thought we'd already met. The one with desserts from Canada Day, right?"

"Yeah, but she's not happy with me, and now I feel like she's looking for ways to be offended."

"I'm sorry."

"Look, I really can't talk now."

"When is your lunch break?"

She glanced at her watch. "In two hours."

"Can I steal you away then? Please?" he added when she seemed to hesitate.

"Whatever it is you have to say must be pretty important."

"It is. Look, I'll be here," he gestured to his grandfather's room, "and whatever you want to do is fine with me. Even if it's roast chicken with the oldies."

"It's roast pork today," she said with a small smile.

"Even better. But please, come and get me? I'm not going anywhere until you do."

"You'll miss your plane."

"I'd miss more than that for you," he said honestly.

She studied him, then finally nodded. "I'll come find you."

"I'll be here," he promised. "Thank you."

"Téa, did you take a photo of Mr. Cash before?" Jackie winced at her abrupt words. How not to get someone on-side. She managed a smile that felt tighter than the leather pants worn by Linc's last co-star. This was probably not the time nor place, but if Téa had taken a photo, it needed to get shut down now.

Téa's chin lifted. "You saw me, so you know I did."

"I thought we had an understanding, and that you'd agreed to not post anything while Mr. Cash was here."

"But he's leaving today, so it doesn't matter."

Her heart panged. Except it did matter. She had told herself it didn't matter, that he was nothing to her, that he was only a friend, but he'd come to be much more. And now, when he'd asked to speak to her, hope danced around that he'd finally say something that she could pin her hopes to. She couldn't risk that being spoiled by a disappointed fan. "But he's not left yet, has he?"

Téa's loud exhalation didn't denote respect. But she didn't have time to deal with her now. Not with a loud alarm coming from Bernard's room. She rushed past Téa to join Maureen at Bernard's bedside.

"He's not breathing!" Maureen said, looking up from checking his vitals.

"Then we need to start CPR." Her voice sounded much calmer than she felt. "Téa!"

"Can I help?" a masculine voice called from the door.

"Get someone to get the facility doctor, and call 911. We need an ambulance right now!"

Jackie's breath came in unsteady bursts as she completed compressions while Maureen squeezed the bag valve mask resuscitator. "Come on, Bernard. It's not your time to go."

"Ambulance is on its way." She felt Lincoln's presence beside her. "Here, let me."

"You know how to do CPR?"

"Yeah. Come on, I'm taller than you so I can do this more easily, so shove over."

Her arms felt like deadweights as she eased back, letting Lincoln take over in a manner that was practically professional.

He clearly had done this before.

"How long was he out?" Jackie asked Maureen, pressing two fingers to Bernard's pulse point on his throat.

"I don't know. He'd stopped breathing and his lips were turning blue when I came in."

Blue? No. Oh, no. There was a sound of rushing feet as more people entered the room. She barely noticed as she prayed and worked and willed Bernard to stay alive. But if he'd already been turning blue...

"Excuse me, who are you?" Dana Monroe, the supervisor, asked Lincoln who was still doing compressions.

"He heard the alarm and came to help."

"We have protocols here. Jackie, take over please."

She obeyed, her shoulder brushing his as he stepped back and Dana asked him to leave. Agitation rose. He'd just been trying to help.

"How long has it been now?" Dana asked. "Jackie?"

"Maureen found him," she gritted out, as she resumed compressions.

"Ten minutes?" Maureen repeated the information she'd shared before.

"Then I think we need to call it."

"But—"

"It's been ten minutes, Jackie. You need to stop."

"But—"

"Now!"

Jackie paused, then glanced at Dana, who wore a scowl.

"We've done all we could. Chances are he was beyond saving, anyway." Dana placed her hands on her hips. "Maureen, you'll need to complete the paperwork. Jackie, I need to see you in my office. Immediately."

Why? Grief at Bernard's passing made her linger at Bernard's side as Maureen began the procedures for when the doctor arrived. She clasped Bernard's fingers and gently squeezed, as if she could instill life into him. "God bless you, my friend," she whispered, as tears choked her throat.

Working with the elderly meant this wasn't unexpected, but it was something that was still hard, and she was so, so tired of loss. And right now it seemed like there were so many hard and sad things to contend with, with too much change and people leaving.

"Jackie, now!"

"She's on the warpath," Maureen murmured.

Which was the perfect topping for an already crappy day.

She cleaned her hands then followed, passing Lincoln who stood with others in the hall. But she couldn't look at him, even though she longed to thank him and knew he must be feeling confused as to why Dana had snapped at him earlier.

"What was that?" Dana asked as soon as Jackie closed the office door. "You know we have policies and procedures, and letting a visitor take part in a situation like that was completely unacceptable."

"He was there, he offered, and we needed help. I called for assistance, but nobody else came."

"You messed with protocols, that's what you did, Jackie." Dana peered at her. "Is it true that he's your boyfriend?"

"What?" She felt dizzy. The five hours of sleep last night hadn't done her clarity of thought any favors.

"I've heard rumors about you and some movie star. I hope that's not true, because the residents here don't need adverse publicity."

"He's not my boyfriend, and I know he would never want to cause Golden Elms any negative press."

"He better not. It's hard enough managing things here without extra challenges." Dana gave another piercing look. "You look tired. I hope you're not coming down with anything. We can't afford for you to get sick and pass that on to the residents."

Wow. Dana was officious, but there was no need to talk down to her like she was a schoolgirl. "I'm not sick," except in the heart, maybe, "but I am weary."

"You have leave in a week or so, yes?"

Thank heavens. She couldn't wait to get away from all of the confusion here. "Yes."

"I hope you'll take time to consider your actions."

On a normal day, Jackie might have enough wherewithal to stand up to Dana's domineering ways. But today wasn't normal, and what little strength Jackie had she needed to complete her duties before she could huddle into bed and cry.

"You're dismissed. I have paperwork, and you have work to do."

She stumbled from the room, accidentally closing the door behind her with more force than necessary—no doubt giving Dana the impression that Jackie was acting like a petulant teenager.

She found the staff bathroom and washed her face, sucking in long, deep breaths as she tried to calm her emotions. Even praying seemed too hard now, her thoughts like stutters that couldn't get past *God, help.*

When she finally judged herself calm enough, she moved back to the hallway, in time to see James Wells, today's on-call doctor, departing Bernard's room. She managed a wobbly smile, glad when he turned to reply to something Maureen said. She hurried past. She couldn't speak. So much for trying to be professional. She couldn't pretend, not even with her friends. Emotions clashed—sorrow, frustration, injustice—begging to release.

The door to Mavis's room opened. "So, Bernard carked it at last."

Jackie's feet paused, as she stared at Mavis, who stood, her hands on her walker, with a smile that spoke of satisfaction.

Mavis whinnied out a laugh. "I always told him I'd outlast him."

Outrage bubbled up. How dare this horrible, horrible woman look gleeful at such a tragedy? Words begged to spill from her lips: *I wish it was you who'd died.* She pressed her lips together to stop them, narrowed her eyes, and kept walking.

"Jackie? Aren't you going to help me?"

No. She felt like a wounded zombie, like one of those half-dead creatures she'd once seen in a terrible movie Rachel had forced them to watch at one of Serena's soirees one time. They'd managed half an hour before Serena turned it off. But it seemed there was no turning off this hollowness, this shivery ache that seemed to be all over her, inside and out.

"Jackie?"

She glanced up. Lincoln.

"Hey, I'm sorry," he said.

Tears smarted then started falling, and she wiped them with the heel of her hand, but her breathing hitched.

"Hey, come here." He held open his arms.

Tempted as she was, she couldn't risk it. People would see. Téa seemed to always have her phone where Lincoln was, Mavis was likely watching, ready to file a report against Jackie, Dana seemed to dislike her. "I…" She shook her head.

"Come on." He grasped her hand and drew her into a nearby supply closet and closed the door.

What? No. Oh.

She closed her eyes as his arms wrapped around her, the comfort of leaning against his strong chest drawing her emotions to spill. Heaven help her, was she the one making a high-pitched wailing sound?

"Hey, it's okay," he murmured, rubbing her back.

No, it wasn't. Bernard had died. She'd been reprimanded. Anna hated her. Lincoln was leaving. She was so, *so* tired. She was supposed to be professional. And this, here, now, was anything but.

He cupped the back of her head in his hand and held her and she leaned into his strength, letting him hold her. Her emotional storm passed, and she clung to him, hugging him like a bear would a tree, as she rested in the circle of his arms.

"You're amazing," he whispered.

"I'm a mess." Good thing it was dark in here, otherwise he'd see her in all her blotchy skin, snotty-nosed, red-eyed glory. And that was just her face. She kept messing up in so many ways, she, who had always prided herself on her calmness and her ability to keep things together.

"You're human." He stroked her hair. "If you didn't grieve the loss of a life then that would show a hard heart. And you don't have that. You have a beautiful heart."

She shook her head against his chest, as the memory of words from long ago taunted like a foul perfume.

"Not everyone can be beautiful," she'd once overheard her old youth leader murmur. "Some people, like Jackie, have a beautiful heart…"

She wrenched from his embrace, wiping at her face. "I'm sorry."

"Hey, you've got nothing to be sorry about."

Oh, yes, she did. She shouldn't have broken down in this way. Shouldn't have let him in as far as she had. Shouldn't even be in this tiny supply room with him! "I need to go." She had rounds. Residents to see. A job to do. "I can't…" She shook her hand at him. "This, no."

Through the dimness she saw his face soften. "We can talk later."

"No." Her voice was firmer now, less wispy-thin. "No, we can't. I don't want to…" Didn't want to continue playing with fire when her heart had already been burned.

"You don't want to do lunch with me?"

She pressed against the headache she could feel forming, digging into her forehead with her fingertips. "I can't. I have work, and I need to get back. I've already been away too long."

"But I'm leaving."

"I know." Oh, how she knew! That knowledge had kept her awake half the night. Her heart started keening again, but she had to be strong. "I'm really sorry, Lincoln. I thought maybe I could be your friend, but I don't want you to call me."

"What?"

"Please don't call me." It wouldn't be good for her mental or emotional health.

"Why not? I'm not leaving forever. I'll be back to visit."

And she'd somehow make sure she wasn't rostered on those days. "It's not that, it's…" She could barely articulate it.

"It's what? Please, help me understand."

"It's you. It's all this. It's too much. You're too much. Everything about you is so big and huge and important and I'm not. I'm just me. I'm not the kind of person you need in your world. I'm not even pretty." She held up a hand to stop his protest. "And I can't even tell if it's real or if you really think you mean it, but whatever it is I know it can't last, so I can't let myself fall for someone who will leave me."

"I won't leave you. I mean, I am, but I'll be back."

"And then you'll go again, and I'll be left wondering if you've really changed—"

"I *have* changed." His face held hurt. "I'm different now—"

"Nobody changes that fast. It takes time, and—"

"I love you."

Her breath fell away. She gulped in air. "You don't."

He smiled and took a step closer, the intoxicating scent of his aftershave wafting near. "I really think I do."

"You're just saying that. You barely know me. You don't mean it."

His breath brushed her skin as his face angled to hers. "Do you want me to prove it?"

Yes. No. Her lips ached to know his kiss—her first kiss—but Lincoln Cash wasn't who God wanted for her. Still, the heady nearness of him made her breathing heavy, her eyelids blink more slowly, as a kind of languor fell over her. Everything seemed to slow, as if even her very pores swayed toward him. Would it be so wrong to know what everyone else already knew?

She placed her hands on his chest to push him away. "I can't—"

"What's going on?"

Jackie jumped as a bright flash filled the room. She spun around. Three faces stared back: Dana, Mavis, and Téa, who lowered her phone with a smirk.

"See? I told you she was ignoring the residents because she found herself a man."

The elderly woman's smugness tore against Jackie's self-control. "Mavis, I'm not—"

"It's my fault." Lincoln's voice, his hand on her arm, stopped her. "I could see that Jackie was upset, and in no fit state to be with the residents, so I brought her in here to try to help. Which clearly has backfired, and doesn't seem to have helped much at all, but I in no way meant to cause her further problems."

"Mr. Cash, it seems you are unaware of our protocols—"

"Oh, I'm only too aware of them, thank you," he interrupted Dana. "But if I could be so bold, perhaps you need to create some protocols where your staff who care deeply about their residents here are not expected to be immediately thrown back on the floor. That seems rather inhumane to me."

"Mr. Cash—"

"I was hoping to make a donation to Golden Elms—"

He was?

"—but I wouldn't want to see it jeopardized if I was to learn that Jackie has been unfairly treated because of today."

"Yes, but while we appreciate that, and heaven knows we could certainly do with more generous donors, you must understand that we have procedures and policies that do not allow for our staff members to become overly-familiar with residents—"

"I'm not a resident," he said.

"Or their relatives."

"Overly-familiar my foot." Mavis sniffed. "They were canoodling! Anyone can see they've been kissing—"

"We have not!" Jackie insisted.

"Maybe all this fuss would be worth it if we had," Lincoln muttered from beside her. His hand slid down her arm, and then he gently touched her hand.

For a second she thought he was going to hold her hand, which was hardly the way to convince the others that nothing was going on, especially with Téa watching like a hawk. But then, he shifted, touched her back and gestured her forward. She obeyed, their forward motion prompting the others to scatter as they emerged from the small room.

She blinked against the brighter light, grew aware there were more people here, people she thought were friends, some of whom now seemed to regard her with sympathy, others with suspicion. Oh, what on earth did people think she was doing in there with Lincoln? Could a day get any worse? She staggered.

Lincoln gripped her elbow, put an arm around her shoulders. "As you can see, Jackie clearly isn't well and should go home. I hope there's something in your protocols about caring for staff who are unwell," he challenged Dana.

"I…"

From under heavy eyelids—she really did feel off-color—Jackie saw Dana's mouth opening and closing like a goldfish. "I'm fine," she mumbled.

"You're not," Lincoln murmured. "You've been working too hard and you need to rest. She needs to go home," he said in a louder voice.

"She can't go home. Who will replace her?" Dana said.

"Perhaps her supervisor could figure that out. Maybe a trainee nurse might finally do more than take photos." He encouraged Jackie to move, holding her in a way that suggested she really was more ill than she felt—and definitely showed they were perhaps more than the mere friends she'd claimed.

They exited the corridor. "What do you need?" he asked.

"Apart from to be by myself?" she muttered.

"Look, I'm sorry for overstepping back there, but you don't seem yourself at all. You shouldn't have come in today."

But she'd had to. Because he'd be here. And he was leaving. "You're going soon."

"I'm not going until I know you'll be okay."

"I am okay," she insisted. "I will be okay."

"You need to go home."

"I need you to stop!" she said. "Lincoln, I appreciate that you care, but I don't want you to tell me what to do. I know what to do. I need to have a rest, but I can do that in the staffroom for a few minutes."

"But you won't rest, will you? As soon as the next emergency comes along you'll be back on your feet, trying to help. When do you take time for you? When was the last time you had fun? Why do you work so hard all the time?"

His words cut, her heart flinching like he threw broken glass. "I don't have time for this now."

"No, because you've got work."

"And so do you. That's why you're leaving, right? You have work there, and I have work here. Your life is elsewhere, while my life is here."

He groaned. "Come on, Jackie. Don't make this harder than it already is."

"But that's exactly my point. It *is* too hard." Oh, she was treading through quicksand, and had to make him leave before she got sucked into breaking down again. "You might say you care about me, but I'm sorry, Lincoln, I don't feel the same about you," she lied. Her heart ached as his face fell. She pushed her fingers into her scalp to relieve the pressure, drew in a deep breath. "I need you to leave me alone. Don't contact me. Don't call. Don't send messages. If you care for me like you say you do, then please leave me alone."

"Jackie—"

"No. Please go," she whispered.

"Just hear me out," he pleaded.

"I can't." Because then she'd stumble, she'd fall, and she found him so tempting she might fall too far and never find herself again.

So she opened the door to the staffroom and went inside, closing it against the famous movie star and all the glittery temptation Lincoln Cash offered. Then rushed to the bathroom, slammed the cubicle door closed, and cried.

# CHAPTER 13

Lincoln's thumb paused on the photo taken last week. How was it possible so much had happened in such a short space of time? It felt like he'd lived a lifetime in mere weeks.

He enlarged the photo, tracing the curve of cheek, the lips he'd never got to kiss, wishing he could see her again. His gut tensed. Had she truly meant it when she'd said not to contact her again? He didn't want to believe it. When he'd finally given up on having her re-emerge, he'd returned to his grandfather's room where Pop had encouraged him to not give up, but to pray for her instead. "And pray about your future. Commit your ways to God and trust Him to direct your paths."

And so he had. There, in Pop's room. He'd prayed and confessed it all and recommitted his heart just like Joel had talked about on Saturday night. Now Lincoln finally knew he was right with God, and felt a peace that undergirded the tension about so many things. Including the interview that would start in ten minutes.

Maybe Jackie didn't believe he'd changed, but he'd show her

he had. And show her less by words and more by deeds. And owning truth and being real was just the least of these.

"Mr. Cash, just lift your chin, there."

He obeyed the makeup artist's instruction as a dab of foundation covered a spot. If only all his mistakes could be covered.

He drew in a breath, slowly released. Actually, with Jesus, all his mistakes had been dealt with. And Linc was trying to trust that God would help him now.

"Now let's just fine tune that hair, shall we?"

"Go for it."

He glanced back at his phone. He had time. A few taps then he added the line and #reallifeheroes.

The next minutes passed as a microphone was fed through his shirt, being careful not to disarrange the artfully sprayed disarrayed hair, then he was led down a couple of cramped corridors to the studio. He nodded to various crew members, shook Jennifer's hand, and settled into the seat as they exchanged small talk.

"You ready?" she asked.

"So ready." See? That was the old Lincoln people knew and loved. Maybe he could do this okay, after all.

He pasted on a smile as she began her opening spiel to the camera then turned to him.

"So, Lincoln, tell us how you feel about your upcoming release."

Lincoln shifted in his seat. How he felt about anything anymore had been trumped by what had happened yesterday. So to sit here and act like he cared about the stupid movie he didn't want to do? "Yeah, can't wait." He tried to inject some positivity into his fake smile.

Why had she rejected him?

His fingers clenched. He was a professional. Acting was what he did. He could do this interview. If only he'd realized it was being filmed. Jolene had been so excited when she'd picked him up from his hotel, explaining that the usual magazine article had transformed into more when a spot became available. "They don't offer TV interviews to everyone, Lincoln, and this is to be a wide-ranging one with Jennifer Jones." She'd nearly squealed in the car seat. "So you need to make the most of this opportunity."

So here he was, making the most of this opportunity with the gargoyle-eyed Jennifer Jones.

"So, Lincoln, are you excited?"

"I'm always excited about the chance to work with great directors," he hedged.

"Yes, but you haven't yet said whether you're excited about working with this director."

Man, walking the line between truth and fiction was so hard. What would happen if he just spoke honestly for once?

He glanced past the interviewer's shoulder-pads and glimpsed Jolene, arms crossed, scowl affixed. Here went nothing, then. "To be completely honest, I was a little surprised that Victor was still happy to have me attached to this production. After what happened in New York, I was under the impression he didn't want to work with me again, so it's nice to know I'm not as much of an embarrassment as I was led to believe."

Jolene's mouth dropped, matching the sag in the interviewer's jaw. He settled back in his seat for more.

"Are you saying Victor told you that you wouldn't be part of this film?"

"I was under that impression, which always seemed a little harsh to me, considering."

"Considering what?"

"Considering he—and it seems many others—have misjudged me. I mean, sure, I'm the first to put up my hand and say I haven't exactly always helped my cause—"

"Like the recent incident in New York?" Jennifer interposed.

"That." He sighed. "That happened because I get migraines

and need medication. I was in the middle of an episode and my migraine was triggered again."

Just as they had been by his return to LA. Just as he'd known would happen.

He gave a wry smile. "Sometimes I wonder if living here in LA just makes them worse." Hey, if he was going to go out with a bang, he might as well make it spectacular.

"Are you saying that you would rather live somewhere else?"

"Maybe. I've recently discovered that I'm rather partial to nature, and it seems to make me feel more at ease. Healthier, too."

"That's right. You've recently been in," she consulted her notes, "Muskoka, in Ontario, Canada."

"Yeah. Visiting family. It was a great escape."

Was Jackie right in suggesting it had been an escape from his reality? Was she right to have been cautious in assuming his feelings for her could not be real? Sure, it had been fast, but living in a fast world meant he was used to making snap decisions, juggling and discerning what was right and what was wrong. And everything about Jackie was right, which meant everything about their break up was wrong. Could it even be considered a break up when they'd never actually really been anything more than friends?

"Lincoln?"

Shoot. She'd obviously just asked him something, but for the life of him he didn't know what. "Sorry. You'll have to forgive me. I'm still readjusting to time zones. Could you repeat the question?"

"Rumors have it that while you were there you were seen in the company of a particular lady."

"She's particular, all right," he said, without thinking. Particular about a man only kissing those lips if he had a WWJD sticker on his car, and wore a cross, and—

"So there *is* someone."

Whoa. Way to go with playing it cool, and not making this bigger than he wanted. Oh, who was he kidding? It was already bigger than he wanted. In for a penny, in for a… "I thought there was, but she didn't want me, so yeah. Good times."

"Are you trying to tell me you were turned down?"

"I'm not trying to tell you that. I thought I made it clear."

Jennifer's penciled-on eyebrows rose.

"So yes, I know all about unrequited love right now." He held up a hand. "Anyone needing another *Notebook* guy, here I am." He caught a glimpse of Jolene giving him two thumbs up. Ugh.

"Well, this is certainly more than what I anticipated today."

He shrugged. "I could sit here and play pretend, but what's the point, really? I'm a guy who has struggles in this world just like the next one. Well, maybe not exactly like the next guy because I get to have all of my problems broadcast for the world to see. Not that I'm complaining. I know I'm blessed in the whole scheme of things. It's just right now I feel a little raw."

"Thank you for being honest, Lincoln."

He nodded. "I've learned a lot lately about the importance of being honest, and I'm really trying to show that more in who I am. Whether it's in my social media or here today, talking to you. I don't want to be on a pedestal or have people think I'm more than what I really am. Even just talking about myself makes me realize just how self-centered I can be. Which is a problem in this industry, isn't it? We live in such a bubble and forget there's a world of people experiencing far greater hardship than whether I got the girl or not. I guess I've come to see that even though the spotlight can shine a little too brightly for me to be completely comfortable, I'm also aware that it can be used for good and show that there are other things in this world that are worth considering too."

"Such as?" she prompted.

"Well, like the beauty of God's creation, or the challenges faced by those who are ageing, or what it's like to care for them.

There are plenty of good and valuable things we can focus on, rather than the love lives of celebrities."

"So are you saying you don't want to comment on the rumors that Natasha is being replaced by Chlolinda Drewe in your new film?"

He bit back an unholy word. "I didn't know."

"And are we to expect any more of those, ahem, passionate scenes that we've seen you do so well in other roles?"

Not with Chlolinda, they sure wouldn't. He thought back to the script and his heart unclenched a bit. "Actually, I don't think this movie has call for that. And honestly, as much as I might personally relate to unrequited love guy, I don't think the love scenes of *The Notebook* are really where I want to see my career going. Sorry." He found a smile. Not sorry. What would Jesus do? Probably not movie scenes requiring intimacy coaches.

"What would be your ideal role? Something more family friendly, I take it."

"You know what I'd really love to do? Something along the lines of *Law & Order*, but filmed in Toronto or Vancouver."

"Police procedural?"

"I really enjoyed my time working in TV. And it'd be awesome to stay closer to family."

"And if my geography is correct, if you were in Toronto you'd be a little closer to your lady friend in Muskoka, right?"

He pushed his elbow on the arm of the chair and propped his chin into his hand. "And convince her to give me a second chance?"

"If she sees this interview, she's certainly going to know that's what you are hoping for."

"I'm not going to deny it. Sure, I'd love a second chance. But then we don't always get what we want, do we?"

"That's certainly true. And then sometimes, like in this interview, we get far more than what we anticipate. Mr. Cash, Lincoln, thank you very much for your time today. I'm sure our viewers will be fascinated by your openness and honesty. I hope that you'll come back again."

"Thanks, Jennifer."

He waited a moment, stupid smile plastered to his face, as the cameras completed the fade away. He then waited a few minutes more as they filmed a few extra shots over Jennifer's shoulder, over his, Jennifer nodding, Lincoln nodding, more fake, fake, fake.

In the background he could see Jolene with arms crossed, her tight expression suggesting she was unhappy about his interview that had been anything but fake. Something she made very clear as soon as he was de-microphoned and released.

"What on earth were you thinking?" she hissed as soon as they were in the safety of the car and driving back along Santa Monica Boulevard. "They're going to have a field day with this."

"Let them. I've got nothing to hide." He downed a bottle of water. Man, all that honesty made him thirsty.

"And what were you thinking disrespecting Victor like that?"

"I didn't diss the man."

"Are you wanting to be fired from the movie?"

Hope flickered. "Do you think they would?"

"Are you honestly telling me you want to see your career implode and you be relegated to doing TV again?"

"I don't want to see it implode," he admitted, "but yeah, I was being honest when I said I wanted to do more TV work."

"You know comments like that are going to set your career back by five years."

But he might feel more sane. More settled. Have more time to do the important things in life. "There are no guarantees in this world," he reminded her. "Anyway, there are lots of movie stars doing TV these days. Look at people like Nicole Kidman or Reese Witherspoon. They balance TV and film."

"I hesitate to point out that you're not exactly on the same level."

"Ouch." He glanced at her. She was staring at her phone. "What?"

She sighed. "Richard saw the interview. You know it was live, right? I did mention that before."

She had? "Oh well."

"Oh well?" She swore. "I can't believe I'm busting my Balenciagas for you when that's your attitude." She stabbed her phone and held it to her ear. "Yes, Richard. I'm sitting right next to him now. Here." She shoved the phone at Lincoln. "You try and talk sense to him."

"Lincoln." Richard's gravelly voice rasped in his ear. "What was that?"

"Honesty?"

"That was—"

Apparently a lot of things, none of them good.

"Well?" Richard demanded. "What have you got to say for yourself?"

"Actually, I found it cathartic. It felt good to be honest for once."

Another long line of foul words filled his ear.

"Come on, Richard. There's no need for that."

"I don't even know why I bother. Do you want to tell me why I should bother?"

"Because you get a cut of everything I do." Man. He bit back a laugh at Jolene's dumbstruck expression. What had been in the water in Muskoka? Truth serum, maybe.

"I've already called the studio and told them they're gonna get sued if they replay the interview in whole."

"Why would you do that? I'm the one who said all of those things and I stand by it."

"But—"

"Look, I'm sorry you don't like it, but I made my position clear. I'm not excited about this film, and I don't want to do it. I hated being put in a position where I felt like I was basically lying."

"It's called PR, Lincoln. Nobody loves every movie they're forced to do."

"But that's the problem. I feel like I've been forced to do this, and I don't want to."

"Well, that's too bad. You signed a contract. *You* signed it. Backing out now is not on."

"You know what? Maybe that's the case, and I'm just going to have to suck it up, but once this is done, I'm going to do the projects I want to do."

Jolene rolled her eyes as Richard bleated, "Fine."

"And, I'm going to continue praying that God stops this film being made somehow."

"God? Since when have you started thinking about God?" A beat. "Oh, don't tell me. This is the influence of your little girlfriend in Muskoka."

"She's not my girlfriend. But I wish she was."

Another blue word. "She's not your type."

"Exactly."

"She'd never fit into your world."

"I don't even fit into my world anymore."

His agent sighed. "Lincoln, have you seen what they're saying online about her?"

"What?" He ended the call, stabbed open Instagram, and saw his latest post had thousands of hearts. And hundreds of comments, and more were being added by the second.

*Is she your girlfriend?*

*And this chick dared reject you?*

*She's not hot enough for you, Lincoln!*

*Woof, woof.*

And worse.

"You need to switch off comments," Jolene said, her gaze fixed outside the window.

He sure did. Before Jackie saw what trolls were saying about her online.

Trolls that only existed because of what he'd done.

∼

"Hello, can I speak to Jackie?"

Jackie slammed the phone down. And she'd thought yesterday was the worst shift she'd had here. All day she'd felt tense, uneasy, conscious of people watching her, as if wondering when she'd next crumple into a ball of emotion again. She'd got the feeling that while Dana had not been thrilled to see her show up today, at least she had been relieved. Until the phone calls asking for Jackie had started and she learned just what some of these phone callers were saying.

Telling her to go hang herself. To do anatomically impossible things to herself. To die.

Her fingers trembled, but unlike yesterday, she'd felt stronger. Sleep had helped. As had the hugs and love from Serena, Toni, and Rachel, who had all dropped what they were doing when Serena had asked in the group chat how Jackie was doing and she'd opened up about the depths of pain and humiliation. Having them arrive last night in her apartment with flowers, chocolates, and hugs had been good. Apart from the fact that Anna's absence had left a great big hole, her silence made all the more obvious when Staci had sent her love with an apology that she was having a birthday dinner for her grandmother with James. Time with the other girls had been good, had reminded her that God's love remained no matter what, that she could trust Him, and that while Lincoln's attention had been flattering, she'd made the right choice in pushing him away.

"If it's real, he'll still care, and you'll see the changes in him. And if it wasn't, then it was a nice dream many women would kill for," Rachel had said.

So Jackie had prayed with them, committed it to God, and had done her best to let it go.

Until now, when it seemed Rachel's comment about women killing seemed awfully close to coming true.

"Jackie?" Maureen placed a hand on her arm. "Was that another of the phone calls?"

She nodded.

Maureen grimaced. "That's enough. You're not answering the phone anymore, understand?"

"Yes."

"You should take the day off."

"You don't seriously think that Dana would agree to that? Not after yesterday's debacle."

"Have you got any idea why this has happened?"

"No."

"Have you posted anything anywhere?"

"I don't do social media." She never posted on Facebook, using her account only for Messenger, which was simply her way of communicating with her friends. Which might be just as well. Imagine if she was findable on social media. She shivered, hot then cold.

"Would Lincoln? No." Maureen's brow pleated. "I didn't get the impression he hated you. Just the opposite, in fact. He seemed like he'd do whatever he could to protect you." She sighed. "Can you think of anyone else?"

Yes. "Téa," she whispered.

"Of course." Maureen rolled her eyes. "Why didn't I think of that? Come on. Let's go talk to Dana." Maureen wrapped an arm around her shoulders.

Jackie was grateful that it was meal-time for the residents, and that Maureen shared her shift today. They moved to Dana's office and Maureen knocked on the open door.

"What is it? Oh." Dana's face held resignation. "More phone calls?"

"They want me—" Jackie repeated word for word some of the things that had been said.

Dana's face blanched. "How dare anyone speak to you in that way?" She gestured for them to close the door and be seated. "How could anyone know you worked here?"

"We've been trying to think about that," Maureen explained. She glanced at Jackie then lifted her chin. "The only person we know who has a grudge against Jackie and would post pictures about her and Lincoln is, I'm sorry to say, but we think it might be…"

"Téa." Dana sighed. "I don't want to believe it of a relative of mine." She pulled out her phone. "Has she posted anything?"

"I'm not on social media," Jackie admitted.

"And I don't follow her, so I can't know," Maureen said.

Dana propped her head in her hands while she looked through her phone. Then she winced. "I'm afraid she has posted a picture of Lincoln, but it's not got you in it, Jackie." She passed the phone over.

Jackie studied the picture of Lincoln and Téa grinning at the camera. She remembered that day. She swallowed. "You're right. There's nothing to link to me at all."

"Except…" Maureen tapped on the screen then enlarged the photo. "See how Téa's name badge mentions Golden Elms? Perhaps they figured it out that way."

Dana snatched back the phone and studied it. "Except that still doesn't explain why Jackie is the one being targeted. I'm actually surprised Téa doesn't have more comments on this. Maybe she's not quite the influencer she likes to think she is."

What was an influencer? Sometimes it felt too hard to keep up with this world.

"Maybe…" Dana tapped her phone a few more times, then gasped. "I can't believe it."

"What?"

She slid the phone across the desk and Jackie saw a picture

of herself and Mac, grinning at the camera, in a post under a name that read lincolncashofficial. He'd written three words: 'Missing these two' followed by a hashtag that read real-lifeheroes.

His post had hundreds of comments. Hundreds of comments just like the ones she'd heard baying for her blood.

"Lincoln did this?" she whispered.

"Honey, he obviously didn't mean to," Maureen murmured.

She peered at the photo. Yep, sure enough she was wearing her name badge with the Golden Elms name and logo, along with her name, there for any eagle-eyed fan to see—and seethe over.

She pushed the phone away. Her head swam so she closed her eyes. Lincoln had done this. Accidental it may have been, and his words were sweet, she couldn't deny that. But he had exposed where she was, who she was, but why people were so vehement against her she didn't know.

"I still don't understand why."

Maureen had her phone out now, then gave her own hitch of breath.

"What is it?"

She bit her lip. "Lincoln gave an interview last night. Judging from the comments here, I think if you watch it you'll see why."

"Wait. I'm gonna put this on the computer and we can see it better." Dana clicked a few keys on her laptop then shifted the screen so they could see it.

Lincoln sat in the chair in a plush studio, fake-smiling she could see. She could tell because there were no laugh-lines near his eyes.

They watched in silence as the interview progressed, until he mentioned Muskoka.

She tensed. Had he mentioned her? No. Only his grandfather. She didn't know whether to be disappointed or relieved.

Then the interviewer's next question stole her breath. "We've heard rumors that you've been seeing a special lady."

He didn't answer at first, and her heart hammered, waiting. Did he think she was special? Would he admit it for all to see?

When he didn't answer, the interviewer prompted him again, this time using the word particular, instead of special.

"Oh, she's particular, all right."

Her heart hollowed in on itself. Had he meant that to sound like she was snooty? Her hand covered her mouth as Maureen gently touched her upper arm.

"I'm sure he didn't mean—"

"Shh!" Dana hushed her.

"—there *is* someone."

He paused a moment, then said, "I thought there was, but she didn't want me, so yeah. Good times."

No, it wasn't. Her eyes filled with tears.

"Are you trying to tell me you were turned down?"

"I'm not trying to tell you that. I thought I made it clear. So yes, I know all about unrequited love right now." His hand lifted. "Anyone needing another *Notebook* guy, here I am."

"I love that movie," Dana murmured. "He'd be awesome in Ryan Gosling's role."

"Shh," Maureen said.

The interview continued, but even though she heard him speak, could see his obvious tension and sadness, she couldn't quite reconcile the fact that this man, this movie-famous man who women of all ages drooled over—even now she was pretty sure Dana was licking her lips—had somehow fallen in love with her. He'd said as much yesterday, but she'd been sure it was just a ploy. And yet this man, this man on the screen talking about the kinds of roles he wanted to do, the fact he mentioned unrequited love—this man was being honest in a way she'd never dreamed. Did this mean he really did like her?

Maureen flapped her hand in front of her face. "I don't know if that was a hot flush or just the effect of that man."

Jackie was pretty sure she was too young for hot flushes, but the man made her feel the same.

"He has such charisma," Maureen continued.

"So sexy." Dana glanced at Jackie. "I probably shouldn't talk like that about your boyfriend."

"He's not my boyfriend."

"Well, this interview makes that clear. I guess we now know why you're getting all those messages." Dana's eyes softened. "I should apologize for what happened yesterday. I don't know what's happened between you two, but it's obviously not been easy. And not made any easier by how you were treated by Mavis and, er, others yesterday."

"It's okay," Jackie whispered.

"I suspect it will be more okay if you don't come into work for the next few weeks." Dana glanced at the rostering chart and frowned. "I know you have scheduled in time away next week, but I think it might be wise if you took that early if we can cover your shifts. Would you be amenable to that?"

Go see her family at long last? Escape the madness found here? "Yes."

"Good. Then consider it done. I'll email you some paperwork so you won't lose pay. We're only talking a few extra days, anyway, aren't we?"

Today was Friday, and she'd been due to leave next Wednesday. "Just Monday and Tuesday."

"I'll clear it, and make it happen." She studied Jackie. "You need to have a rest, and no, I'm not saying that to be kind. I'm saying that because we need you here, and I want you to take time to be refreshed and do things that will be fun. A burned-out nurse cannot nurse well, and you know this place will not operate nearly as effectively if you're not doing well." She peered over the top of her steel-rimmed glasses. "I suspect part of yesterday's meltdown was an overreaction due to overwork. It's not wrong to have some fun in this world, you know."

"I know."

Maureen patted her arm. "And maybe you and Lincoln can patch things up, too."

With his talk about blessings and God's creation, maybe he had experienced some genuine heart change. And maybe she did need to go and rest and take time to lean on God again. There had been so much happening lately, she knew she needed to re-calibrate her soul and find peace. A few days off could be just the thing. She could go into hiding, just like he had, and not switch on her phone. Just take her Bible, her cross-stitch, the paperback advance copy of Staci's new clean read, and just be.

And maybe she could find out just what God wanted her to do next.

# CHAPTER 14

*L*incoln tossed the script aside with a loud groan. He glanced out the apartment window where the Pacific Ocean glowed with afternoon haze. Of course, that could just be the general haze that hung around all of LA. Maybe that was what had caused the increase in migraines of late. Or maybe they'd been caused by his own stupid actions.

Why hadn't he thought things through before posting that picture of Pop and Jackie?

He didn't know it would escalate into a feeding frenzy like this. Thank God he'd turned off comments when he had, but apparently that had not been enough to turn off the vitriol Jackie was facing. He talked to his grandfather, who said she'd been receiving death threats at the nursing home, and had taken leave for a while.

Death threats? Was the world crazy? Who were these anonymous people who thought they had a right to intrude into his life like this? Or was that him pointing a finger in blame while three fingers pointed back at him? After all, if he hadn't posted that picture, if he hadn't been the one doing that interview, nobody would be any the wiser.

It was his fault she was in pain.

It was his fault she'd been forced to go into hiding.

He'd called Joel Wakefield, knowing he couldn't very well call Jackie, as much as he might want to. He was trying to show that he was different, that he respected others, and part of that meant respecting her boundaries and her desire for him to not contact her. So while it killed him to not talk to her, he'd do his utmost to make sure that she was safe. Hence the call to Joel last night when he asked how she was doing, and Joel had said that she'd taken time off and had gone to visit family.

Lincoln was half tempted to contact a private detective to make sure that she was safe, but he refrained. His fans couldn't be that stupid to hunt her down, could they? A private detective might also help him discover where Jackie's parents lived, so that he could call them and make sure she was doing okay, but he wasn't sure if this would break the no contact request she had made of him, so he'd refrained. So far.

Joel had reminded Lincoln that the best thing he could do was to pray, so he spent another moment now asking for God to be with Jackie, to protect her, to surround her, to give her peace and wisdom, to know she was loved. Then he prayed almost the same for himself.

He needed wisdom, and peace to know the way forward. And protection from the machinations of others as he worked to trust God for his future.

His interview had made waves. More tsunami-like than gentle ripples. Apparently that was the effect of undiluted honesty.

Victor had *not* been pleased, so Richard had reported, giving Lincoln a blow-by-blow account of Victor's pithy opinion of Lincoln's character and his low estimate of his talent as an actor. "Apparently the only good thing he says about you is the fact that the ladies love you so if you're in this movie they'll insist on making their husbands and boyfriends watch it with them."

Woo-hoo. Joy.

"I told you this would backfire," Richard had continued. "Lucky for you I had negotiated in it at contract so they can't get rid of you."

Awesome.

"Lord, help me."

He closed his eyes, trying to be still and to focus on God. During their twice-weekly Zoom calls, Joel had been coaching him in this, in trying to learn to rest while in the middle of the whirlwind, to be still so he could hear God's voice.

"It's one thing to read your Bible," Joel had said. "It's another to do what it says. So when you're quiet, and actively listening for what God might be trying to say, you can be sure it won't be the opposite of what God says to do in His word."

So he listened now, waiting, waiting for a small voice to speak. Or a big one. Lincoln didn't mind.

God. The creator of the universe. God, who loved Lincoln and Jackie, both. God, who saw all that had happened, all that was happening, all that would happen. God.

He breathed in, and felt a measure of peace within his soul.

He didn't sense anything more than that God was near, God was here, and that He could be trusted. "Lord, help me to trust you," he prayed for what must've been the hundredth time since the weekend. "Show me what to do, what not to do. Open the right doors, close the wrong ones. And Lord, you see what's happening with this movie. If there's any way you can make it stop, then please do so." Moisture welled against his eyelids. "And Lord, be with Jackie. Heal her heart. Bless her." That prayer he must've prayed a thousand times.

A scent like jasmine wafted through the room, and he opened his eyes. Sometimes he wondered if God sent this perfume just to buoy his heart with hope of her. It was one of the things he remembered most about her, the fragrance of her hair as he'd held her. He'd always loved the scent of jasmine, its sweetness like it held the promise of tomorrow. Jackie was like that. Like she held the promise of all things good.

He picked up the script. Maybe part of God's plan was for Lincoln to do the film. He'd assume so, until otherwise. And if that was the case, then he'd best do what he could to make his fans happy and prove himself as a man of his word.

And maybe one day Jackie would see him as a man who could be trusted, too.

∼

"Jackie, darling!"

Her mother's arms slipped around her and gently squeezed. It had been too long. Far, far too long. She drank in the comfort to be found in her mother's arms.

"I'm so glad you arrived safe. That's such a long drive to do on your own."

But driving had allowed for a stop halfway in Montreal, at a cute bed and breakfast not too far from the St. Lawrence River. She knew some French, enough to get by, and to be in a place where nobody knew her, where she could spend her days by herself, alone in a city, was rare. It might not have had all the charm of escaping to Lake Muskoka, but her days of visiting places like the botanic gardens and the Notre-Dame Basilica in Old Montreal had reminded her of different kinds of beauty in this world. In fact, praying while gazing upon the botanic garden's Jardin Japonais had filled her with ease for the first time in days.

And now she was here, having enjoyed her three days of respite, knowing she still needed more to meet the Rachel and Serena-approved amount of days for fun, but it had been enough to help sustain her for the next few weeks at least.

"Come on. Bring in your bags."

She obeyed, following her mother's directives to ascend the staircase to the little attic room that had been her bedroom when she was a girl. She'd been tempted to find alternative accommodation, but there really wasn't any point in coming all this way to help her mom if she wasn't here to be a part of what really mattered.

She returned downstairs and found her grandparents, hugging them as they exclaimed of their delight at her return, and her mother made cups of tea.

"I'm sorry it's taken so long," she said. "Work has been busy."

Her grandmother placed down her china cup. "Work will always be there."

Guilt gnawed. Unsaid was that her grandparents wouldn't.

"How is Golden Elms going to manage without you?" her mother teased.

Good question. She didn't have to return until mid-August, so while this month-long vacation should prove a good break for her, it would also prove a good challenge for the others. "I'm sure they'll manage."

"Now, tell us, Jacqueline," her grandfather said. Her grandparents were the only ones who called her by her full name. It was strange when Granddad couldn't remember her mother's name, Marie. "What has been happening in your life recently?"

So she filled them in, editing certain details to not scare her mom or her grandparents, and not sharing anything about a certain movie star who'd chosen to avoid the spotlight by hiding in Muskoka. Time away might allow her to forget. Especially if she didn't turn on her phone or watch the news or look at newspapers or magazines. The past few days of avoiding all that had helped. It was amazing how much better she felt when she didn't have the clutter and chaos of the outside world always intruding. Some days it almost felt like Lincoln Cash was a myth, that he'd slip into the kind of impossible dream status that Rachel had mentioned. She prayed so, anyway.

"You have no boyfriend?" Grandma asked.

"No."

Her mother looked at her—maybe she heard the strain in Jackie's voice too—but said nothing. "There may be a nice man here for you, Jacqueline," Grandma said. "We ask our friends, oui?"

Listening to her grandparents, she was reminded why Grand Falls was considered by many to be the most bilingual town in Canada. Settled by the French known as Acadians, so close to Quebec, three quarters of the population spoke both languages. It was why she spoke some French, too.

"You can ask, but I will not be here for too long. I have to return next month."

"But if you meet the right man, you will stay, non?"

*Non.*

"If she meets the right man, she wouldn't let something like a few miles get in the way, I'm sure." Mom patted her arm, her serious eyes holding words she didn't say.

Jackie's heart twitched. Mom knew. How?

"We'll talk later about such things," her grandmother said, before embarking on a lengthy monologue about the challenges of healthcare and getting old.

Jackie nodded, offering sympathetic murmurs, before catching her mother's gaze again, as if she had questions she couldn't ask in front of Grandma. Her heart tensed. She wasn't looking forward to this conversation.

Later, that night, after her grandparents had gone to bed, she found her mother in the living room, the TV muted.

"Come, sit beside me." Her mom patted the sofa. "I want to know what has put that look of sadness in your eyes."

"I'm not sad, Mom."

"You're not happy, either."

"I'm trying to be."

"It is that man, isn't it? Lincoln Cash. Is that his name?"

His name on her mother's lips wasn't something she expected to ever hear. "How did you find out?"

"I have friends on Facebook. They told me about him. And you."

She swallowed. "What did they say?"

Mom chuckled. "That you broke the heart of a movie star."

"Oh, Mama." She snuggled into her mother's side, and through tears, told her the truth of what had happened. This time she left little out, save the horrific messages wishing she was dead.

"So he broke your heart, too."

"It's not broken." She still remembered her mother's sobbing, night after night, her heart and trust shattered when her husband—Jackie's father—had abandoned them when Jackie was just five. Jackie had kept her father's name even though her mother had reclaimed her maiden name. Perhaps that was why the rabid fans hadn't found her yet. Robichaud was a fairly common last name around here.

Jackie smeared away her tears with the back of her hand. "I'm doing better. But I'm so glad to get away. I need time to sort through what's happened, to get my heart whole again."

"Prayer helps with that."

"It does."

"And good food."

"You know I've been looking forward to your cooking."

"I can tell. You're way too skinny, honey. We need to fatten you up."

"Happy to be fattened." Maybe she'd regain some curves again.

Her mother laughed. "It will be fun to be together again."

"So fun." She snuggled into her mother's side. "So, what are we watching?"

"Okay, let's start."

The round table—in actuality a circle of tables—held Victor Drewe, various producers, several of the eight-person writing team—now did that say something about the challenges of the script or what?—and the various actors and actresses who had signed up for this gig. Actresses including Chlolinda.

As Victor introduced her, Lincoln caught the subtle rolling of eyeballs from various cast members, people who, like Linc, had needed to fight the hard way, via auditions and screen-tests and hard graft, who hadn't the magical coat-tail ride of being related to the director. But he gritted out a smile and worked to get his heart in line with what Jesus would do. Which according to Joel—and Lincoln's new Bible which he was reading each day—was to love the unlovely. Which apparently included Chlolinda. So even though Linc didn't want to be here, and the space movie would likely prove a dud, as Joel had pointed out, it was a paying gig, and until God told him otherwise, this was where Linc was meant to be. Here, to be the salt and light Jesus talked about. Even though Linc was pretty sure his light was plenty dim, and at times he still felt rather salty about being forced to do this. He was trying, though.

The script reading commenced, and he whacked on a smile, conscious of the rolling cameras. The launch of a production needed media opps like this, the more the merrier to try and lodge the film in the minds of the audience. He needed to look like a team player, even if he resented playing.

He said his first line, sipped from his water bottle, tried not to cringe at the lame dialogue, and waited for his next turn. And read more, and prayed. Read more, and asked God to bless Jackie. Read more, and asked God to soften his heart and attitude. Read more, and asked God to bless Joel and Serena. Read more, and relaxed. Read more, and started trusting.

. . .

"I don't know how you do it."

The breathy voice made him freeze, then he relaxed. Nothing could happen. They were here at the long buffet table grabbing lunch along with a hundred others. And Chlolinda had looked like she was struggling at the reading earlier. What would Jesus do? Have a listening ear, at least. "Do what?"

"Things like this." Her bare arm bumped his.

He inched away. He didn't want any gossip about her and him. "You mean the read through?"

"Don't you find it intimidating having all those executives looking at you?"

"Sometimes," he admitted. They were the ones who bankrolled the production. Movies happened because of money, because people hoped people would buy a ticket and watch the thing. Add in merchandise, potential sequels, gaming opportunities, and more, and everything was carefully calculated to avoid a repeat of those flops that had ended directors' careers. Judging from some of Victor's pointed comments today, maybe he was having second thoughts about having cast his daughter in a major role.

She paused, her plate suspended above the fake-meat platter. "I just don't know if I'm cut out for this."

Whoa. Was this his moment to say, "Maybe you should talk to Daddy about quitting?" He bit back the words. Tried to think what to say—oh, heck, just pray, already. *Lord?* Words crystallized. "Why do you say that?"

He stepped back from the table, his plate filled with protein and salad—his trainer would be proud of him—and waited as she gazed wistfully at a bread roll. He knew how that felt. Wanting something until it was all you dreamed about. Denying yourself and then binge-eating something ten times worse. "Just take it."

She did, plopping two gold-paper-wrapped pats of butter on her plate as well, following slowly as he moved to a table with a couple of older actors at the end. He nodded, then chose the seat at the foot of the table so she couldn't sit beside him.

He shoveled in a forkful of lettuce. Yum. What he'd give for another of Jackie's drool-worthy burgers. Even if the aftermath had made him look like a five-year-old.

Chlolinda sighed.

He knew that was his cue to ask her more, but he *really* didn't want to. Still, the fact was that he wasn't trying to live for himself anymore. "What's going on, Chlolinda?"

"This." She ripped apart her bread roll. "I just feel like an imposter sometimes."

Whoa. She recognized that too? He'd have to give the girl more credit. "I think we can all feel that way sometimes," he said cautiously.

"Come on. You don't, do you?"

He could lie, or he could admit the truth. This one was easy. "Yep. I often feel like that." Feeling like he fell short, that he'd never be good enough. Muskoka—Jackie—had shown him just how blind he'd been before.

"Wow."

Yeah, he couldn't believe he'd admitted it aloud either.

"That's not what I thought you'd say." Her head tilted as she chewed her bread. "There's something different about you, and I don't know what it is."

He could tell her it was Jesus. He hesitated.

"I mean, I saw your interview. Who hasn't? But I can't believe a girl has done this to you."

"Done what?"

"I don't know. That's the thing. I can't put my finger on it. All I know is that the Lincoln I knew back in New York had a kind of swagger about him but never seemed at ease. You always seemed restless, like you were looking for the next thing.

And now you seem confident, but more at peace. What's changed?"

He nearly choked on his turkey breast. Okay, so maybe God did want him here for a reason. "You asked before about imposter syndrome, about balancing other people's expectations with the feeling you're not good enough."

"Yeah."

"I guess I've learned lately that I don't know as much as I thought I did. And yeah, the girl I met helped me see that."

"She sounds like a—"

"She's actually the nicest person I've ever met. She's like gold. And she helped me understand that all of this," he pointed to his face, then gestured to the buzzing scene, "doesn't really matter in the whole scheme of things. Yeah, it does to some degree, but there's only one person I really should be concerned in pleasing."

"Her," she guessed, her nose wrinkling.

"Jesus, actually."

"Jesus who?"

"Jesus Christ."

She blinked. Swore. "Are you a Christian?"

"Yeah. I am."

"I can't believe it."

"It's true. And I've found that giving my life over to God's purposes means I don't have to keep stressing about what comes next. God's in control, so I'm trusting Him with it all."

"Including the girl?"

"Especially her." *Lord, bless Jackie. Help her, heal her.*

"Huh." Her eyes were wide with fascination. "Do you go to church?"

"I'm still looking for a good church around here." Joel had mentioned there were some where celebrities attended and weren't hassled by the public. "So maybe when I find one I'll let you know, and you might check it out too."

"Why?"

He settled back in his seat. "Because I think you could do with learning more about God, too."

July passed into August with a round of cooking, chores, and medical appointments. Jackie loved her grandparents but understood her mother's weariness at the drudgery of it all. So she researched respite opportunities, and found a home cleaning service that didn't cost a bomb but could help with clearing out some of the clutter that her grandparents' hoarding tendencies had made so challenging.

And she prayed for God to heal her. For God to help her mom and grandparents. And for God to touch Lincoln's heart, too.

"And how is the weather in Vancouver?" Linc asked his mom.

"Raining, would you believe." She sighed. "We've only been back a few days, but Muskoka seems a lifetime ago. It's funny how quickly one can settle back into normality."

True. He'd been back in LA for two weeks now. Muskoka seemed like a fairy tale.

"It was good to see your grandfather again," she said.

"How is he?"

"Doing okay. He kept talking about his time with you. Crossword puzzles, Lincoln? Really?"

"They kill the time while I'm waiting on set."

He longed to ask her about whether somebody else was back, but knew that if he did, he was signaling his interest in a girl in a way he'd never really done with his mother before. Then again, he'd never admitted on live TV how his heart had been broken, either. He swallowed. "So, did you meet some of the staff there?"

A beat. "Are you beating around the bush about Jackie? Is she the mystery girl on that interview?"

No flies on his mom. "Yeah," he admitted lamely.

"All your grandfather would do is talk about her. Apparently the two of you were caught in a closet or some such nonsense. Is there anything I should know?"

"I like her, Mom. She's so different. So good and yet so real."

"And something of a local hero, if the reports I heard are to be believed."

"She's the real deal. She doesn't need to put on a cape and a suit."

"And she rejected you."

"Yeah."

"Is that a first?"

Maybe. Probably. "Yeah."

"Well, I think I like her already."

Huh? "Mom, you're supposed to be on my side."

"So what are you doing about it?"

"I'm trying to be better. She always teased me about being arrogant, and—" He stopped at the sound of his mother's laughter. "What?"

"Yes, definitely a keeper."

He groaned. "That's the thing, though, Mom. She doesn't want me to contact her, and I'm trying to respect her boundaries, but I feel like I'm dying inside."

There was a long pause on the other end of the phone.

"Mom?"

She cleared her throat. "I don't know if I'm supposed to say this, but I always hoped there would be a woman who would make you feel this way. I feel ashamed to say it, but you've had it easy, Son. And to hear you now, you really seem to have changed."

"That's not just because of Jackie," he mumbled.

"No. Your grandfather told me about certain other... things that occurred. And I can't say I fully understand those things, but I am glad that you seem to be wanting to settle down." She chuckled again. "Maybe I'll finally see some grandchildren at long last."

"Mom, stop. I need to actually see her, then convince her to give me a second chance. Or a first one, I don't know. But she doesn't want me to, and so I'm trying to respect that."

"Then talk to her friends, see if they know if she's ready to see you." His mother laughed. "Oh, she sounds like someone I really need to meet."

"Get in line," he grumbled. "Not that I know when it can happen, with this movie schedule that I'm on."

They talked about his latest film, then the phone call wound up.

But as he lay on the sofa and prayed for his parents to find God, his own heart now beat with fresh hope.

"I don't know. There's something about a man that can be too handsome, can't there?" Serena's voice filled Jackie's ear as she stared at the frozen screen.

Lincoln Cash stared at her, moody, brooding, frozen in a scene where he stared out as if he could see her. She shivered. "For sure."

She'd finally switched on the phone, had balked at the dozens of missed calls and emails. Then deleted all the non-essentials. Serena's messages of concern she considered essential.

"So, are you having fun?"

"Yes." Sometimes, anyway. Re-connecting with her family was wonderful, even if she was tired sometimes. Eating her mom's food was good—she'd put on some weight, and was pretty sure she'd gained a cup size, which wasn't bad. Her mom had insisted on watching some of Lincoln's films, so this had become their evening ritual. Watching Lincoln, seeing him so remote and different from her world. It served as a reminder that he'd obviously been under some spell in Muskoka, otherwise fabulous him would never consider plain and ordinary her.

The lack of any messages suggested that too, although she couldn't help but wonder if he'd taken her 'don't call me' line seriously. Whatever. Watching Lincoln was good, getting him out of her system, like a kind of detox for her soul.

A sound came in the background. "Oh, I better go," Serena said. "Toni is out with Matt and I'm baby-sitting."

Her heart grew soft. "How is Ethan?"

"He's walking!"

He was? And she hadn't been there? She pressed her lips together.

"In other news, we still haven't seen anything of Anna. I mean, we see her, but it's like she's ghosting us. She hasn't been in church for weeks now."

"I'm praying for her."

"Me too." Serena paused. "Speaking of praying, Joel has been catching up with Lincoln. Did you know that?"

"No." Hurt cramped within. "I… I didn't know Lincoln had gone back to Muskoka." And he hadn't tried to contact her?

"No. They catch up on Zoom."

Relief pinged. But, she questioned, "Why?"

"Lincoln apparently thinks of Joel as his pastor."

"What?"

"He's changed, Jackie. I really think you could give him a chance."

"I want to, but I'm scared," she whispered.

"I know. But God hasn't given us a spirit of fear, has he?"

But of love, power, and a sound mind.

Another squeal.

"Sorry, hon, I really need to go. Give my love to your mom."

"I will. Thanks for talking."

"Thanks for answering my call. At last."

Jackie heard the tease in her friend's voice as the call ended. She sat on the sofa, puzzling over what Serena had said. Was Lincoln really taking steps to grow as a Christian?

What did that mean? What could it mean? Lincoln meeting regularly with Joel sure didn't sound like an act. Which meant maybe it was real. Which meant maybe he'd meant what he'd said before too. Her heart trembled. Could a future with him be a possibility after all? *Lord?*

Her mom returned, carrying bowls of yoghurt and berries. "You finished your call? How is Serena?"

"She's good. Says hello, and sends her love."

"I always liked that girl." Her mom gestured to the TV. "So, are we going to watch more or what?"

More of Lincoln, who just might be someone she could love.

Her mother pointed at the screen. "Come on, honey. We don't need to keep watching the same shot. He's not that handsome."

"Nope, not at all," she mumbled.

Her mother laughed. It was good to hear her laugh. It had been too long.

Just like talking to Serena had been.

Just like seeing Ethan, Anna, and the others.

Just like it had been too long since seeing Lincoln in real life, too.

## CHAPTER 15

"Yeah, it wasn't quite what I remembered church being like, but it was cool. And I recognized a few people, got invited to a group that meets online."

"I'm glad." Joel smiled. "Christians need all the support they can get."

Sure did. Lincoln cleared his throat. "I even wondered about taking Chlolinda sometime." He shrugged, conscious that Joel was looking at him with a slight frown through Zoom. "She seems open to talking about God."

"As long as it's not some ploy to get your attention," Joel cautioned. "It wouldn't be the first time someone has pretended interest in God or church because they're interested in impressing someone instead."

"Do you think that's what Jackie thought about me?" he asked.

"Maybe. Maybe at the start, anyway."

It felt impossible, this distance between them, not knowing how she was doing, simply praying, and fighting to trust God to protect her. "Has anyone spoken to her recently?"

"Funny you should ask," Joel said, smirking. "I happen to

know a certain somebody in this very house did just a few days ago."

His pulse ratcheted up. "And how is she?"

"Serena says she's fine."

"Where is she? She's still away, right? Pop would've told me if she'd gone back to work." He called his grandfather at least once a week now. Apparently the replacement staff 'weren't much chop' in his grandfather's words.

"She's still visiting her grandparents," Joel said slowly.

"Where do they live?"

"New Brunswick."

Panic made him blurt, "But where?"

Joel took several beats to answer. "Look, I know you want to be in touch, but I just don't know if she's ready."

"Can you find out? Is Serena there? Would she know?"

Joel regarded him seriously then finally nodded. "I'll go get her."

"Thanks." He exhaled, shoved fingers through his newly-cropped hair. The role demanded it. He looked like he was ready to join the military, but at least it had kept him cool in LA's heat. Not that it was helping right now. He felt hot, then cold, his nerves tensing within. He was about to speak to Serena, who'd recently spoken to Jackie, and who might know how Jackie felt about him. *Lord, help me cope with whatever gets said.* He swallowed. *And give me grace if it's a no or not yet.*

Serena appeared, they went through the usual helloes, then she got down to business.

"Joel mentioned you wanted to know how Jackie is doing."

"Look, Serena, I really don't want to cause her any hurt. I just want to know that she's okay."

"She's okay," Serena said softly.

"Good." Relief gushed in a long sigh. "So she's safe? Nobody has tried to hurt her?"

"She's safe, Lincoln. You don't need to worry."

He pressed his face in his hands. Except he couldn't help but worry about her. It was like she'd broken off a piece of his heart that would never be healed until he saw her again. *Lord, thanks for keeping her safe. Help her to find happiness again.*

"Are you okay?" Serena's voice came.

"Yeah." He rubbed a hand over his face. "Just praying."

Silence ticked. Then she finally said, "You really have changed, haven't you?"

"I'm trying. I'm not great at trusting God, but I'm praying for her all the time, that He would bless her."

"Me too." Her voice was soft.

"I'm sorry. It's late, and I should let you go. You're probably busy."

"She's in Grand Falls, Lincoln. Her grandparents' last name is Robichaud. Her mom's name is Marie."

What?

She gave the address of a street, and he rushed to write it down.

"Why are you telling me this?"

"Because she misses you."

"How do you know?"

"Because she as good as told me. And Joel and I have been praying for you both, and regardless of what happens, you need to talk to each other and finally set things straight."

"I know."

"She needs to see that you have changed, that you are following Jesus. And she's not going to see that when she's not on social media."

"She isn't?"

"Come on. She barely watches TV, Lincoln. She likes to do cross-stitch, and read, and talk with people. You've seen her in action. You know nobody is better than her at empathy."

So true.

"And I don't know if you know this, but I love a good wedding. Just sayin'."

A wedding? His heart hammered. He'd be happy just to see her again. "I hope Joel knows what a prize he has in you," he said.

"I let him know every day."

He laughed, his heart lighter than it had been in weeks.

"God bless you, Serena. You and Joel are the best."

"Actually, Jackie is the best. So, go get her, Tiger."

"I promise I'll look after her."

"You better. Otherwise you'll have to deal with me. And I *will* hunt you down."

He grinned. "I hope you do. But you don't need to worry. Jackie is really special to me."

"I know that. But the person you have to convince is Jackie."

And he could only really do that in person. Which meant somehow finding time off-set to allow a trip across the continent. "So that's exactly why we need your prayers."

The high summer sun made her wish she'd thought to bring a cap. Good thing the spray from the waterfall kept her cool, the gush of water in spring melt nearly the equivalent of Niagara Falls, or so the nearby plaque said.

Rainbows shone through the water spray, shimmery images, there one minute, gone the next.

It seemed a dream, a mirage that belonged to the fantasies of a too-skinny girl from another world. Jackie shoved her hands in her shorts' pockets, doing her best to make the most of a scene she'd forgo next week. Mom was finally going to get some respite, and between Jackie and her mom's efforts, and the cleaners Jackie had organized, her grandparents' home was finally starting to look like something safe for the elderly to live in. Next week she'd return to Muskoka, which meant she needed to make the most of whatever time she had remaining to fit in the activities which the others might count as fun. Sure, a walk by a waterfall in the center of a town might not be everyone's idea of a good time, but at least she wasn't sitting at home watching Lincoln on TV, wishing, dreaming…

"Lord, if there is any way…"

She didn't dare finish that prayer. Surely it had to be selfish to pray that way. But the yearning to see him only grew, even though it was impossible. She tried to pray it away, tried to lean on God more, to find contentment, to be thankful for the little things. Little things like sparkly rainbows that glimmered, and showed beautiful things still existed in this world, that sometimes a person just needed to move into the light to see things a different way…

"Jackie?"

She paused. No. She was really starting to imagine things. Lincoln Cash not only filled the TV screen and her dreams, but now her ears were playing tricks on her too.

A crunch of gravel came from behind her. She couldn't move. She gripped the handrail, peeking down at the rushing water as a shadow moved closer.

"Jackie."

His voice was husky, cautious, deep.

"Your mom said you were down here. It took a while to find you."

She drew in a deep breath, willing oxygen to fill her lungs and spark sense to her brain. Was this reality, or did she share her grandfather's onset of delusions?

"Jackie."

Her knuckles were white. "How did you know I was in Grand Falls?"

"Serena."

She closed her eyes. Of course.

When she opened them, she saw his hand on the railing next to hers. Could smell the delicious tang of his aftershave. Could feel her hairs on her arm stand to attention, like a sunflower moved with the sun.

"She thought you might not mind a visit from me."

She'd been right.

"Are you ever going to look at me?"

"I can't."

"Why not?" Humor laced his voice.

"Because I don't know what to say."

"You don't have to say anything. But I needed to see you. I was dying without you. And I just had to tell you that I miss you, that I think you are someone special. So special."

She'd long felt like she'd been secure and contented in God's love, but the thought that Lincoln thought she was special made her heart tremble.

"It killed me to have to leave you the way I did, and especially when everything hit the fan like it did. I'm so sorry about that. So sorry."

His voice broke, carving away yet more of her defenses.

"I never meant to hurt you," he continued. "And I've been praying for you every day."

He had? Oh, God had changed him. Was changing him. Could this finally be? *Lord?*

"Look, I know you wanted space and didn't want me to contact you, so I'm sorry if me being here upsets you." He gave a chuckle, deep and raw.

She froze. Why was he laughing? This wasn't a joke, was it? He couldn't be that cruel, could he? She barely dared turn around.

"I don't know if you've ever seen the movie *Notting Hill*, but right now I feel like Julia Roberts' character." A beat passed. Two. "See, I'm just a guy, standing next to a girl, wondering if she could ever love him."

She couldn't speak. Her heart was in her mouth.

"Do you want me to leave, Jackie?"

"I want," her voice wobbled, "I want…"

Seconds ticked away. Oh, why couldn't she articulate this?

"Okay," he said slowly. "I'll leave. It was nice to sort of see you."

His arm moved, she heard the sound of gravel as he walked away.

She turned. "Lincoln," her voice was soft, breathy, unlike hers. "Lincoln!" she called more loudly.

He turned, then paused, and her heart spasmed as he drew closer, closer, closest, and she was in his arms and he in hers. She tucked her head into the curve of his shoulder, breathing in his scent as he kissed her forehead and squeezed her tight.

Oh, she was breathless with longing, with gladness, with emotions she could barely describe. But she knew in this moment this was right, this was good, that this man was good.

He cuddled her, rocking her slowly from side to side as if she was his human teddy bear and he'd been longing for the comfort of her embrace. Her hands slipped up his broad back, finding the muscles bunching there. He lowered his head, and his baseball cap fell off.

"You've cut your hair."

"It's for the space role." His blue eyes sparkled at her. "I don't hate it."

"You look older."

"More mature?"

"You are."

His lips tweaked to one side. "You look beautiful."

"You're obviously so old you can't see properly anymore."

He shook his head. "I've missed the sparkle of your brown eyes, your skin," he traced her cheek, "your hair," his hand slid down the length of her ponytail, "and these lips," he whispered.

The pad of his thumb brushed her lips softly. Her heart thundered louder than the waterfalls beside her.

"Oh, Jackie, I missed you something fierce, and I've been begging God for the chance to finally see you, but I knew you wanted me to stay away. Not that I even knew where you were until two days ago."

"When Serena told you?"

"When Serena told me, yes." He eyed her seriously. "You don't mind?"

"Not at all."

"Not at all?"

"No." She smiled.

His grin lit up his face, and he looked set to swoop in and kiss her—oh, why hadn't she brushed her teeth before her walk?—when a group of loud teenagers drew into view.

"Come here." He picked up his cap and shoved it back on, and shifted so they were now both facing the water, her back to his front, his arms around hers.

She drew in a moisture-laden breath and slowly released, savoring his nearness, this sense of protection and security, even as she prayed that their pose meant Lincoln wouldn't be recognized.

"Hey, man," one of the teens said to Lincoln. "Good day for it, eh?"

She felt his posture tense, then relax. "It's the best," Lincoln said, his hands caressing hers.

"Check out the view. It's awesome."

"It's beautiful," Lincoln said, before bending until his stubble grazed her cheek as he leaned close. "So beautiful," he murmured, and she was certain he wasn't talking about the view anymore.

The kid said something else she couldn't quite hear, her ear against Lincoln's bicep, then the group disappeared, and she finally relaxed.

"You don't think they recognized you?" she asked, pulling from the serenity of his arms.

He shrugged. "I'm probably not the first person they'd think to see in Grand Falls."

Laughter borne of relief escaped. "Imagine how disappointed they'll be when they discover *the* Lincoln Cash was here in town." She grinned. "Are you disappointed to not be recognized?" she teased.

"You and I both know the answer to that. I don't want anything or anyone getting in the way of this."

"Of what?"

"This." He drew closer, closer, so close she could feel his breath on her cheek. She closed her eyes, waiting for her first kiss.

"Jackie O'Halloran," he murmured, his breath on her mouth. "Can I kiss you?"

She nodded, tilting her face until her lips found his. His lips were firm, warm, and seemed to soften the longer she clung. She heard a sound like a chuckle in his throat and pulled back. Had she done it wrong?

"Jackie."

Her name was but a breath and then he kissed her again, hands cupping her face, before one slid into her hair as the other stole around her waist, tugging her even closer.

She was melting, fire scorching every vein, as he took his time. Oh, the man knew how to kiss.

She was dazed by the time she pulled away, hands on his chest, as she gazed up at him shyly.

He leaned his forehead against hers, and she closed her eyes. Why wasn't he saying anything? "Was… was that okay?" Nerves rushed her to say, "I've never kissed anyone before," she confessed.

He pulled back. "And you saved your first kiss for me?"

More like she hadn't had opportunity. But maybe, a quiet

voice protested, it was God who had kept her heart from being truly touched until now. Until her love could show this man just how loved he was. God didn't see Lincoln's past, so neither should Lincoln focus on it either.

"I don't know what to say," he rasped.

Were those tears in his eyes? Her throat constricted. "You don't need to say anything," she said, nestling closer.

"I don't deserve you," he murmured. "You're so good, and I'm not."

"I'm not very good," she admitted. "But I think you're good enough for me."

"Good enough?"

"More like perfect, actually."

"I'm definitely not that."

"But God is working in you, and that's what makes you perfect for me."

His eyes were beautiful, like he might cry again, which drew new softness in her heart and hastened her to say, "I think that's enough talking. I need you to kiss me again. Because obviously I need lots of practice."

"Oh, sweetheart, you don't. I might have more experience than you, but I've never felt this way before."

"And how's that?" she asked, half eager, half concerned. Was he amused by her lack of expertise?

"You don't need to look like that," he said, caressing loose strands of her hair then tucking them behind her ears. "It's all good, I promise."

"It is?"

He nodded. "I just meant I've never," he swallowed, "never known what it is to kiss someone I truly love before."

"Do you love me?"

"I do." He smiled. "I really do. And so when I kiss you, it's like every kiss is a promise for the future."

Her heart stuttered. "Is that a line from one of your movies?"

"It's good, isn't it? But no. It's a line from my heart and my soul. I love you, Jackie. You make me a better man."

She wrapped her arms around his neck. "I think you better kiss me again."

"Gladly."

And as his mouth met hers, so was she.

"So this is the young man about whom all the fuss is about."

He grasped the elderly lady's hand. "My name is John Lincoln Cash. It's a pleasure to meet you."

"Hmm." She turned to her daughter and granddaughter. "I thought you said you didn't have a boyfriend?" she said to Jackie.

"I didn't." Her cheeks were pink. Adorable.

"But now you do!" Her grandmother clapped her hands as her mother grinned.

"Now you do?" he asked Jackie, his voice husky.

"Maybe I do."

"I think definitely you do." And he reclaimed her lips with his own.

It still amazed him to think that she deigned to kiss him. That she thought him worthy enough to touch her lips. Which might sound all mediaeval princess-in-a-tower kind of thing, but honestly, he felt that way about Jackie. She was beautiful, untouched, unspoiled by ordinary things. He felt like a lesser mortal who'd been gifted a wondrous gift in her affection.

The rest of the day passed with him trying to assuage Jackie's mother's fears and concerns about the house and the meagre offerings she could give him. He solved it by insisting on taking them out for dinner, and that he didn't need them to go to any trouble, especially as he'd been so rude as to force himself upon their hospitality.

"Where are you staying?" Marie asked.

"I rented a little place by the river not too far away." It was the nicest he could find at short notice. He had used his Christian name, and hadn't been recognized. Yet.

He glanced at Jackie. He'd never grow tired of seeing her again. "I was hoping that you might be able to take a day or two off and we could do something together."

"Like what?"

"Something fun."

Her nose wrinkled. "You always thought I should do more fun things, didn't you?"

If having fun meant doing more kissing, then he was totally up for that. But he didn't want to push things, not when he was trying to do things God's way. And anything more than kissing was probably something he needed to be careful of around her. He got the impression she didn't know she was fire that made him want to be burned.

"You know the expression. All work and no play makes Jackie a dull—hmm, no. You couldn't ever be dull. But I don't want you to run the risk of burning out again—"

"Again?" her mother asked.

He glanced at Jackie, pushed his eyebrows up. "You didn't tell them?"

"I didn't burn out. Things just… got a little difficult."

He caught Marie's look of concern and nodded. Yeah, she had a right to look like that. "Anyway, whatever it's called, we need to make sure you have more balance in your life, don't we?"

"Yes, Mr. Cash," Jackie said like a schoolgirl.

"Which is why I hope to take you out on a date. If that's okay with your mom, of course."

Marie beamed. "You can take my daughter on a date any time you like. Just make sure you treat her right."

"Of course. I wouldn't dream of doing anything less than

what she deserves."

THE NEXT DAYS were filled with everything from zip lining down the St John's River to dates at the best restaurants Grand Falls offered. Which might not be too grand, but were cozy enough to allow for conversation. Of course, the best conversations were had by his cabin beside the river, where they talked about the past few weeks, and he explained about his renewed commitment to God and how that had changed his life.

He admitted to inviting Chlolinda to church, trying to get her into a women's group with the pastor's wife, that he had joined a Bible study on set.

"It's so weird, you know? I'm in this fake world, doing this movie I really don't want to do, but I'm just getting opportunity after opportunity to show a little bit of God's love. It's really weird to be talking with some of these other people, like camera crew and others, about real things when we're in this artificial world. But it feels really good too."

"You're amazing."

"God's amazing," he said. "You know, Chlolinda said she'd noticed I'm not so edgy anymore. And it's funny, even my migraines have cleared up a lot, too. I really feel more at peace these days."

She sighed. "I'm so glad." She threaded her fingers through his. "So, what happened about the movie? How did you get time off to be here?"

"There was some hiccup with the budget. I don't know. I'm just grateful for the chance to come here." He grinned. "I didn't realize just how long it would take."

"Did you stop over?"

"Toronto." His heart pricked.

"What's that look for?"

He exhaled. "So, I talked with my agent, and I don't know if I ever told you, but I really want to do a police drama TV show."

Her smile was wry. "You didn't tell me. You told the whole world in your interview."

Ah. That. But wait—"You know about that?"

"I was lucky enough to have Dana, my supervisor at work, show me."

He pressed his lips to the back of her hand. "I hope you know I never meant to get you into trouble."

"You can't be responsible for what your crazy fans do."

"But I should've been more careful. I will be more careful in the future." He squeezed her hand. "I won't let anything bad happen to you."

She nodded, her eyes saying she trusted him.

Gladness sang within. He'd prove worthy of that trust all his days.

Her lips curved, echoing his. "You were saying about the police drama."

"Yeah, that's right." He shifted in his seat. "So anyway, there were some network people who saw the interview and reached out to Richard, my agent. Apparently there'd been interest in doing a police drama in New York, but they found it more cost-effective to do it in Toronto, and they wanted to know if I was interested. I've looked at the script and it seems really good. It's gritty, it's not sleazy, and I'd be a just-widowed cop, so there's no love interest. Anyway, I'm interested, but thought I'd mention it to you and see if you had any interest in reading through the script and making sure you thought it would be a good fit for me. And for us."

"Us?"

He nodded. "I'm in this for the long haul, Jackie. I am not going to accept roles that could cause a problem for us. I don't want to be some sort of sex symbol, not when the only person I want to see me that way is you."

She laughed.

He stared at her. "What's so funny?"

"Oh, bless. I know you didn't mean it to sound like that, but I was just getting vibes of the Mr. Movie Star arrogance from before."

"Hey, I just meant—"

"Oh, you're fun to tease."

"You're having fun, are you?"

"Yes, I am."

He didn't care if he was the butt of her jokes for the rest of his life. She was having fun. She was more at ease. "Well, you know what happens to people who make fun of arrogant movie stars?"

"What's that?"

"They get tickled."

"Oh, do they?"

Before he knew it, she jumped up from her Muskoka chair and was running away along the riverbank. He took his time in chasing her, loving the sound of her laughter as it drifted on the air. He caught up to her, she dodged and weaved, and he soon had her wrapped up in his arms, tickling her to her shouts of laughter.

"Stop it! Stop it! Oh, I'm laughing so much I'm getting a stitch!"

"Stretch it out," he said.

She obeyed, then smiled at him. "I don't think I've run that fast for some time."

"Hey, there are still openings in the Muskoka running club."

"The what?"

"Joel and I and Serena, oh, and apparently your author friend and her boyfriend too, all like to jog. You're welcome to join us, next time I'm in town. Or even before."

She giggled. "That's really sweet, but I'll have to see how I go."

"I'm hearing a declined invitation."

"Your hearing is good." Her head tilted. "So, when do you next think you'll be in Muskoka?"

"When do you return?"

"Next week. My shift starts Wednesday."

"Then I guess I'll be back as soon as I can after that."

She placed her arms around his waist. "You can get time off from the movie?"

"We're still in pre-production mode, and haven't started filming yet, so yeah, there's some time." He winced. "I did hear a rumor that we may be shooting part of it in Morocco."

"Morocco?"

"They needed a place with a moon-like environment and there was a choice between Morocco or outback Australia. I would've preferred to have gone to Australia, but hey, Morocco will be nice." He smiled. "Maybe you could come visit me on a set one day."

"In Morocco?"

"Sure, why not? I can arrange for flights and accommodation for you, and your mom, or Serena, or whoever. It'd be nice to see you."

"It'd be nice to be seen," she murmured.

"Be nicer still if the Toronto thing comes off, though. Then I could come see you every weekend, or you could come see me."

"I like the idea of seeing you regularly."

"You and me both." He kissed her. "You and me both."

## CHAPTER 16

"Are you ready for this?" she asked, hand poised at the door.

He nodded.

"Are you sure? It's not too late to back out."

"Jackie, honey—"

Her heart sparkled at his words.

"—if this is what you need to do, then I'm happy to be a part of it. I want you to be happy."

The sparkles turned into fireworks. She'd seen the same genuineness in his words and serious expression many times recently. She wasn't expedient to him, and he actually wanted to be with her. If he kept on with showing such things, these feelings of deep liking could soon tip into something more serious.

"Okay. Don't say I didn't warn you."

She knocked, then waited, her nerves easing as he moved closer and threaded his fingers through hers. "You've got this," he murmured.

"Shouldn't you be saying break a leg?" she tried to joke.

"You're funny." His lopsided smile said it was true.

Some of the nerves abated as they waited. Why didn't Anna answer the door? Her car was here, so she was inside. Staci had even been so obliging as to call her and let her know when she'd seen Anna's car pass by. Seeing Staci was in her grandmother's house at the time, and had called only five minutes ago, Anna couldn't have got too far.

Jackie knocked again. "Anna? Please answer the door. It's Jackie. I want to talk with you."

Still nothing inside.

"Are you sure she's in there?" Lincoln whispered.

"Do you think I should check out the back?"

"I'll go." He pressed a kiss to her cheek and hurried around the side.

Jackie knocked again. "Anna? Please. Don't you think this childishness has gone on long enough?"

Funny how since she'd started dating an actor, she suddenly noticed words and phrases from movies and the like. She was pretty sure that line was similar to something Gilbert said to Anne of Green Gables.

But it was true. Anna's childishness had gone on long enough, and it was at Lincoln's instigation that she had finally found the nerve to confront Anna. The others had said that Anna wasn't going to church, accidental encounters in the street were met with frost and prickles, and even at the medical clinic where Anna worked as a receptionist the interactions with her were like talking with iced glass. Jackie hurt over it. So when Lincoln had suggested going to see her—"I've learned you've got to be honest with how you feel"—she'd finally agreed.

She'd hoped having him here with her might be the x-factor that finally got an answer.

"Anna? I know you're in there. Please open the door. I miss you, my friend."

Lincoln returned to her side, palms up in defeat. "I didn't go in the back. I figured that would look creepy and someone might call the police."

"I thought the police were fans of yours," she teased.

His lips curved ruefully. "Did I ever tell you about that?"

"I don't believe you did. Lucky for you, others have."

"Look, it was only twenty k's over."

Her eyebrows rose. "Should I be worried about your driving prowess?"

"Never." He traced her cheek with the back of his fingers. "Besides the fact that I never would put you in a second's danger, ever since that police officer was kind enough to let me get off with just a warning and make that safety video. I now have a reputation for safe driving that I need to maintain."

"Poor you."

"Not poor. Not with you by my side," he murmured, bending to kiss her.

She eased away to his mild protest. "I'm going to try one more time. Can I...?" She raised her eyebrows.

"Okay." He mock-sighed. "If you must."

"Thank you."

"I'll be the one here praying," he whispered.

She'd sensed his prayers these past weeks. Oh, she could very well fall into love. She knocked on the door again. "Anna? There's someone else here who wants to see you." She swallowed. "It's Lincoln. Lincoln Cash."

"Anna?" Lincoln said, adding his own knock. "Please? There's something I need to say."

From within there came a sound. Jackie glanced at Lincoln, and he clasped his hands together in a praying gesture. She nodded, adding her own prayer for good measure. *Lord, please help her, soften her heart...*

The door inched open, and Anna's post-work appearance shocked her. "What?"

"Anna." More than that she couldn't say. It had been a while since she'd seen Anna, and the other girls had said she looked different, but Jackie hadn't expected her to have gained twenty pounds and look unwell.

"What?" Anna repeated, her gaze on Jackie hard like granite, before it drifted to the man standing beside Jackie. Her smudged-mascara eyes widened.

"Hi, Anna," Lincoln said quietly.

Anna pressed her lips together.

"Anna," Jackie reached out a hand, but Anna shifted away. Okay. "Anna, it's good to see you."

"What do you want?"

The near-snarl in Anna's words made Jackie want to back away. She planted her feet more firmly. "Anna, I hate that we don't have much to do with each other anymore. Please, let me come in. I want to talk and clear the air between us."

"No." Anna moved protectively, as if she didn't want Jackie peering behind her. Was she trying to hide something?

"Okay, we can talk here. That's okay. It is good to see you," Jackie said. And it was. Even though something felt, looked, a little—a lot—off.

"What do you want?" Anna repeated.

Jackie silently exhaled. "I want you to forgive me. I don't know exactly what I've done wrong, but whatever it is, I'm so sorry that I've upset you. Please, please talk to me about it. I miss you, everyone misses you, and Serena is having another soiree tonight, and I hoped you might want to come, because they all want to see you, and—"

"No." Anna moved to shut the door.

Jackie braced her hand against the wood. "Please?" Emotion swelled and she blinked back tears. "Anna, I love you. You're one of my dearest friends, and I miss you, and—"

"Why would I want to go someplace and be the only single person there?"

"You won't be," she assured. "Cherry, Serena's assistant is coming, and Staci said Brandi—you know, from the bookstore?—well, she might come too, and—"

"Oh, that's right," Anna continued, as if she hadn't heard. "Because I don't like being picked on."

"Picked on?"

"By my so-called Christian friends."

"Anna, please. You know what I said was because I care about you—"

"Yeah, it's easy for you to say I should stop looking for a man when you've got someone like that"—she pointed to Lincoln—"waiting for you."

"Anna, stop. You know that's not true. This," she gestured to Lincoln, "took me as much by surprise as it did you, and everyone else. And you know I've talked with you about this frustration you're feeling long before Lincoln ever showed up in Muskoka."

"I know you think you're better than me, and—"

"That's not true."

"It *is* true. You always have, and you always will, Pastor Jackie." She spat the words. "I don't want to see you or the others anymore. I've got my own life. So stop bothering me."

"Anna, wait—"

The door closed with a loud thump, leaving her shell-shocked. "Anna?" She banged on the door. "Anna, please!" Their friendship couldn't end like this. It *couldn't*.

"Hey." Lincoln wrapped an arm around her. "She's obviously upset and not wanting to listen."

She drew in an unsteady breath. "I don't know what I did wrong."

"I suspect she doesn't really know, either, and the frustration that she feels is as much about feeling frustrated with herself as it is about everything else." He hugged her. "You can't take that on board. You've done like what it says in the Bible. As far as it depends on you, live at peace with others. You've done your best to reconcile, the rest is up to her."

She leaned against his chest. "I feel so bad."

"Hey, you can't control what another person thinks." He smiled crookedly. "Ask me how I know."

She appreciated his willingness for self-deprecation, but Anna's words haunted her still. "I still can't believe she thinks I act superior. Do you think I act like I think I'm better than others?"

He chuckled softly. "It's a good thing you're not insecure, right?" His gaze grew serious as he looked deep into her eyes. "Jackie, it's hard for me to answer this, because as soon as I met you, I knew I was way inferior to you. Your character shines like a diamond, and it means you have this quality that others see that can maybe seem intimidating. So if someone is struggling, they might try to lash out at that. But you and I both know it's actually Jesus who is shining through you. And if people are rejecting your values, then that says a lot about where they're at with God."

Tears trickled from her eyes. "You're so sweet."

"I know."

His laidback humor drew a smile as she wiped her tears away. "I just really miss her, you know?"

"I know." He gently squeezed her shoulders. "Come on. We'll need to trust that God will continue to work on her heart, and leave her in His capable hands. Now, let's go meet these scary friends of yours again."

"Scary? You know them all."

"Well, not all of them. You threw a few names out there of people I haven't met yet." His face wrinkled in concern. "Are they superfans to be afraid of?"

"I guess you'll have to wait and see."

Lincoln heaved out a breath as he glanced around the room. The room that had fallen silent as they entered, hand in hand. He got the feeling Jackie wanted to release his hand, to not seem like a show off. She didn't understand he needed to hold her hand because she was like a lifeline. His grip tightened.

"Hey there."

"Oh my gosh!" someone whispered. "Is that really Lincoln Cash?"

"It's like a dream," someone else whispered.

Awkwardness filled the room, then Joel moved close. "Hey, Lincoln. Good to see you again."

Lincoln had to let go of Jackie's hand then as Joel clasped him in a hug. Instantly the tension in the room dropped about twenty points, as a wave of squeals and girlish giggles encased them. He found himself hugged, squeezed, and gushed over, as Serena introduced two new ladies, Cherry, her assistant who worked with her at the Muskoka Shores resort, and Barbie-lookalike Brandi, who apparently owned a bookstore in town.

Staci, the author woman he was pretty sure, wrapped an arm around Brandi. "If ever you write a book, then Brandi is the best at putting on a shin-dig here in town."

"I'll keep it in mind," he said politely.

"It's so good to see you," Rachel said—he remembered her, she was the cocktail lady, who was kinda hard to forget.

"Yes, and you." Jackie hugged her. "Work's been manic since I started on Wednesday. I'm so glad it's the weekend."

So was he. The budget delays had stretched on, allowing more time to stay north, which naturally meant more time with Jackie. And fueled hope that maybe the budget issues might be of a permanent nature.

"And I'm sorry we're later than expected, but we called in at Anna's." Jackie's voice was wobbly, and he moved to her side, placed a hand on her back. "She didn't want to see me."

"Oh, Jackie." Serena hugged her.

"She looks really different, doesn't she?" Toni said. "I saw her at the clinic a few days ago and almost didn't recognize her."

"She's put on weight," Rachel said. "And not in a good way. Unlike some." She grinned at Jackie. "Girl, you've got curves."

Lincoln swallowed. Yeah, he'd noticed that too. It made their hugs more... fun.

Jackie pinked, and she was dragged away to speak with some others. He watched her go, feeling the loss of her presence.

The other guys—the investment banker Matt, Dr. James, Rachel's builder husband Damian—drew closer, offering a beverage as he tried to make small talk. It felt kinda weird, feeling like they were trying to act normal, trying not to be awed, and he wondered what to do to put them at their ease.

"Have you ever seen this man eat a burger?" Joel said, before whipping out his phone and showing the picture from Jackie's apartment.

"You mean that wasn't staged?" Damian asked.

"I'm trying to keep things a little more real."

"That must be a challenge, given the line of work you're in," James said.

"You know, it's had its moments, that's for sure."

"Tell me about it." The doctor's voice was wry. "I'm going out with an author and I'm never sure if what I say will end up in a book."

"Are you disparaging your fiancée?" Staci demanded.

"What?"

There was another round of squeals and congratulations, as Staci showed off the fat diamond cluster on her left hand.

He glanced at Jackie, saw her smile, then the way her gaze caught his. Time slowed. Yeah, maybe one day he'd look as proud as James did there. Except he'd be really glad to just skip all the fuss and elope. Maybe Joel knew someone who did impromptu wedding ceremonies. Then he and Jackie needn't be apart…

"So, you and Joel seem tight," Damian said.

Lincoln nodded. "Joel and I have been doing regular Zooms these past few weeks. He's basically my pastor."

"Wow." He caught a few of them glance at Joel with what looked like respect.

"So, are you planning on taking our Jackie here to any fabulous Hollywood parties any time soon?" Rachel asked.

"Actually…" Lincoln glanced at Jackie.

"Ooh, he is!" Rachel clapped her hands.

"It's not in Hollywood, but there is a special announcement coming up that involves a party. And Jackie, I'd hoped to ask you this privately, but seeing it's happening here—"

"Here? In Muskoka? Are you filming here?" Rachel demanded.

"No. I'm getting to that."

"I'm only asking in case we need to have a girls' shopping trip to get Jackie a dress. I'm up for any excuse to go to the city and make a splash."

He didn't doubt that for a second.

"I have a friend who owns a great boutique in Toronto," Serena said. "She could cut you a deal."

"And if you can't find anything there, then I know a couple of fantastic places in Chicago or New York," Staci added.

"What's the party about?" Jackie asked him.

He rubbed his hands. "Okay, so this is hot off the press. I got an email today from my agent who said that the Toronto police drama is going ahead."

"It is?" Jackie's eyes lit.

He nodded. "So after this movie is done, I'll be living in the city for a while. Two hours away."

"It's not that far once you get used to it," Matt said.

"Congrats, man." Joel thumped him on the back. Joel had been praying with Lincoln for this to come off.

"There's still a lot to happen," like finish a space film, "but yeah. I'm starting to see how God is making my paths straight."

"God is good, huh?" Joel said.

"All the time," came an echo from around the room.

Lincoln grinned. He liked this crew at Muskoka Shores.

Jackie drew close, and he snagged her hand, leading her out to the patio. "Are you doing okay now?"

"Yes. Thank you."

"Anna will come around. We'll keep praying, and God will soften her heart."

"You're so good." She wrapped her arms around his neck and kissed him.

After another oh-so-enjoyable moment, he drew back, his breathing ragged. This woman had no idea the effect she had on him. "What's a four-letter word for holds in deepest affection?"

"Like?"

The teasing sparkle of her brown eyes drew his smile. "Deeper. As in, gives meaning and purpose to one's life, held a man on a cross, inspires millions of songs, inspires me to want to do all I can to be a blessing in your life."

Her hand lifted to caress his jaw, her expression soft.

"I love you, Jackie. You're everything I could've dreamed, but never knew I needed."

"Is that another line from a film?"

"It's another truth straight from my heart to yours."

She nuzzled closer. "It's a good thing," she murmured.

"What is? That I love you?"

"Yes. Because I suspect I might love you too."

His grin could power a hundred electricity stations.

"I have a good feeling about us," she murmured.

And as his lips closed on hers, so did he.

THE END

If you enjoyed this book, then make sure you read the next in the Muskoka Romance series,
*Muskoka Holiday Morsels*
and Anna's story in *Muskoka Promise*.

# A NOTE FROM THE AUTHOR

Thank you for reading *Muskoka Spotlight,* the fourth book in the Muskoka Romance Christian contemporary romance series. This book is based on my visit to the beautiful Muskoka region of Ontario, Canada, and springs from *Muskoka Blue,* the sixth book in the Original Six contemporary romance series, that enters on Sarah and Dan's romance story (grab your copy of *Muskoka Blue).* If you've enjoyed this book, please check out the pictures from my visit to Muskoka on my website at www.carolynmillerauthor.com

~

Reviews help other readers find new-to-them authors, so if you can spare a moment to write a quick review at Goodreads / your place of purchase, I'd be very grateful.

Enjoyed this taste of Muskoka? Then make sure you read the next books in the Muskoka series, *Muskoka Holiday Morsels* and Anna's story in *Muskoka Promise.*

If you enjoy Christian contemporary romance you may want to check out the books in the Original Six hockey romance

## A NOTE FROM THE AUTHOR

series, a sweet & swoony, slightly sporty Christian contemporary romance series.

The Breakup Project<br>
Love on Ice<br>
Checked Impressions<br>
Hearts and Goals<br>
Big Apple Atonement<br>
Muskoka Blue

Romance and hockey fans may also want to read *Fire and Ice*, the first book in the new Northwest Ice series.

I'd love for you to check out my other books and to sign up for my newsletter at www.carolynmillerauthor.com where you can be the first to learn all my book and contest news, and discover more behind-the-book details and photos. Newsletter subscribers can also get an exclusive bonus book free, so grab your copy of *Originally Yours* here.

Big thanks to Brittany, Becky, Rebekah and Kaye for your eagle eyes, and the ladies in my Facebook group, Carolyn's Books & Friends, for all your support in helping promote my books.

# ABOUT THE AUTHOR

Carolyn Miller lives in the beautiful Southern Highlands of New South Wales, Australia, with her husband and four children. A long-time lover of romance, especially that of Jane Austen, Georgette Heyer and LM Montgomery, Carolyn loves to write contemporary and historical romance that draws readers into fictional worlds that show the truth of God's grace in our lives.

To find out more about Carolyn's books, and to subscribe to her newsletter, please visit www.carolynmillerauthor.com

You can also connect with her at

## ALSO BY CAROLYN MILLER

<u>The Original Six hockey series</u>
The Breakup Project
Love on Ice
Checked Impressions
Hearts and Goals
Big Apple Atonement
Muskoka Blue

<u>Muskoka Romance series</u>
Muskoka Shores
Muskoka Christmas
Muskoka Hearts
Muskoka Spotlight
Muskoka Holiday Morsels
Muskoka Promise

<u>Northwest Ice hockey series</u>
Fire and Ice
The Love Penalty

<u>Three Creeks Ranch Romance series</u>
A Cameo for a Cowgirl

<u>Trinity Lakes collection</u>
Love Somebody Like You
Tangled Up in Love

### The Independence Islands series

Restoring Fairhaven

Regaining Mercy

Reclaiming Hope

Rebuilding Hearts

Refining Josie

### Historical:

### Regency Wallflowers

Dusk's Darkest Shores

Midnight's Budding Morrow

Dawn's Untrodden Green

### Regency Brides: Legacy of Grace

The Elusive Miss Ellison

The Captivating Lady Charlotte

The Dishonorable Miss DeLancey

### Regency Brides: Promise of Hope

Winning Miss Winthrop

Miss Serena's Secret

The Making of Mrs Hale

### Regency Brides: Daughters of Aynsley

A Hero for Miss Hatherleigh

Underestimating Miss Cecilia

Misleading Miss Verity

'Heaven and Nature Sing' from the Joy to the World Christmas novella collection

'More than Gold' from

the Across the Shores novella collection